THE TEMPLE TREE

Jamie Hannaker, a British Board of Trade aircraft accident investigator, and Melanie Grey, the young air stewardess, both waiting at an airport in Ceylon for the routine night flight back to London, are immediately attracted to each other. Their awaited jet aircraft, coming in to land in bad weather with eighty-one passengers and a secret consignment of gold on board, undershoots the runway and crashes into the jungle close to a Hindu temple. There are no survivors . . . and the gold is missing. The Colombo police and the Sinhalese Air Safety Bureau seem only too ready to attribute the disaster to 'pilot error'. But where is the gold? . . . Hannaker's experience and intuition lead him to suspect sabotage, and he fears a repetition of the disaster. His love for Melanie and concern for her safety intensify his determination to find the real cause, and he comes up against some devious characters in his lone fight to penetrate the curtain of native superstition and religious mysticism which cloaks the truth. There is a terrific build-up of tension, the pace accelerating to a final tremendous climax. This story dramatically illustrates the contrast between East and West and between the older civilizations and that of the jet age.

THE
TEMPLE TREE

★

DAVID BEATY

THE
COMPANION BOOK CLUB
LONDON

This edition, published in 1972 by
The Hamlyn Publishing Group Limited,
is issued by arrangement with
Martin Secker & Warburg Limited

THE COMPANION BOOK CLUB

The Club is not a library; all books are the
property of members. There is no entrance fee
or any payment beyond the low Club price of
each book. Details of membership will gladly
be sent on request.

Write to:

The Companion Book Club,
Borough Green, Sevenoaks, Kent

*Made and printed in Great Britain
for the Companion Book Club
by Odhams (Watford) Ltd.*
SBN 600871479
5.72/247

To B, as always

NEW MOON

Ammawaka

'YOUR AIRCRAFT, SAH, will be landing in two hours time.'
The Sinhalese company representative pressed the palms of
his hands together and bowed low. 'I pray you will not mind
sharing taxi-cab with crew member and Chinese gentleman?'

Jamie Hannaker shook his head and thanked the man. Then
he shut his briefcase, put it next to his old green panic-bag
beside his chair, leaned across the table for his whisky and
water and for want of anything better to do watched a fair-
haired girl emerge from the lounge and start walking across the
polished parquet floor of the hotel foyer.

Outside, the monsoon rain was still sheeting down. It re-
glazed the wide windows into huge distorting lenses that made
weird patterns of the scenery beyond—the sea blended with
white and green convolvulus, the frantic coconut palms curled
now into peacock-tailed snakes, the beaches blown up by the
wind, running their sands over all the other colours like yellow
paint.

Inside the hotel, the atmosphere was oppressive. People
talked in soft muted voices. The air was heavy with something
sweet and aromatic like incense or sandalwood, the mustiness
of old furniture mixed with overlush tropical flowers, and that
indefinable smell of any place east of Alexandria.

Hannaker knew it well enough, yet it always awakened in
him a curious irrational uneasiness. Perhaps uneasiness was the
wrong word. A kind of wariness, a prickling at the back of the
neck, an inexplicable sensation of some fourth dimension.
Perhaps he felt it because he always came here on the tail end
of a disaster. A disaster which the whole Eastern way of life
made more difficult for him to unravel.

Hannaker was fond of the East. It attracted him but he mistrusted it. Maybe his job made him that way. Times, dates,

7

hard facts, sworn statements, those were what his job needed. No maybes, tomorrows, possibilities, perhaps.

He wasn't the only one who felt that way. 'If they used the stars for navigation instead of casting horoscopes, and blamed Allah less and maintenance more, half your lot would be out of a job.' Those were the words of the station manager at Simbanzi, where Hannaker had just been investigating a take-off accident for them, and hence this six-hour stop-over in Ceylon waiting for the British Oriental Airways scheduled flight to London. As always on an inquiry out East, people had tried to complicate matters by bringing in things like unlucky days and local superstitions. When he had proved conclusively that the cause of both engines failing immediately after take-off had been the fact that the engineers after an inspection had put one fuel valve round the wrong way, they had resisted such a simple Western-style explanation. Hannaker had felt he was trying to swim against an invisible current in a slippery green river as endless as time.

Or perhaps the explanation was also simple, and that he himself had a thing about time.

Above the soft murmur of Sinhalese voices, he could hear the tapping of the girl's heels.

Time. Time spent. Time wasted. The exact time. In a way, he had a right to have a thing about time.

There was just time to catch the post if she hurried, Margaret had said. She could drive to the post box in the village in ten minutes flat. She had timed herself. And that counted getting in and out of the car and actually dropping the letter in. Hannaker remembered looking up from his notes, the same sort of notes that were in his briefcase now. The same briefcase, come to that. What was the hurry anyway? He remembered smiling and catching her hand. It was a summer Sunday, and the post was collected early. Fine summer Sundays meant speeding traffic, but neither of them had remembered that. She must get the letter off to her cousin in Cornwall.

The letter was so unimportant. God, how unimportant! More than most people, he should have known the power of the trivial to topple the world.

8

Over the rim of his glass, Hannaker went on watching the girl. She seemed to cleave her way gracefully and coolly through the heat and confusion and the clutter. As she passed under the huge fan, rotating ponderously like some old Anson propeller, the current of air caught at her hair making it sparkle like the Sinhalese women's saris. She was wearing a pink cotton dress with a very short skirt, and her straight hair came down to her shoulders. Hannaker guessed her as English or American, as incongruous as he was amongst the saris and the silk.

He didn't know if she was pretty or not, except that she walked confidently and carelessly as a pretty girl does. Not that, since that summer Sunday four years ago, he cared whether she was pretty or ugly.

He watched her walk up to the reception desk. The Sinhalese clerk bowed and smiled to her. A favoured guest? A rich American heiress perhaps, spending a vacation in the quaintness and the sun?

The desk clerk unhooked a key and handed it to her. He must have made some remark, for the girl looked at her wrist watch, nodded and laughed. Then she turned.

As a disinterested observer, Hannaker was pleased to see that she was indeed pretty. Then her eyes met Hannaker's. The smile vanished. The eyes, Hannaker decided, would be blue. They were frostier now than the ice clinking in his glass. He smiled, ruefully, apologetically. The frosty expression melted, but she didn't smile back. She walked diagonally across the foyer towards the lift, her head held high, the long blonde hair swinging reprovingly behind her back. A curious contrast Hannaker thought, to the provocative swing of the short, short skirt.

She kept her back to Hannaker while she put her fingers on the lift bell. A slender back springing gracefully from a narrow waist. No rings that he could see on either hand. Aged, he would guess, about twenty-four.

She was now examining the monstrous Albert Memorial of a lift shaft as if its gilded mesh and golden leaves and stylized flowers held a hitherto unrevealed fascination for her. It was yet another relic of the heyday of the Empire when visiting royalty had stayed in this hotel, and was set a little to one side of where Hannaker sat.

With her, Hannaker raised his eyes, and watched the fairy cabin descend. It was made almost entirely of panes of plate glass loyally embellished with Prince of Wales feathers in nineteenth-century wire-cut, of a kind that would have fetched a fortune in a King's Road antique shop. In contrast, as it descended, it made a high whining noise like that of an aircraft's flaps coming down. It stopped with a long-drawn-out sigh. The gilded mesh of the gates clashed open. Without a backward glance, the girl stepped inside.

Hannaker watched her being gathered up like Moses to the regions above. Just before her head was chopped off by a line of cherubims with trumpets, the girl's eyes met Hannaker's again.

A surprising current of sympathy seemed to pass between them. Amusement crinkled up her eyes, and curved the corners of her mouth, as if she saw the momentary ridiculousness of her situation through Hannaker's eyes. Then with tantalizing slowness, she disappeared, shoulders, waist, hips, legs, neat small feet, till Hannaker was left smiling at nothing but the empty lift shaft.

Hannaker shrugged his shoulders. A face passed in the crowd. He remembered wishing that it had been a face appearing instead of disappearing.

Automatically his hand went down to touch the green canvas of his panic-bag, just to make sure that it, too, had not disappeared. It was there all right, lying like a faithful dog just beside his feet, as always accompanying him everywhere. Inside there was a Pentax colour film camera, pencils, wax crayons, a compass, magnets, a magnifying glass, a microscope, gumboots, medicines, tie-on labels, tools, spanners, dental mirrors, two torches. This was his constant companion, a movable distillation of the vital things he might need at any moment, its product the contents of his twelve years' experience investigating aircraft accidents.

He had taken an engineering degree, then spent three years with an aircraft manufacturer before coming into this line of government service. Most top investigators he had found were ex-pilots who were more interested in the flying errors—after all, sixty per cent of all aircraft accidents were caused by them —than in the jig-saw built up of small pieces of shattered aircraft that he found so fascinating. Twice he had built up the whole fuselages of four-engined aircraft out of bits no bigger than three inches square on a frame of chicken wire. His office was a Madame Tussaud's filled with murderers—fractured bolts, burnt tyres, the time fuse of a bomb, cracked windows, metal plates scarred by fatigue, a defective selector, a broken piece of wire.

That his work was aircraft accident investigation he saw, not as any irony, but as a relief and an opportunity. Always painstaking and accurate, he brought now to every inquiry a bitter obsession. The long careful sifting of an accident's cause from muddle and rubbish—the worn shaft, the fuel leak, the misread instrument, the hair crack in a bolt—eased something in himself. As if he had made yet another attack on the world's vast armies of needless miseries.

There was so much to do—and so little time to do it. Waiting and doing nothing was such a waste—and besides it let thoughts into your mind which were best kept away.

The gilded sunray clock on the wall above his head struck its liquid chime seven times. Another twenty minutes before pick-up. More vehemently, Hannaker cursed the time spent kicking his heels, and the deluge of the monsoon rain outside.

Just before the twenty minutes was up, the girl was back. He hardly recognized her at first. As the lift whined down he glanced across hopefully. The legs had looked familiar, but then he had almost turned away again. The rest of her was clad in a neat blue uniform. Gone was the pale swinging hair, scooped up now decorously under a high perched forage cap. She carried a matching bag over her shoulder, and a suitcase in the other hand. As she stepped out of the lift, she walked in that exaggerated manner which all stewardesses seem to acquire. As if, Hannaker thought, they carried a water bottle on their heads. Not the beautiful stone jar of the Arabian women, but a squashy plastic affair that they had to keep balanced by the constant mincing and convoluted wiggling of their hips. Hannaker was simultaneously pleased and disappointed.

Only the face remained the same, and the slight tentative smile she gave him as she passed. He watched her walk up to the desk. There was a whispered consultation between her and the company representative.

Then the two of them were walking over to the Chinese gentleman still sitting quietly and decorously by the potted palms. A little porcelain miniature making a perfect still life for some amateur water-colour artist. After a moment, the girl detached herself and approached Hannaker. She kept her eyes lowered as she came near. Only the faint colour under her skin showed that she remembered noticing him before.

'Mr. Hannaker?' And without giving him time to reply, a little breathlessly. 'I believe you're travelling with us tonight?'

Hannaker struggled out of the deep low chair, and stretched himself. For some reason he was pleased that he towered above her, and that she had to tilt her now sculpted head slightly to talk to him.

'That's me,' he said smiling. 'Flight 708 to London. It's still an hour late?'

'So I'm told.'

Hannaker grimaced at the wind and the rain beating on the plate glass of the windows.

'I must say I'll be glad to get out of this.'

'It's only just broken, the monsoon. Up till last week it was marvellous. Sunshine, blue sky, swimming.'

She shrugged her shoulders as if remembering the feel of it on her body.

'I'll believe you.' He tucked his briefcase under his arm, picked up his panic-bag and smiled.

'I hope you don't mind about the taxi,' she said, preceding him across the foyer. 'They're so erratic, it's safer to use mine. The rest of the crew have already gone out to the airport.'

'You're the crew member we'll be sharing with?'

'Sorry, I should have introduced myself. I'm Melanie Grey, the stewardess.'

'I'd gathered that,' he said gravely. 'The stewardess bit, I mean.'

She smiled over her shoulder, but said nothing. And then she asked with professional politeness, 'Have you been in Ceylon for long?'

'Six hours to be exact. In transit from Simbanzi. I'm just catching a connection here.'

Together they paused for a moment to collect the Chinese gentleman and his multitudinous small bags. 'You left yours at the airport, did you, Mr Hannaker?'

Hannaker nodded, and she began counting the Chinaman's bags, bending her head this way and that to see they were labelled. A wisp of hair fell loose from under her cap. It made her look very young and somehow vulnerable, as if all this dressing up and show of efficiency were all some act, as indeed it probably was.

'Tell him he'll probably have to pay excess, will you?' she murmured to the company representative, and then to Hannaker, 'My Chinese doesn't run to that.' She smiled. 'We can put all this in beside the taxi driver, and then we three can sit at the back.'

'Sounds reasonable to me,' Hannaker said. In the old days, before Margaret, he would have made some crack about sitting squeezed up tight with a pretty girl. But not now.

A sudden gust of air, warm and moist and sea-scented, blew briefly across the foyer. In through the plate-glassed entrance doors came a man wearing a royal blue uniform with a peaked cap heavily encrusted with gold braid.

'Ah! there's the taxi now!' Miss Grey said with relief. 'Wait till they load up first. That usually takes about five minutes.'

'I see you have it all taped.'

'One has to. That's my job.'

'Do you like it?' He watched the bearers tucking the small heavy-looking bags under their arms, and the porcelain figure of the Chinaman come to life, running after them, every line animated with acute anxiety.

13

'The job? Oh, yes. Very much.'

She stared at him intently for a moment and he wondered if she was going to ask him if he liked his. In general, when he was travelling by air he preferred not to give his occupation, and perhaps she sensed his reticence, for instead she made some vague remark about her job, about it being fun to see the world, the usual line these stewardesses gave.

'Don't you get tired of dashing hither and yon?'

She shook her head. 'Anyway, we have rather a good arrangement on this line. We're based in Ceylon for six months at a time. A semi-permanent slip crew really. We take the outbound London flight on to Hong Kong. And the Hong Kong home-bound to London.'

'You get the best of both worlds.'

'In a way, yes.' She smiled up at him. It was an endearing, slightly crooked smile which enhanced her youthfulness and awakened in Hannaker a curious weighty feeling of despair. 'That's what everyone tries to do, isn't it?'

'With varying success.'

The expression of her blue eyes changed at the slightly bitter note in his voice. An understanding? A shielded sympathy? Something anyway beyond the polite professional hostess interest. He shrugged, impatient with himself. 'How many of the six months have you done?'

'Three and a half.'

'So you've got to know the island pretty well?'

She made an expansive gesture with her hands. 'I don't think if you stayed for thirty years you'd know this island well.' And then in a different, brisker tone, 'Ah, they're ready for us.'

The taxi driver had reappeared in the doorway, rain dripping now from the fine peaked cap, dark splashes staining the royal blue uniform. The company representative hurried forward, all nods and smiles, eager for their little party to be on its way.

Together Hannaker and Miss Grey walked across the foyer towards the main doors. Beyond its liquid panes, the rain still cascaded down. Sky and road were the same colour of drenched ochre.

'Where's the Chinese gentleman?' Hannaker asked.

'Already in the taxi, I imagine. Making sure about his baggage.' She smiled faintly.

'Bon voyage. Au revoir. A very pleasant journey, sir, miss.' The company representative flung the doors wide open, averting his head from the snatch of the wet wind.

A handful of rain, a flurry of torn blossoms blew in their faces like sodden confetti. Miss Grey paused and removed a wet petal fastidiously from the lapel of her blue uniform before walking unhurriedly down the steps. Belatedly, a *podian* (house boy) came running after them with a multi-coloured umbrella.

Drawn up in front of the steps was an old London taxi-cab, the front part half-filled with the Chinaman's luggage. As they approached he leaned forward anxiously, his round face floating behind the wet windows.

'Wonder what he's got that's so precious?' Hannaker murmured.

'Customs will no doubt find out.' She smiled. Hannaker struggled with the catch of the taxi door. The Chinaman had huddled himself in the far corner. Miss Grey sat herself in the middle. The taxi driver slammed the door shut as soon as Hannaker had climbed in.

Surprisingly, the engine started up straight away. In a cloud of steam and a bow wave of yellow water, they pulled away. Miss Grey murmured a few words of what seemed to be intelligible Chinese, for the Chinaman nodded, smiled and gazed out of the window at the deserted roadways, the blown trees, the grey ebbing sky.

'What did you tell him?' Hannaker asked. 'Weather fine . . . aircraft serviceable . . . looks like being an excellent trip. The usual hand-out?'

'Something of the sort.' She laughed, took off her cap, shook the rain water on to the floor, and replaced it carefully.

'I suppose after a while you come to believe it?'

'Not even after a while. Mostly it's true.'

'Like today.'

'Oh, we'll soon get out of this.' The taxi driver hurtled round a corner. This time the bow wave splashed a muddy map across the window. Hannaker held Miss Grey's arm to steady her. He removed it again quickly as soon as the taxi righted itself.

She laughed. 'The most hazardous part of any trip.'

'I believe you.'

They were on a straight stretch of road now between high closely packed palms. There was no sound except the rattle of the wipers, the wet motor-boat-like chug of the vehicle over the concrete joins, the slush of the rain. Hannaker was uncomfortably aware of Miss Grey's legs close to his, her fastidious very English profile cameoed against the dark green of the jungle whipping past on either side of them. He fancied he could smell her perfume too, clear and fresh in the welter of tropical foliage and flowers, some bitter aroma that exuded from the Chinaman's corner, and the mouldy smell of old upholstery. He felt it imperative to maintain some sort of conversation. Besides he wanted to talk to her. Minutes were draining away, faster than the rain through the gutters. He wished again that he wasn't just leaving.

'D'you think he'll be able to land in all this?' He jerked his head up towards the sky.

'They've got an instrument landing system!'

'And I should hope so too! Still, I imagine you've been in worse.'

'Much worse.'

'Ever get scared?'

'Often.' She laughed. 'No, that's not really true.'

'You've got confidence in the crew?'

'Yes.' She glanced at him sideways. 'Don't you have?'

Hannaker sighed deliberately. 'Let's say my job tends to diminish confidence.'

Strange, he thought, that usually he stonewalled questions about his job, and here he was now, inviting her curiosity.

'Which is what? Your job?'

'Accident investigation.'

'Aircraft?'

'Yes.'

She didn't shudder or make any exaggerated exclamation.

She said in a low voice, 'Yes, well, I imagine it would.' Sympathetically she added, 'Isn't it rather depressing?'

'Maybe I'm not the sensitive type.'

She turned and looked at him curiously. Her cool blue eyes travelled unhurriedly over his face. 'I wouldn't have said that.'

He was disproportionately pleased. Those few words warmed him more than any flattery. He was about to ask her how long she would be stopping over in London, how often she came there, with the idea of leading up to a date, when he became aware that the chug-chug of the taxi down the long straight road had become laboured.

The driver had hunched his shoulders and was moving himself backwards and forwards in his seat as if he was trying to encourage a mule. Without success.

Speed slackened. The driver took one hand off the wheel and banged angrily on the dashboard, wiped the steam from the inside of the windscreen with the cuff of his sleeve, and switched the headlights off and on. The engine gurgled, coughed and gave up. In the middle of nowhere, the taxi came to a slithering halt.

'What on earth?' Miss Grey jumped up in her seat. The Chinaman rubbed a patch clear in his window pane and peered out, murmuring unanswerable questions or complaints. The taxi driver threw off his cap, leapt down, splashed through the brown puddles, and lifted the bonnet. A little fluster of steam hissed out and died away again under the steady torrent of the rain. Fumes from the engine mixed in with the smell of tropical vegetation, and the sickly sweetness of forest flowers. On either side of them the palms, shadowy and colourless now as darkness closed in, sighed and swayed in the wind.

'As you so rightly said,' Hannaker got up, 'the most hazardous part of the journey.'

He pressed down the handle. He had to shove hard against the wind to open the door. He jumped out. Walking forward was like pushing through a bead-curtain of rain. Torn-off sodden leaves made the tarmac slippery. Trapped water from the sides of the road was flooding over the low camber in little ochre whirlpools.

Miss Grey wound down her window, and crinkling up her eyes against the blow of the wet wind called, 'This is where you come into your own. You'll know what's up. *He* won't!'

'Don't bank on it.'

The rain ran off the end of his chin and down his nose. Determinedly, he bent over beside the driver. He poked a finger round the rust-caked engine. He felt in his jacket and produced his torch. Contrary to Miss Grey's belief, he was not an expert in the workings of a motor car. He loathed the things anyway. And his interest lay in altogether subtler and more delicate instruments.

The white beam of the torch showed dirt, rust, neglect. The trouble might be anything or everything.

'How far away are we?' Hannaker held up his hand for the driver to stop talking. 'How far from the airport?'

The driver shrugged. Rain slicked down his hair, stained his uniform. 'The airport?' Hannaker repeated, pointing, 'About five miles, eh?'

'Yes, sah.'

'Miss Grey,' Hannaker shouted into the car, 'How far to the nearest telephone?'

She cupped her mouth with her hands. 'Three miles . . . four miles. Lord, why?'

'Don't know if we'll make it under our own steam.'

'What's the trouble?'

'I'm not too sure yet. Leads might be soaked. Might be the distributor.'

'Can't you *do* anything?' Some of the smooth poise had disappeared. Without the enamel-hard air-hostess veneer, she looked appealing and helpless.

He was about to return to the bonnet and do a meticulous elimination of all possible sources of trouble when, far out in the grey wet darkness, he saw a couple of lights. Car head-lamps coming down the straight stretch of road from the direction of the airfield, throwing white cones of reflected light on the glistening surface. Coming fast, too, expanding, closing the gap between them, the wind catching at the engine noise, magnifying and diminishing it by turn.

Inside Hannaker relief and disappointment mingled. The taxi-driver was already out in the middle of the road signalling wildly for the car to stop.

It began to slow. The powerful beams picked out the figure of the Sinhalese prancing like a devil-dancer. The other vehicle came to a quiet halt. The headlights dipped. A low-slung racing car—a white Porsche, expensive and cared for.

The window of the car wound down. A slow voice, quiet and authoritative, was replying to the driver's flood. Then the car door opened. A large broad-shouldered man got out and walked towards them, his now distorted top-heavy shadow flung ahead of him by the light of his own headlamps. Yet for all his size he moved lightly on his feet, unhurriedly, one hand thrust in the pocket of his raincoat, head up, as if he didn't feel the wind and the rain. He stopped beside Hannaker, rested his free hand on the roof of the taxi and smiled.

'You seem to be in trouble. If that's not stating the obvious.'

The slow voice was unmistakably English. He bent his head to smile and nod to Miss Grey. A big handsome head, Hannaker noticed, with the automatic pigeon-holing reflex he had acquired over the years. Aged, at a guess, thirty-eight. Maybe more. Brown hair, greying very slightly at the temples, swept back in a thick wave from the broad furrowed forehead. Eyes light green or grey.

Miss Grey sighed. 'I'll say we are.'

'Perhaps I can help?'

'Oh, yes please!' There was immense relief in her voice. 'Do you know anything about the inside of a car?' Not entirely guilelessly, she turned her large fine eyes up to him. Hannaker had never ceased to marvel at the way a woman knew immediately that she was being admired. 'We simply came to a full stop. Here, of all places. Mr. Hannaker has just been having a look-see. . . .'

Miss Grey spoke quickly and nervously, partly from fear of being late for her flight, partly, Hannaker thought, because of the curious intent way this man stared at her.

'Mr Hannaker? That you, sir?' The big man turned, his brows raised questioningly. 'Perhaps I should introduce myself. Laughton's the name.' He glanced down at Miss Grey as if that information ought to mean something to her. 'Roy Laughton.'

'Melanie Grey.'

'Delighted to meet you, Miss Grey. Even,' he ruefully shook the rain off his head, 'under these circumstances.'

'D'you live here?' she asked, as Hannaker stood beside him, uncomfortably aware of the wet now trickling down inside his collar, of the rain drumming against the sides of the taxi.

'I do.' Mr Laughton smiled and sighed simultaneously, 'I have for my sins a small factory south of here.'

'Of course,' Miss Grey exclaimed. '*Now* I remember! I've heard a lot about you.'

'Good, I hope?'

'Very. I knew your name rang a bell. I know about your factory, too. Sinha Radio. Isn't that it?' And in explanation to Hannaker, 'It's the most modern factory in Ceylon.'

'That,' Laughton smiled modestly, wiping the rain off his face, 'isn't saying much.'

'We actually took a tour round it once, didn't we? There was a delay over an engine change!'

'You're Oriental Airways, are you? I thought so. It's difficult to be sure of uniforms in this light.' Laughton took the opportunity to peer through the taxi window and look more closely at her. 'Yes, you did send a tour round. But I don't remember seeing you. I should have remembered if I had.'

'I didn't go.'

'Pity.' He smiled, 'Perhaps you'll come some other time? Without there being an engine change.'

'Thank you.'

As if now for the first time aware of the passage of time, Laughton thrust out his hand and looked at the luminous hands of his wrist-watch. 'Well, this won't do at all, will it? Let me see inside that engine. If there's nothing I can do, I'll turn round and give you a lift. To the airport, I take it?'

'Won't that be an awful trouble?'

Stepping backwards reluctantly towards the bonnet, ardent eyes still fixed on Miss Grey, he brushed her protests aside. 'I've just come from Tallaputiya myself. Been seeing a rep of mine off to Hong Kong.'

'We're taking the incoming Hong Kong flight on to London.'

'An extraordinary coincidence,' Hannaker remarked dryly.

'I don't believe in coincidences,' Laughton hunched up his shoulders against the storm. 'Let's see what the trouble is.'

He turned to the driver, huddled in the shelter of the upraised bonnet, and asked him something in Sinhalese. He brushed the driver's reply aside.

'No mechanical sense, these chaps.' He shouted at Hannaker. 'I find that out every day. Would you like to hold that torch for me, Mr . . . er . . . ?'

'Hannaker.'

'Over there if you don't mind, Mr Hannaker.' In the beam of his torch, Hannaker watched the big hands move deftly and unhurriedly. 'Mmm, distributor leads are wet. You just visiting our beautiful country, Mr Hannaker?'

'Not even that. Just in transit.'

He glanced sideways at Laughton's absorbed face, faintly illuminated in the reflected light from the torch. In this soft effulgence a curious broad flat face, not so handsome as in profile. A short nose, long upper lip, eyes narrowed now in concentration. A closed-up, enigmatic face.

'Pity!' Laughton brought out a handkerchief and unscrewed the rusted radiator cap, throwing over his shoulder some irritated Sinhalese at the driver. 'And Miss Grey is your air hostess for the flight?'

'Yes.'

'Have you met her before? Could you hold the beam steady, Mr Hannaker? We want to get this fixed as soon as possible.'

'No. Why? Is that better?'

'No reason. Yes. Much better. Well, that seems O.K. and the battery's all right. You know it might simply be those distributor leads. This bonnet leaks like a colander.'

'I was beginning to suspect that.'

Laughton took a handkerchief and thoroughly wiped each plug dry. 'Might be. Might not be. Anyway, let's see what

21

that does.' He spoke to the cab driver, who went leaping over the puddles, pulled open the door and thankfully got into the cab.

The driver turned on the ignition and pressed the self-starter while Laughton went on checking.

Nothing happened. Laughton frowned. For some sour reason Hannaker was glad.

The Sinhalese tried again. This time just a wheeze.

'Third time lucky,' Laughton said, watching the driver's face as he pressed the starter again.

The engine kicked then all right, throbbed, shook the whole chassis, wavered a little as if it might give up, and then caught, going into a steady harsh throb.

'If he lets it run a bit, that'll do the trick.' Fastidiously Laughton wiped his fingers one at a time on his handkerchief, then he pulled down the bonnet and wiped them again.

'You're a wizard,' Miss Grey exclaimed in a flood of relief, as still in his irritatingly unhurried way Laughton stepped up to her window and leaned his hand on the door.

'Doesn't your rich company run to better transport for its precious cargo?'

He was not, Hannaker knew, referring to the Chinaman or himself.

Miss Grey smiled, shrugged her shoulders and said in an earnest business-like tone, 'I really am most grateful. I don't know how to thank you.'

'Well, don't try now. It would take much too long. You'd better be on your way. Try to thank me some other time, eh?'

Even in this uncertain light, the colour in Miss Grey's cheeks darkened. She seemed unsure of what to say.

'Have lunch with me, perhaps? Come and see the factory? I could pick you up at your hotel. Mount Lavinia, isn't it?'

She nodded, trying at the same time to slide her left hand forward so that she could peep at her watch. The car still shook with the throb of the engine. Laughton retained his grasp of the door.

'By the way.' Laughton suddenly stabbed a finger at the stewardess. 'April.'

'April?'

'You're an Aries girl. Early April. That's your birthday, isn't it?'

'Yes, But how did you know?'

'Ah! Just a hobby of mine. I'll tell you how it's done next time I see you.'

Reluctantly and only because Hannaker thrust a determined hand forward, Laughton tried the handle of the door. Showering drops of rain over the skirt of Miss Grey's uniform, Hannaker stepped inside.

'O.K., driver . . . *paliangpo*.' Laughton banged imperiously on the side of the cab. As the driver released the brake, he called, 'I'll come round for you one day.'

The revving engine snatched them from him. Hannaker turned round, caught a glimpse of Laughton, one hand still upraised, silhouetted against his own headlamps. He stood for a moment, apparently satisfying himself that they were all right, before getting back into his car. When Hannaker looked again, there were just two red rear lights rapidly dwindling into nothing.

'He'll find the bird flown if he does,' Hannaker remarked.

Miss Grey turned her face to him, brows raised. 'What was that?'

'I said that chap will find the bird flown if he comes to the hotel tomorrow.'

'Oh, was that what he said?' She shrugged. 'He's obviously not familiar with airline schedules.'

'He's also rather obviously taken with you,' Hannaker said, thinking how odd and unused and old-fashioned the words sounded, like articles taken from some dusty attic.

Miss Grey shrugged and said nothing, her body swaying slightly to the rough movement of the taxi over the road, her eyes fixed on the hypnotic sweep of the wipers over the drenched windscreen.

On either side the jungle was thinning. The sky to the left glowed like a drowned sunrise with the reflected lights of the airport. Hannaker was instinctively aware that the dwindling journey was for him an opportunity gone.

23

Yet all he could think of to say was, 'I thought he was a bit odd.'

She grinned. 'Why? Because of what you said before? That he seemed taken with me?' Her repetition of his outdated phrase refreshed it.

He shook his head. 'No, I didn't mean that.'

'I know you didn't. Maybe,' she frowned thoughtfully, 'because he made it a bit obvious?'

Hannaker was surprised by her perception.

'But then,' she added judiciously, 'I think he's English but not English. A cosmopolitan, eh?' She smiled sideways at Hannaker, and meeting his sombre stare, turned her eyes back to the windscreen. 'More Sinhalese than the Sinhalese.'

She interrupted her assessment of Laughton to tap the Chinaman on the arm, and point out the great green stalks of the threshold lights, indicating that any moment now they would be turning in through the airport gates.

'That kind usually are,' Hannaker said. 'Like converts.'

'But he's a good man. Very kind, apparently. You saw that. He's got tremendous influence here.'

Hannaker forebore to say that if he had enough money to hand around the influence would be automatic. With a great jerk of the steering wheel the taxi wheeled round into the pro-mised entrance. Water spurted up on either side of them. A policeman inside a glass booth raised his white-gloved hand to his Australian-type slouch hat, but remained in shelter.

'Well, we're not too late.' Miss Grey peered at her watch. 'We have a full passenger list. I might not see much of you, Mr Hannaker. Hope you enjoy the trip.'

They were slowing up now in front of the flight of concrete steps that led up to a new terminal building.

'Hope you enjoy your trip to the factory.'

'If I go.'

'I expect you will.'

Porters hurried to collect their baggage. The taxi doors were opened. The Chinaman and his impedimenta were assisted out.

'Would you mind,' said Miss Grey, glossy stewardess smile lacquered back on her face and with something that sounded to Hannaker like relief in her voice, 'checking in immediately at our Traffic counter? This is where I leave you.'

From his office window opposite, the British Oriental Airways Station Manager watched the emergence of the old taxi out of the rain-filled darkness, and let out a long sigh of relief.

The last twenty minutes of his fifty-year-old life had been fully occupied with fretful complaints that two passengers were missing and frantic inquiries from Catering about the where-abouts of the Chief Stewardess. The previous two hours had been fully occupied with the service from London which Captain Dewhurst had brought in and handed over to Captain Mason to take on to Hong Kong. Forty passengers disembark-ing, fifty-one passengers embarking, incoming crew and slip-crew milling around, Dewhurst in one of his pale bloodless nit-picking moods over the slowness of Ceylon Customs, had hardly laid the foundations for smoking a quiet pipe of peace.

It was always the same at Tallaputiya. The least thing that went wrong—and he heard about it. Delegate—that's what they had emphasized at his managerial course, and being a precise and careful student, delegate was what he had tried hard to do here in Tallaputiya. But delegate in theory and delegate in practice he had found were two different things. Anything he delegated had a habit of boomeranging back, inflated by inaction or wrong action.

That was why there was always around him a sweet-smelling aura of mint, and why his waste-paper basket contained numerous small rectangular pieces of opaque wrapping paper.

Digestif Rennies, said the packet which now again he reached for, *quickly relieve indigestion, acidity, heartburn, flatulence, dyspepsia, biliousness.*

He was conscious that none of these disorders actually described his own condition, but nevertheless gratefully he unwrapped another tablet and slipped it in his mouth.

The round wire-meshed loudspeaker on the wall above him suddenly erupted into a crackling waterfall of slow drawling English.

'. . . Whisky Echo crossing the coast in cloud at Flight Level 140. Estimating Tallaputiya at 13.45 GMT. Request clearance to descend.'

And then, the high-pitched over-quick reply from the Sinhalese controller. 'Whisky Echo clear to descend to cross Tallaputiya Beacon at 10,000. Wind . . . south-west twenty-five knots . . . visibility one mile in heavy rain . . . altimeter setting 994.'

'. . . altimeter 994.'

Reeves looked at his watch and saw that he had at least half an hour. It would take Captain Coates ten minutes extra to bring the 707 down through the bad weather on instruments. In spite of the slowness and inefficiency of his Sinhalese staff, in spite of the waywardness of passengers and the pranks air crews got up to, he had again succeeded in assembling fifty-one London-bound souls in nice time to connect with the incoming jet-liner from Hong Kong. He swallowed his Rennie thankfully, and taking a large white handkerchief from his uniform pocket began as delicately as a woman with a powder puff to dab at the round globules of perspiration on his round pink face.

It was easy to see why his nickname (intended affectionately, for he was basically kind) was *Kala*, the Sinhalese for pig. For a pig was what he looked like. Not the dirty farmyard variety, but one of those immaculate pink jolly effigies that smile from grocery windows advertising plastic boiled ham and tasteless sausages. He had a bunchy wide-nostrilled nose, and small blue eyes which blinked very rapidly when he was worried, which was nearly all the time.

He had been in Oriental Airways ground service for twenty-five years, almost all of it in developing countries in Africa and Asia, and the experience had made him put his head in the sand. 'I never saw fit to ask,' was his favourite expression. It stemmed partly from a lower-middle-class upbringing with an expectancy of being told what to do. Partly these days it stemmed from a genuine fear of what he would find out if he did.

For developing countries were particularly touchy, and you

26

had no protection from your own country if you or your subordinates did anything tactless. Her Majesty's Government was too busy washing itself clear of the stain of colonialism to risk the slightest allegation of racism. You just didn't ask questions like why none of the plumbing worked in the newly built terminal in the Tonjit Islands, why the taxi service in Palang was run exclusively by government ministers. Like the three monkeys, you kept your ears covered, your mouth shut, and your eyes closed. Otherwise, Oriental Airways might find its licence to operate from such countries in considerable jeopardy.

At the same time, the experience gave you a considerable insight into why practically every developing country that had gained independence had had to end up with a dictatorship, and usually a military dictatorship at that. Of course Ceylon was different. Reeves liked the Ceylonese. With their brown eyes and their black hair they were amongst the most handsome races in the world. They were pleasant to deal with, and he could have forgiven them almost everything—the inefficient telephone service, the execrable trains, the holes in the road disarmingly explained as "sleeping policemen to wake up car drivers,' the radio system which would have been more effective in the hands of the town criers, even for so unaccountably building this new aerodrome so close to the hills—if only they would stop the in-fighting.

This was his second tour in Ceylon—the first was ten years ago during the massacres between the Tamils and the Sinhalese. Of course things were better now, but the animosity, as he knew only too well, was still there. The Tamils were still in the lower-paid jobs like tea planting. The aristocracy and the politicians and the big landowners were mainly of the race of Sinha the Lion.

They practised different religions too—the Tamils were Hindus and the Sinhalese Buddhists—which didn't help. He had to be very careful with his local stewardesses to get them to do their job amicably and keep the peace. But at least Ceylon still had a democracy of a sort. Inefficient though it might be, there was still no dictator in sight. There were times when

Reeves privately considered that for Ceylon's own good (and the world's) a dictator might be no bad thing. To make the quite incomprehensible wormy wrigglings of Sinhalese the number one language instead of the internationally understood English might satisfy nationalistic yearnings but was fatal commercially. And astrology and fortune-telling might be all very well in women's magazines, but to bring it into running the country was something else altogether, and though Reeves disliked the English Sunday as much as the Ceylonese, to change it into a movable weekly rest called Poya-day that depended on the erratic moon calendar so that one was never exactly certain of when it was, seemed altogether the height of lunacy.

'. . . Whisky Echo reporting over the beacon at 10,000. Request clearance to make an instrument landing system approach.'

'Tower to Whisky Echo . . . cleared for an ILS approach to runway 28. Wind twenty knots, gusting thirty. You're number one to land.'

There was a pause. Then Captain Coates' voice from the aircraft, irritable and quicker.

'Hey—this thing's deteriorating, isn't it? Coming down in buckets up here. What's the latest visibility?'

'Latest visibility . . . ?' A long, long hesitation. Then: 'Wait!'

'Hell . . . d'you think I'm at a bus stop? I want the visibility *now!*'

A fearful thought pierced through the pink skin of Reeves's forehead. Immaculate pink fingers with perfectly clean lighter pink nails reached for the Rennies. Coates was going to divert! He was going off to land at his alternative, Madras in Southern India! And as it was one of these special flights—they were particularly worrying, what with the precautions and the police and so on necessarily laid on since the contract started one month ago—there would be even greater problems and confusion.

Looking at his watch, he saw there was no time to wait for the Tower to produce the visibility—he would have to go and see that his staff were not snarling up the boarding passengers.

He crossed his fingers, slipped another Rennie into his mouth and two more as emergency rations into his tunic pocket, and left his office for the main Passenger Hall.

From the British Oriental Airways Traffic counter, Hannaker watched the typically European figure come into the chrome and glass and polished wood of this temple for air passengers.

Airports, he reflected, like the poor were the same the whole world over. Except for the brown faces, the soft slip-slop of bare feet, the preponderance of saris over suits and dresses, these long lines of counters, the uniforms, the metal-and-antiseptic smell, the Tannoy, the familiar initials BOAC, TWA, PAA, KLM could have spelled Orly, London, Kennedy, Montreal instead of Tallaputiya. Even this Station Manager who had now stopped to talk to him could be duplicated a hundred times in the airports of the world. That same effortful calm enamelling the pink anxiety of his face, that same false charm of the inquiries put on as automatically and as meaninglessly as a gramophone record.

'Been in Ceylon long, sir?'

'Precisely six hours.'

'Oh, I see!' The same standard laugh. 'Just in transit. It is rather a bore hanging around, isn't it? But not long now.'

'How long?'

'Oh, just a few minutes. He's overhead now.'

'You don't reckon this stuff,' Hannaker jerked his head in the direction of the rain pouring over the window, 'might make him divert?'

'Oh no, sir, no, sir, no!' said Reeves fearfully and vehemently. 'We'll get you back to London dead on time.'

'Good.' Hannaker smiled.

'Got an important engagement in London, have you, sir?'

'Not really. Just a spot of leave. First for quite a few years.'

'Where?'

'Scotland. The Tay. Trout fishing.'

'There are some excellent trout at Nuwara Eliya,' Reeves said, automatically advertising the Company's package holidays. 'You should try a holiday here one day. And now, sir, you've been cleared at the Traffic counter, have you? I wonder if you would mind going on to Passports.'

The Station Manager had already left without waiting for a reply, busy sheepdogging his other sheep into the correct pen. Humping his briefcase in one hand, and his panic-bag in the other, Hannaker joined the queue at Emigration, waited patiently while his passport was interminably examined, got his Customs clearance, thus finally winning his certificate from the Sinhalese traffic girl—the Embarkation Card that enabled the bearer to proceed into Limbo, where duty-free liquor was available, where music softened the sound of the monsoon rain outside, where the doors were locked between Heaven and Earth.

Once inside, Hannaker surveyed his fellow travellers on Flight BA 708/13: three tall Englishmen, pale as their light-weight suits, a high-caste Tamil lady, cool in a rich golden sari, the round red mark of the Brahmin between her carefully plucked eyebrows, her husband small and incongruous beside her in western clothes: a Sinhalese husband and wife and five children, their skins lighter than the Tamils, two Nigerians in traditional white robes, a Turk in a fez, three shrouded Arabs, and a bunch of American tourists gathered round their guide.

Self-consciously, they all waited. Nobody said anything to anyone else. Even the children were quiet. More to encourage himself than anything else, Hannaker murmured to the Chinaman, 'Not long now!'

The Chinaman smiled inscrutably.

Hannaker lit a cigarette, walked over to the window, and stared out into the rain-filled night. High on the wall above he could hear the click of the electric clock.

'Waiting is always difficult, is it not?' An elderly woman with powdered cheeks and bright blinking eyes spoke to him in thickly accented English. Dutch, Hannaker guessed.

'The worst part.' No, that wasn't true. He had found waiting unbearable only since that Sunday afternoon. Before then, he had always told Margaret that he had a system for waiting. Very masculine and superior. If you're worried about

30

someone, give them a bit of time. Another ten minutes, another half hour and if they don't turn up, then *do* something.

That's what he'd done that Sunday afternoon, when she'd just gone down to the village to catch the post. Given her another ten minutes. Another ten. Then just ten more. He worried too much, Margaret always said. She wouldn't believe his excuse that he felt like a walk. He had sat at his desk imagining her laughter. 'No, you weren't just going for a walk. That I refuse to believe! You! On Sunday? You imagine things. What on earth do you suppose could have happened? On a peaceful Sunday afternoon?'

In the end, he had waited forty minutes and then begun the two-mile walk up the lane. He had his excuse, his smile even on his lips, just waiting for the little white car to come zooming round every bend of the lane. Till that last one. Before he'd seen anything, before he'd turned that corner, he had known. What was it? A voice encased in surrounding silence? A man's sob? The green hedges muffling something? Or had it been telepathy, a sixth sense?

'Are you going home, too?'

The Dutch lady again. The same use of home as all expatriates have. Husband was probably in tea or oil and they would be going back into the bosom of a big family in Amsterdam. Hannaker forced his mind back to the present.

'Yes, I'm going home.'

'We've been away five years. One gets impatient.'

'Of course.'

'He's later than ever.'

'Just a few minutes.' I'm beginning to sound like that Station Manager, Hannaker thought. The man had said exactly those same words how long—he looked at his watch— nearly half an hour ago.

'One wants to say *do please hurry*.'

'Yes!'

'Not that it does any good.'

'No.'

A normal instrument landing would only take about fifteen minutes at the most.

'It's very bad out there.' The careful smile, the unhurried voice did not match the anxious expression in her eyes. 'You don't think he won't be coming?'

'Well——' Hannaker began uneasily, conscious that diverting was exactly what he thought the 707 captain had done. 'You can't see much and he may think Madras——'

'Madras . . . no, no, no! He will be coming here . . . to Tallaputiya!' A sing-song up-and-down voice chimed in the conversation as the Sinhalese husband joined them. 'He will be landing here . . . that is for certain! Tallaputiya is very up to date. The pilots like it very much . . . very much indeed.' There was a sudden flash of strangely white palms as though the Sinhalese was showing there was nothing hidden there. 'Good runways, everything to hand, you know. We have just built Tallaputiya . . . specially for Jumbo Jets.' It was clearly very much a matter of local pride. 'Oh, he will be coming in for us, all right . . . I can promise you that!'

'But the weather?' said the Dutch woman.

'The weather?' The Sinhalese looked astonished. 'It is always like this in Colombo in south-west monsoon. We get as much rain here in two hours'—clearly here was another example of local pride—'as you do in England in half a year. We are used to it, you see.'

'But how will the pilot be able to see?' persisted the Dutch woman.

'Tallaputiya is the finest airport in the world. Tallaputiya——'

The Dutch woman stared disbelievingly at the windows, at the misty darkness and the rain sluicing down over the glass.

'I can see nothing.' She shrugged her shoulders and sighed.

'Oh, but the pilot doesn't need to see, lady.' The milk-chocolate-coloured hand went shoulder-high and began to descend slowly in front of them like a conjuror's wand. 'He will be following the radio beam. His instruments will tell him everything.'

'Well, I wish they would tell *us* something,' said the Dutch lady with sudden asperity. 'Here we have been waiting for over an hour and nobody has told us anything.'

'Airports are the same the whole world over,' Hannaker said.

'Except Tallaputiya,' said the Sinhalese.

In this glass-lined no-man's-land, the passengers went on talking, snoozing, reading, smoking—every now and then looking at their watches and shaking their heads.

Ten more minutes went by. Then another ten.

Hannaker swore under his breath, cursing the monsoon, trying to burn out with irritation a curious sense of apprehension. Someone by now should have told them *something*. He knew only too well the discomfort a diversion at this stage could create for the passengers. Being shunted around here and there, being asked to 'rest' in the lounge, being given free and flustered meals, apologies and the odd drink if they were lucky.

Any moment now the Tannoy would break its silence to say *British Oriental Airways regret to announce . . .*

But there was nothing. Even the murmur of voices around Hannaker seemed to die down. He walked over to the locked door through which he had come and was just going to address another remark to the lady from Holland when something about the scene on the other side of the glass struck a chilling chord in his memory.

Momentarily in the long bustling Passenger Hall, life had halted. For a fraction of a second, the figures in there were preserved as though in isinglass. Now there was no sign of the Station Manager, but a traffic officer sat with a telephone receiver half-way to his ear. A cream-faced traffic girl was stopped dead in the middle of a mincing step. Sinhalese porters stayed still as stone statues. An engineer officer stood petrified at the counter. Then, like a jammed movie reel abruptly re-started, everyone began talking, running, waving their arms. Even through the thick glass and the sound of the storm he could hear the note of high shrill voices.

Hannaker knew then. Just as he had known that Sunday afternoon.

He put up his hand to cover his eyes. An English summer

hedge merged in his mind with the dripping jungle beyond the airport. Like a child's puzzle, somewhere beyond them both the timeless horror waited. Here is a pretty scene, see if you can spot the missing articles. Tommy's whistle, Mary's slipper, the wrecked car, the broken aircraft. Hannaker dropped his hand and looked around him. The other passengers were still grumbling amongst themselves. One or two had walked over to the window. The Sinhalese paterfamilias was drawing a lion with his fingertip in the condensation on the glass. The Dutch woman was resting her head on her husband's shoulder, her eyes were closed. Hannaker said nothing to any of them. Only the Chinaman, silent, detached, seemed to notice Hannaker walk over to the other door—the one that gave access to the aircraft ramp—open it, and slip out into the rain and the darkness.

Seeing a uniformed official, Hannaker called out, 'What's happened?'

'Please, sah . . . nothing.' Under the dripping peak of a cap, a face forward, eyes wide, glistening cheeks slack with the same contagious touch of horror. 'Just slight delay.'

'Where did it crash?'

'Nowhere, sah. Just very slight delay.'

Angrily Hannaker pushed past him. Head down against the wind, splashing through invisible puddles, he began running towards the main entrance.

Behind him, high above the sound of the storm, came the wail of an ambulance siren. He turned, rushed out in the path of the yellow headlamps, waving his arms. It swerved past him, sent a wave of black water over his legs, and disappeared, its blue light blipping and fading, its klaxon mingling with the sob of the wind. Hannaker ran on till he reached the lights of the main entrance. A bell sounded and a fire-engine crystallized in glittering raindrops skidded out round the corner ahead of him.

The car-park was deserted, except for the same ancient taxi that had brought them here, the driver curled up quietly in the darkness with his head on his chest.

Hannaker jumped in beside him. The slamming of the car door woke the driver who automatically began chanting,

'Colombo thirty rupee . . . Mount Lavinia Hotel twenty rupee,' and then recognizing Hannaker, stared at him uncomprehendingly.

'See that van?' Hannaker pointed at the red tail lights of another ambulance fast disappearing in the rainy distance. 'Follow it!'

The Austin shuddered into protesting life, jittered forward into the night, slipped sedately along the drive, skidded out into the main road—and began slowing up.

'Mount Lavinia Hotel, sah?'

'Follow those lights!'

'No lights now, sah.'

'*That* way!'

The taxi went swishing along the road which was now a river. The headlights reflected against a glassy wall of water. The driver slowed.

'Hurry!'

'Where to, sah?'

They had come to a cross-roads. Hannaker made a calculated guess and said, 'Right.'

Ninety-nine to one the 707 had crashed on the approach, probably dead in line with the runway—an undershoot, the cause of so many fatal landing accidents. Following the lead-in lights—Hannaker could see one on its pole above a dark bush of rhododendrons—was the best way, like a tracker following spoors or blood, of being guided to the crash.

That road was a dead end. Turning round again, back to the cross-roads they went, this time taking the road ahead. This one was better. It more or less followed the lead-in lights, before curving round to the left.

'Follow those lights!' Hannaker pointed to another white muzzy blob on the top of a pole.

'Sah . . . no road.'

'Then keep as close to them as you can!'

The rain, pouring down, enclosed them in a dome of glass. Along the side of the road the long necks of palm trees, flamingo-like, swayed and twisted, tossing the feathers of their huge leaves. A huddle of brown palm-thatch houses, dark and

35

empty except for a golden paraffin flare flickering over betel nuts and mangoes, momentarily seemed to shake itself visible, then slid back into the rain.

As though in a black maze, the taxi turned, circled, accelerated, braked, went forward again, slowed down, stopped.

'Mount Lavinia Hotel, sah?'

'Those lights. I said follow those lights!'

'No lights, sah.'

'Nonsense . . . there's two over there!'

'No road, sah.'

Hannaker looked at his watch. It must have been at least an hour ago since the aircraft crashed. They had been milling around for well over an hour. At this rate and in this rain, they would go on all night. Help would have reached the aircraft a long time ago—it was difficult to see what use he could be. He was on the point of telling the driver to go back to the airport when just round the corner on the left, he saw a white smudge come glittering out of the dripping black and green of the forest, and belting down a rough road, its light flashing, its klaxon wailing, an ambulance skidded round onto the road, and then at full speed went hurtling towards Colombo.

'There we are, driver . . . up there!'

'Bad road, sah.'

'Go on!'

'Holy place, sah!'

'Hurry!'

'Sacred to Skanda, sah.'

'And quickly.'

Reluctantly, the front wheels of the taxi angled over to the left. Very slowly, the springs banging, the taxi proceeded over the bumps and dips of a rocky unmade way through the jungle. Hannaker was aware that the road was going upwards, towards a small hump—a hillock with trees on the top of it, the most likely place for an aircraft to crash on approach. Begonia bushes, aramantha plants and thornweed scraped against the side of the taxi, making the driver hesitate.

'Go on, man! Go on!'

The track itself in the darkness reared and fell; red sand

swept down in runnels of brown water; pools splashed up mud as the wheels lurched forward.

The driver started a spiel of Sinhalese, punctuated by the one recognizable word *temple*. And then hopefully, 'Mount Lavinia Hotel?'

'Go on!'

Tilting and groaning, splashing and skidding, the taxi jerked on upwards till, rounding a corner, suddenly the headlights reflected on a long white-washed wall. Hannaker could see pillars beyond it, a courtyard and a small bell-tower. High on a rock face opposite was carved amongst the mosses and lichens a gargoyle frieze of gods and devils, under which grew bread-fruit and paw-paw trees, their fat fruits glistening in the electric rain.

'Sah . . . *look* . . .'

The driver's indrawn breath broke off into a frightened sob. He pointed over to the left, away from the temple, where the whole forest was alight and glowing under water. Weird blue-white beams flared through a glowing lacework of incandescent green. Red lights bobbed. The wet sky above the melting green was fingered with lights, through which figures ran back-wards and forwards, flickering like smoke shadows. Bathed in the combined headlamps of ambulances and fire engines, a huge aircraft glittered silver like some enormous insect clawed down from the sky.

The 707 lay half on its side, its back broken, the starboard wing tilted high, the port wing twisted underneath the fuselage, the left engines crumpled almost flat. Scatterings of tail-plane, wings, doors and windows like bits of Christmas tinsel hung high in trees that still stood on either side of an enormous swathe cut out of the forest. Firemen stood by with hoses, pouring foam over the fuel tanks, Sinhalese officials shouted, stretcher bearers were bringing out shapes covered in woollen blankets—while high above everything, jumping and swinging from branch to branch, frightened monkeys squealed and gibbered.

'Christ!'

Hannaker jumped from the taxi and ran over to the aircraft

main door. He was just going below its crumpled metal lintel, when an arm came out from the darkness, barring his way.

'What are you doing here?'

Hannaker turned and saw the same pink perspiring face under the uniformed cap that he had seen in what now seemed another world, centuries ago.

'How did it happen?'

'Passengers,' Reeves went on, rain dripping from the peak of his hat, 'are not allowed.'

'Oh, for God's sake...' Hannaker could feel his heart hammering so fast he could hardly speak, while this man appeared almost on the point of asking for his Embarkation Card. 'I've come to help.'

'The authorities——'

'I'm a Ministry accident investigator.'

'Even so, until the Ceylon government ask——'

Hannaker had begun to push past the Station Manager, when Reeves said, 'They've got everybody out.'

'Alive?'

'All dead.'

'How many?'

'Eighty-one.' Reeves paused. 'They're in the temple now. Ambulances are taking them to the Colombo mortuary.' He said the words listlessly, as though all the little worries of his everyday work had been crushed to nothing by this huge disaster, so that he too seemed hardly alive. He wasn't even chewing his usual Rennie. He couldn't. In spite of the drowning rain, his own mouth was dry and parched. 'Nobody can help anybody now.'

Hannaker was still trying to get inside the aircraft, while Reeves was still barring his way.

'You mustn't go in without authority.'

'But I told you ... I'm an accident investigator!'

'Seneratne wouldn't like it. He's the Ceylon aircraft accidents man.'

'It's vital to check things *immediately*!'

'He's been here already and got the Flight Recorder. That'll tell us what happened.'

Seeing that Reeves was quite adamant in maintaining the regulations, Hannaker allowed himself to be led away from the aircraft door. He was aware only of a stunned paralysis, beyond consciousness and pain. He could no longer feel the beating of his heart or the wet cling of his clothes. He followed Reeves through the rain to the steps that led up the rock to the temple.

'This is the Bharratu shrine,' Reeves said. 'Holy of Holies for the Tamils of Ceylon.'

'My driver said something about Skanda.'

'The temple's dedicated to Skanda, the local reincarnation of the god Siva.'

The steps were shallow and whitewashed—cut in the grey lichen of rocky outcrop. There were sixteen of them, leading to a wooden gate on which were carved five-headed cobras and devil-dancers in high headdresses. Beyond was a small court-yard, in which grew a single temple tree or frangipani and further away was the shrine itself, its plain verandah supported by stone pillars. Flares were burning at the entrance, spluttering in the heavy rain.

When they reached the verandah, Reeves gestured to Hannaker to remove his shoes. On wet stockinged feet they went across the rough earth into the vestibule beyond, lit by a single oil lamp, its light flickering over the walls, bringing life and movement, it seemed, to the murals of temple girls, their big breasts bare, their brown arms and ankles fettered with brass bracelets, appearing to be dancing in their ornamental flaring skirts.

A thick cloud of incense smoke enveloped them as they entered the temple. Partly because of this, partly because the only light came from tiny candles set in little saucers of votive offerings, betel leaf, dried fish, chillies, meat and rice, gold ornaments and coins, all Hannaker could see at first were grey shadows moving.

Then his eyes began to get used to the darkness.

Hannaker had been nerving himself, but even so, as slowly he began to see, the sight still caught him vulnerable and unprepared.

High above everything, carved out of living rock were the

39

Hindu Trinity of Brahma the Creator, Vishnu the Preserver and Siva the Destroyer. And painted on the wall opposite in egg-bright glaze were the eight positions of the Kama-Sutra above the carved marble column of the *lingam*. On the left sat Ganesh, the god of wisdom, elephant trunk arched over pot-belly, large stone eyes wide open and protruding. And beneath the carvings and the paintings—as still as the idols themselves —were the rows of bodies covered in gay woollen blankets from the aircraft.

Creation and dissolution, the spirit of sex, life and death were here captured and crystallized.

'This is the main hall,' Reeves said, 'Skanda is kept behind that gold screen. Only the priests are allowed.'

In between the rows a solitary figure in a cloth, a saffron string hung with charms round his neck, moved slowly—head bowed, open palms held tightly together, lips moving in prayer. No hint of surprise or terror or weariness at his task showed in his bearing. Only a calm acceptance of all the night had brought.

'The Brahmin . . . high priest of the temple,' Reeves whispered, following Hannaker's sombre gaze as the holy man completed one row, turned and began walking down another.

The single flickering lamp flung his shadow on the uneven wall, now pointed and demoniac, now rounded, shrunk and gentle, a nurse ministering to the rows of shrouded bodies, who seemed in this darkness simply to be asleep. The heavy fumes of incense, the reek of the smoking candles, subjugated for the moment the insidious smell of death.

Hannaker felt dizzy. The weird scene spun. Reality trembled, re-shaped, faded, like the holy man's shadow on the wall. These strange unknown rites of death numbed his pain as no familiar ritual could have done. He could almost believe that the disaster had never happened, that all this was part of some incense-filled dream.

'Wouldn't have suffered,' Reeves said. 'Couldn't have felt a thing.'

Those familiar words to soothe the suddenly bereaved, to assuage grief, to cast out guilt, brought Hannaker back sharply to reality. To the last syllable exactly the words the police officer had used four years ago. Eyes averted from Hannaker's face, fixed on a flock of crows high above the tree tops. No pain, hardly a mark on her. Pretend it never happened. Dead yes, but doesn't know it. Killed humanely. Absolutely nobody's fault. . . .

But this *was* somebody's fault. The grief for Margaret multiplied eighty-one times in eighty-one homes. The words thundered in Hannaker's head. He was afraid he had shouted them out aloud. He glanced sideways at Reeves. But the Station Manager was surreptitiously counting the bodies that remained, working out the number of trips the ambulances had yet to make.

Unable to bear the place any longer, Hannaker turned abruptly and went back to the verandah.

He stood for a moment, staring out at the night. The pale reflection from the headlamps below still faintly illuminated the courtyard, silhouetting the stumpy branches of the temple tree, making the waxy blossoms glow like spent candles.

Hannaker rested his hand on the cool wet stone of the parapet. Gratefully he felt the rain stream down his face. He drew in a deep sobbing breath. But instead of the healing smell of wet earth and sodden leaves and kerosene, the air was heavy with the fragrance of the blossoms of the temple tree.

Hannaker shuddered. He felt very sick and tired as if he had been on a long journey and had finished up where it all began. He wished he could get the cloying honey-sweetness out of his nostrils. Far more potent than the charnel house from which he had just fled, more immediate even than the scent of an English hedge, those blossoms would now for ever crystallize for him the smell of death.

FIRST QUARTER

Pura Attawaka

'YOUR TEA, SAH! Good morning, sah! And a very good morning it is!'

The sing-song voice came to Hannaker down a tunnel of haunted sleep. At first he couldn't remember where he was. He half opened his eyes. The bedroom was filled with a pearly underwater light. Soft feet slip-slopped across the polished floor. There was a click, and the blinds went up, and the bowed figure of the Sinhalese bearer stood, one hand upraised, smiling like a genie revealing the brilliance of a calm hot morning.

Sunlight flooded the room, glittered on the silver tray beside Hannaker's bed, splintered on the bearer's brass buttons, staining the white linen of his jacket with rainbow drops.

Hannaker smelled the fragrance of fresh tea. He raised himself on one elbow. His muddied shoes were now clean and set neatly by his bed. His suit was pressed and dried. It hung on an old-fashioned wooden valet, waiting for the former Hannaker to get up and occupy it again. All was as before. Nothing remained of last night. Only the nightmare of fragmented pictures that had haunted his sleep.

'Shall I pour your tea directly now, sah?' The bearer stood by his bed again. 'Please?'

'Yes, thank you.'

He watched the sunlight touch the man's smiling face. The stewards on the 707 had worn white monkey jackets like that, still unmarked, as immaculate as his.

'Well,' Hannaker said, shutting out the vision of last night and taking the cup from the bearer's hand, 'the weather's certainly changed.'

'Yes, sah. Weather changes very quick here, sah, in monsoon time. But when rain comes, comes at night-time. Very lucky.'

The bearer hovered. 'You will be staying with us, please, another night?'

'No. 'Fraid not.' Hannaker was just about to say he hoped to be on the next flight out, when the bedside telephone rang.

Bowing, the bearer withdrew. Hannaker put down his cup and lifted the receiver.

'Good morning Mr Hannaker. And a very lovely morning it is, too. This is British Oriental Airways at your service.'

It was a conspiracy, Hannaker told himself, to blot out the irremovable visions of last night.

'We are pleased to tell you, sah, that we think we have secured you a place on tonight's Pan American departure. If you would call at our desk in the hall, sah, at your convenience of course, we should in minutes have the confirmation through.'

'Thanks. Will do.'

Hannaker put down the receiver, and got out of bed. Framed in the large window, the palms now were as still as painted stage prop trees. There were striped umbrellas on the hotel lawns and all along the pale crescent of sand. The sea was a straight pure mathematical line across a sky only one shade lighter than its own intense blue. It was all very eerie, Hannaker thought, pouring himself another cup of tea and sipping it thoughtfully. It was like having been inside a glass snowstorm scene which now some all-powerful hand had set the right and sunny side up. Padding through into the bathroom and turning on the shower, he decided that it was not his sort of environment at all. Just as well that he was getting to hell out of it.

Still frowning, Hannaker dressed and went downstairs. In the foyer, too, all was as before, except that the rain had gone. Now only sunlight assaulted the big windows. But within the bamboo blinds and filmy decorative curtains all was dusky and quiet. The same waiters moved quietly among the tables. The same voices as yesterday seemed to murmur. The same fragrance hung in the air.

This morning the doors to the garden terrace were open. White-clothed tables were set for breakfast. Coffee cups tinkled, trolleys were trundled. Tiny spurts of blue flame

43

flickered from the fresh fish grill. Hannaker paused by a marble and gilt console table filled with the morning papers, all discreetly folded. He picked up the *Ceylon Daily News*, and opened it.

British plane crashes at Tallaputiya. Sabotage suspected.

The old story, Hannaker thought bitterly, tossing it aside. He decided he wasn't hungry. He walked over to the Oriental Airways desk.

'Got my seat confirmed yet?' he asked the same little man behind the counter.

'Yes, sah. It is just through now. We are empowered to make the booking. Departure is at twenty thirty. Pick up here at eighteen thirty.'

'And the Chinese gentleman?'

The desk clerk smiled apologetically. 'He has cancelled his reservation, sah. He prefers, it seems, to go by sea.' And changing the subject quickly, 'You will have nearly the whole day here now, sah. Is there some entertainment we might arrange for you perhaps, sah?' He reached under the counter, produced a clip of highly coloured excursion pamphlets and licking his thumb, flicked through them. 'May we book you on a motorcoach tour to Ratnapura, city of gems? Or a tour of the ruined cities of Anuradhapura and Polonnaruwa? A trip to Sigiri? A taxi to Kandy? A visit to Peredeniya Gardens?'

A vision, alien and unreachable, of a day spent quietly with Melanie Grey tantalized him momentarily. Had it not been for the fact that she might come out of duty to a passenger or, worse still, pity for a lonely one, he might have asked the clerk to call her room number.

Instead he shook his head. 'No, thanks. Nothing. I've some work to do.'

He was about to move away, when like the crystallization of his own thoughts, he heard her name in the sing-song voice of the bell-hop. 'Paging Miss Grey. Miss Melanie Grey, please. Miss Grey wanted at Reception.'

Hannaker transferred his sombre gaze from the bell-hop in the white ducks and the pillbox hat towards the big reception desk. He already had a shrewd idea of whom he would see

44

there. Yet the sight of Laughton, handsome now in a cream silk suit, struck in him a chord of misery muffled, but resonant.

Laughton was leaning, apparently idle and relaxed, one elbow resting on the reception counter, chin cupped in his hand. Yet his eyes kept up a careful scrutiny of all possible entrances, as if he didn't want to miss the first glimpse of her, and there was beneath the surface carelessness a tension and concentration about him, like a gun-dog pointing.

Hannaker was still watching him when Miss Grey appeared. He knew she was there by the expression on Laughton's face. This time she came down the mezzanine staircase. She wore the same cotton dress as yesterday and her hair was loose. She looked paler, but she still walked with the same determined jauntiness down the last few steps into the foyer, beaming herself for some strange reason towards Hannaker. A thin mesh of sunlight piercing the bamboo touched her face and spangled her hair. She began to smile slightly, the colour came up in her cheeks as she walked towards the Oriental Airways desk.

Then she seemed to come within the orbit of Laughton's stare. She turned her head, and saw him. The smile and the colour deepened. She tossed her fair hair behind her shoulders and hesitated.

Sometimes, Hannaker thought, one's whole life could be contained in the bursting bubble of one second of time. He turned away and said to the clerk, 'Well, I'll be in the garden or the pool if there's any change in the booking.' When he glanced over his shoulder again, Laughton had come forward to claim the girl. The sound of her high heels touched off that sad muffled chord again.

Then behind him, he heard her voice saying, firmly but laughing, 'It won't take a moment. I must always tell the Company where to find me. What did you say the phone number was? Mahara 356. Fine! Then I'll go straight away and fetch my swim things.'

She put a hand gently on Hannaker's arm. 'I hear they've got you on the Pan Am flight, Mr Hannaker.'

Close to, her face had a transparent pinched-up look. There was a curious cold fixed shadow behind the blue eyes. But the bright smile was up like a lipsticked flag. 'I'm sorry about this.' And not giving him time to express any sympathy in return, 'I hope you have a good flight with Pan Am. I'm sure they'll look after you.'

'When are you going yourself?'

'To London? Not till tomorrow. So I don't suppose I'll see you again.' She put out her hand. 'I'll say goodbye.'

Before Hannaker had time to grasp it, Laughton stepped forward. Half humorously, half impatiently, he put his big hands on her shoulders and turned her round. 'No, please. It is very unlucky to say goodbye twice for the same journey. Now run along! Quickly, dear girl! Go and get your swim suit! Instead of wishing Mr Hannaker goodbye, we shall both wish him a smooth and happy departure.'

'No,' Melanie said in answer to Laughton's teasing remark as she settled herself into the sunwarmed leather of the white Porsche, 'You're wrong. Somehow I knew it was you as soon as I heard myself paged.'

The roof of the car was rolled back. Sunlight flooded down, bathing her in a comforting warmth.

'Mmm . . . I wonder.' Laughton shouldered his way out of his jacket, and draped it over the back of his seat. He adjusted the driving mirror with a fine precision—but first, she noticed with a faint distant amusement, examined his own face in it. A handsome face, she thought, glancing at his profile: heavy, inclined to be fleshy, but possessed of a certain distinction.

The engine leapt into life with a muted roar. 'What can I say about last night?' he said. 'Simply that we are not going to talk about it. Nor, Melanie, are we going to think about it. Except for just this.' His voice dropped to an earnest compulsive pitch. He has a great range of voice, she remembered thinking, as if he could communicate without words, just with tone. 'Only this,' he repeated. 'What is done *is* done. What has happened *has* happened.' He lifted his right hand from the wheel and sliced it down sharply sideways as if severing the head of time past. 'One thing the East has taught me is to

46

accept.' Then in an abrupt change of voice, laughing now and self-deprecating, one eyebrow raised in mock apology, 'Am I preaching at you?'

'Yes,' she said, and laughed.

'Nevertheless for today will you do just that? Accept . . . please . . . what I have planned for you?'

'I can think of nothing better.' She half closed her eyes and tilted her head back against the warm backrest. Sunlight glued her lids down. The mingled smell of mimosa and jacaranda was like some soporific syrup. She was filled with a sense of well-being, seductive and illusory.

Still with her eyes half closed, she watched Roy Laughton put the car into gear and slide it away from the portico, the tyres gently squealing. The white bulk of the hotel fell behind them as he nosed the car amongst the lorries and the bullock carts towards the long black ribbon of the coast road. The ocean breeze, sharp with the smell of the sea, cooled her cheeks. She felt a sense of guilty escape, as if Laughton were sliding her away from reality. From the misery, the tangled wreckage that lay only a dozen miles beyond the green flanks of Mount Lavinia.

'I'm not sure that acceptance is right though,' she said, opening her eyes suddenly. 'Otherwise,' her voice faltered, 'things would never be discovered. Then we wouldn't be able to stop them happening again.' She had a sudden vivid vision of Hannaker, shabby, sombre-eyed, pursuing his strange, lonely, meticulous destiny. She wanted for some reason at this inappropriate moment to cry.

'My dear serious little girl!' Laughton reached over and squeezed her hand. His touch was firm but curiously dry. 'Have you been pondering my stupid remark all this time?'

'Not really.'

'And I have confused you. Of course, do whatever you can. But accept those things which one can't do anything about.' He smiled, and gently but continuously pressed his foot on the accelerator so that the car leapt forward. And the sheer exhilaration of speed seemed to whip her misery away behind, along with the blossoms and the fallen leaves dried out now

47

after last night's rain. When he saw her smile again, he eased his foot up. 'You were still thinking about the crash though, weren't you?' he asked reproachfully.

'Then?' She sighed. 'Indirectly, yes.'

He shook his head, slackened speed still more till the engine was no more than idling, and coconut palms and thatched huts and wayside shrines passed by at a leisurely tourist pace. As if bowing to the inevitable, he added, 'Think about it if you must.'

'I don't want to really, Mr Laughton.'

'Oh, Roy, please.' He touched her hand comfortingly. 'But it still puzzles you?'

'No. Not even that.'

'They know what caused it, then?'

She had spoken to Dewhurst, the Flight Captain, last night, and remembering what he said, her face clouded over. 'I think they have some idea.'

Laughton wrinkled his brows, but said nothing. With an almost apologetic gesture he pointed out the sight of a fleet of catamarans, cupped in a blue goblet-shaped inlet some fifty yards to the right.

'One day we'll go down there and swim. The water's like glass and the reef's full of semi-precious stones. It's like Aladdin's cave.' And in almost the same sentence, 'Marvellous how they find out what causes a crash'—he snapped his fingers—'just like that!'

'Yes.'

'Was it some sort of mechanical trouble? Maintenance out here can be a problem.'

'I don't think so. They reckon the pilot undershot. He came down too low on the approach.'

Roy Laughton shook his head, frowning. 'Frightful business.' Then slowly, in a quiet, genuinely worried tone, 'Does this happen often?'

'No. But it *does* happen.'

'More than it should?'

'Well, I'm no expert. You should have asked Mr Hannaker that.'

48

'Hannaker?'

'The passenger with me in the taxi.'

'Oh, him! The chap we've just left?'

'Yes. He's an aircraft accident investigator.'

'Is he now? But he's on his way to England, isn't he?'

'That's right. Going on holiday, he told me.'

'How will he get there?'

'They've booked him on tonight's Pan Am flight.'

'You must forgive me for asking all these questions. I know so little about flying.' And then doggedly returning to the subject, 'It isn't likely to happen again, is it?'

She pressed her lips stubbornly together. 'No.'

'How can you be sure?'

'I can't.'

'There . . . you see! You can't be.' He sounded angry. 'It might.'

'But,' she spoke slowly and softly, 'it's something I can't do anything about. One of those things I must accept.'

'You could give up flying.'

At first she thought he was joking, but no, when he turned to her, his light grey eyes were very clear and direct and earnest. To change the subject, she asked him about the village they were just going through. 'Oh, nowhere of interest.' He continued to frown ahead, absorbed in his own thoughts.

'And where are we going? Am I allowed to ask?'

'The Sinhalese say,' he smiled sideways at her, 'one is allowed to ask anything. But one is not allowed to expect an answer.'

'Do I get one this time?'

'Certainly.' And sloughing off with an obvious effort his mood of anxiety, he announced with mock ceremony, 'I am taking you to my bungalow near Mahara for a swim in my pool and then to lunch.'

'Not the factory.'

'Not today, no. That can wait. Today we decided should be simple and quiet. We want you to see where I live. Only six miles away now. The most beautiful part of the island, I think. Besides,' he smiled shyly, 'I have instructions.'

'From whom?'

He opened his mouth as if he were going to tell her, thought better of it, and then once more taking his foot off the accelerator so that the car purred idly forward, said softly, 'You said you had heard about me? What had you heard?'

She shrugged her shoulders. 'Just what I told you. About the factory. And about you being a model employer.'

'Grossly exaggerated! I'm terribly strict. I run the place like the army. But that's what they need. They lap it up. No, I mean what did you hear about *me*?'

'That's all.'

'Nothing about my private life?'

'No. Except,' she hesitated, wondering if he were about to announce that in the bungalow she would meet up with a harem of wives, 'that you're more Sinhalese than the Sinhalese.'

He laughed. 'And now you wonder what that means.'

'Of course.'

'Alas for your scandal! It simply means I love Ceylon.'

'Oh.'

'Disappointed?'

'No . . . reassured. I thought I might find half a dozen females.'

'You're thinking of Mohammedans. And I haven't half a dozen. Only one.'

Melanie was suddenly acutely embarrassed. It had somehow never occurred to her that he might be married. 'Your wife?'

'No.' He smiled. 'But she was the one who insisted I bring you over. And at once. Now how can I describe her? The mistress of my household? My *apu*? My guardian angel? My private magician? My evil genius? My conscience?' He laughed and added softly, 'Ceylon itself, maybe.'

'I can't wait to meet her.'

'Nor can she wait to meet you. And not to tease you any more . . . she was my Ayah. She brought me up when my mother died. She is more to me than any mother could ever be.'

'And you told her we'd met last night?'

He paused to watch a red and green parrot swoop across the road and on to a branch of a wild rubber tree. 'No. She told me . . .' he smiled at Melanie's puzzled face '. . . she told me in fact before we met. As I said, she is my private magician. Everyone in Ceylon is a magician.'

'That is how you guessed my birthday?'

'Perhaps.' He covered Melanie's hand with his. 'But Ayah has her horoscope cast every week. Mine too, I suspect. Yesterday, it was foretold, I would meet my golden girl. Today, Ayah, too, wishes to meet her. As simple as that.' A deprecating smile curved his lips, but his eyes were untouched by it.

He more than half believes it himself, Melanie thought, wishing for the first time that she hadn't come. Then abruptly he laughed. A deep reassuring sound. 'Now my serious girl, don't take me *too* seriously.' He pressed his foot on the accelerator. 'We are going too fast for you to bale out now. And where but my place could you go? I tell you this only because Ayah believes it. And she does, I promise you. Out here they live in a different dimension to us. The Prime Minister himself, the politicians, big business men would take no decision without their horoscope. So why not my little Ayah? Why may she not have hers?' He sighed. 'Besides, it has stopped you thinking of last night, hasn't it?'

'Yes . . . it has.'

'And now we are here!'

He grinned at Melanie's raised brows. On either side was jungle. Ahead nothing but the narrow road curving away ahead.

'Wait and see!'

Impatient for her reaction he pressed his foot down. The Porsche covered the last mile in a flash, rounding the curve. Immediately ahead the road was barred by high double ornamental gates flanked on either side by stone pillars, surmounted by a carved figure of the lion of Ceylon—curling tongue, protruding eyes, forked tail stretched.

'Is this it?'

'Yes.' A teasing smile still hovered round his mouth. He

51

eyed her sideways as without unduly slackening his pace he drove forward. She put up a hand to shield her head from inevitable impact. But when the bonnet was a few yards away the iron gates suddenly swung open.

Laughing and covering her hand apologetically, Laughton said, 'One of the few advantages of knowing something about radio!'

'There she is now! On the bungalow steps! Can't wait to lay her hands on the pair of us!' Roy Laughton swung round the pink gravel sweep in front of the large white bungalow, and lifted his free arm to wave.

At the top of the verandah steps, dwarfed by the lemon tree in a stone urn beside her, stood a tiny barefoot Sinhalese woman, wrapped tight in a plain white cotton sari. Only the little shrunken face showed, the skin very cracked and brown, the mouth lost in a mesh of wrinkles. Were it not for the large liquid eyes, she might have been a mummy.

At the foot of the verandah was a paved patio inset with beds filled with flowers. Beside and behind the bungalow, Melanie glimpsed ornamental walks and arches and steps, the apex of a fountain just visible over a clipped orange bush hedge.

'You're right,' she breathed, 'this must be one of the most beautiful places on the island.'

But Roy was already out of the car, and striding round to open the door for her. Then holding Melanie's hand but keeping ahead of her, he ran lightly up the verandah steps, and with his free arm lifted Ayah off her feet, high in the air, and down again.

'There! I've done what you commanded me! You old dragon, you!'

Two little gnarled hands thrust out of the folds of the sari and cupped Laughton's face tenderly. The liquid eyes glittered. The lost mouth disclosed itself in a huge brown-toothed grin.

'Isn't he a silly boy, Miss?' Ayah spoke for the first time as Laughton set her down. The voice was husky and deep, the accent cultured. The little brown birds of hands fluttered over her sari, tweaking it into place, ripping back its folds. Then she took one of Melanie's hands in both hers. 'Welcome to Sinhala, my dear. It is very good to see you. I am sorry I didn't greet you first. It is the fault of this naughty boy. You must try to excuse him. I don't know why he behaves in this fashion.'

'Because he loves you, I expect,' Melanie said gently.

'Does he? Oh, perhaps. No, I really do not think so. Besides,' she tweaked an unsatisfactory fold in her sari straight, 'we love where we have to love, do we not?'

Over the tiny woman's head Roy winked at Melanie. 'What she means is that I am very spoiled and I do *not* appreciate her in the least.' He dropped his hand on to the ayah's shoulder.

'But then, Miss Grey, he was scarcely two years old . . . so everyone spoiled him. . . .'

'And now, dear Ayah, you have someone else to spoil. A guest. We are going to swim. We shall want towels in the changing-rooms. There . . . you will not have thought of that.'

Once again Roy winked at Melanie as the old woman bridled.

'They are already there, Master Roy.' Ayah clapped her hands. Immediately a smiling servant came across the polished tiles of the hall behind. 'Go with Master Roy to the changing-room, and collect his shoes and suit. I myself will go with you, my dear. It will be pleasant after all this time to have a little chat as we walk along.'

She still held on to Melanie's hand, leading her across the threshold into the hall. The little hard fingers had no warmth, no feel of flesh. They seemed to act like a metal cage. Like the iron gates clashing softly shut.

'After all what time?'

'After all the time when Roy has shown so little interest in anyone.' Ayah stared at Melanie boldly, and yet with a tiny flicker of approval in her eyes.

Melanie was glad when the old woman let her hand fall and began walking a little ahead of her across the tiles of the long hall. Brightly embroidered tapestries hung on the walls. Seeing

53

her staring at them, the old woman paused. 'These tell stories from our history. Master Roy is an expert.'

'He seems to be an expert on many things,' Melanie smiled.

'And so he must be,' the old woman inclined her head graciously, and moved on past glass-fronted rosewood cabinets filled with jade miniatures and ivory netsukes, little ebony tables holding silver bowls of exquisitely arranged flowers, gilt sofas upholstered in silk.

'It's all very beautiful,' Melanie said warmly. 'Those marvellous flowers. Did you arrange them?' She nodded towards a vase, Ming surely, filled with a mixture of roses, and frangipani.

'I did them in your honour. I hoped you would like them.' Ayah shot her a quick triumphant look, lowered her head again, and led the way down a flight of stairs at the end of the hall. The wall here was made of sliding glass panels, and opened on to a rear hall and another patio.

'Wait! Stay a moment.' Ayah stopped, then stood on tiptoe so that she could hook a lock of Melanie's hair in her forefinger. 'You are so fair.' She let it fall again. 'You must shield yourself from the sun. At first.' She opened a door on the right, disappeared for a moment and came back with a straw hat. 'Put this on, my dear. Master Roy would never forgive me if anything happened to you.' And when Melanie hesitated, 'Please. He has suffered so much in the past . . .'

Melanie did as she was told. The old woman nodded and smiled.

'You will notice the great heat from the flagstones,' she murmured, gliding ahead of Melanie on to the patio. It was edged by a low wall filled with some yellow flowers in thick bloom. More lemon trees in tubs flanked another flight of steps down to the sun terrace and the swimming pool. Tiny lizards, interrupted in their sleep, flickered along the flagstones and disappeared in the cracks of the wall.

'I see what you mean about the heat,' Melanie said, 'It's a complete sun trap.'

'That is how Master Roy designed it.'

'Don't you feel it hot on your feet?'

The old woman shook her head. 'Besides, I am not important now. I have done what I had to do . . .'

'You've been wonderful,' Melanie said warmly, thinking how inadequate her words sounded, 'Roy told me on the way here . . .'

The old woman paused in the shadow of a lemon tree, and looked earnestly up into Melanie's face, "Did he tell you that I brought him up?'

'Yes. He also told me you had been more than any mother. . . .'

'How foolish,' the old woman said sharply. She moved forward again, resting her hand on the head of another little stone Sinhalese lion that guarded the head of the steps. 'That is all done with. Now I think what a long way he has come from then. A little tin bath—that was all Master Roy had.' She began to descend the stone steps. 'His father was only a schoolmaster, you know.'

'I didn't know.' And because the old woman obviously wanted to talk, 'What kind of man was he? Roy's father?'

'Oh, a very nice gentleman. He was handsome. Like Roy. But timid. Not like Roy. Very religious. He came here from England with the Baptist Mission. Oh, I got on well with him. But *her* . . .'

Melanie walked down three more steps in silence. She was not sure how Roy would like these confidences. She felt disloyal for listening and yet too sorry for the old woman to stop her.

'Oh, don't think please, Miss, that I did not like her. I was devoted to her. She was a fascinating woman.'

'When did she die?'

'Die? I don't know. Is she dead at all? Maybe not! No one knows. She simply disappeared.' The old woman waved her hands wide and let them fall.

They had reached the sun terrace now, with the pool and changing-rooms at the far end. The sun flung tiny rainbow reflections from its surface over the marble flagstones of the terrace. But the depths of the pool were an indigo blue.

Uncertain of how to reply to Ayah's last piece of information,

55

Melanie made some remark about the pool. She watched their strange foreshortened shadows, Ayah's and hers, move like silhouettes on some old blue Chinese porcelain, down its depths, till they came to the changing pavilions—miniature white bungalows with big frosted windows and green striped blinds.

Ayah produced a key and unlocked the ladies' pavilion. 'It is necessary, I am afraid,' She held the door open for Melanie to precede her. 'Servants here do not have sufficient respect for property. Other people's property.' She closed the door, and stood with her back to it. 'That,' she added softly, 'was something *she* could not understand.'

'Who?' Melanie was about to walk into one of the cubicles, when Ayah said, 'There is no need. No one else is here. It is my privilege to help you.' She held out her hand for Melanie's holdall. 'Who? Why, Roy's mother of course. She could not deal with servants.'

Imperiously she crooked a finger, and Melanie began to unbutton her dress.

'Why did she disappear?' Melanie asked, embarrassed by the woman's glowing, assessing eyes on her.

'No one knows, my dear. Least of all me. But I remember it so well. Roy had just had his first birthday. And not very much for it, either. A few days afterwards there was a scene. One of so many, *I* thought. No one confided in me then. I was just a humble ayah. But one heard . . . things. She hated Ceylon. She wanted to go home. She said the servants laughed at her. She was even afraid of handling my Roy. If she did anything for him, she could not be trusted. Always, I had to watch her. I did everything for him, even before she left.'

'When did she leave?' Melanie stepped out of her dress, which Ayah took and smoothed, and hung carefully on a hanger. Then she glided behind Melanie. The hard little fingers struggled with the hooks of her brassière. They were as cold as beads.

'When? The day after the scene. She walked out of the bungalow. No one ever saw her again.'

'How awful!' Melanie folded her arms over her half-naked

56

body, as still with those glowing eyes on her, the old woman folded the brassière, and placed it on a table beside the dress.

'Mind you, there was a Bibby boat in the harbour then. Bound for England. They were easy-going men, those sailors. Maybe they took pity on a beautiful woman.' She held out her hand for Melanie's waist slip. 'For she was a beautiful woman. Though not as beautiful as you, my dear.' She studied Melanie with a curious cool dispassionate stare. Then she lowered her eyes.

'After that, of course, old Mr Laughton . . . I say old, and then he seemed old, though he could only have been about thirty-five . . . became quieter than ever. He did not hear when you spoke. A year later,' Ayah waited for Melanie to step out of her pants, 'he too was dead.'

She stood between Melanie and her holdall, eyes half closed, apparently half in a dream.

Melanie shivered. 'Could you pass my swim-suit, please?'

Slowly, reluctantly, Ayah unzipped the bag, took out the swim-suit, shook it and held it out by its straps.

Melanie took it hastily from her and began to put it on. 'What did he die of?'

'Meningitis, the doctor said, but often I wondered.' Ayah spread a hand, withered as some old parchment fan, across her left breast and sighed. 'A broken heart, *I* thought. Or perhaps he took poison. Who knows? After that . . . it was Roy and me. The school closed when Mr. Laughton died. So there was nobody here to help us.'

She stepped behind Melanie and pulled up the zip. A hand trailed the skin of Melanie's back.

'What did you do?' Melanie's eyes were fixed longingly on the sunlit rectangle of window.

'We went home to my village. Hambantota, just south of here. We lived in a palm-thatched hut. Roy and me. He went to the Buddhist school there. He speaks Sinhalese and Tamil as well as he speaks English. Ask him one day to tell you our glorious legends. You saw the lions on the gate when you came in. See now!'

She pointed down to where, entwined in the cream and

57

reds of the mosaic were the same stylized lions. 'He has taken them as his symbol.'

'Very suitable. The lion is the British symbol too.'

The old woman shrugged and took a hair-brush from Melanie's bag.

'May I, please?'

'No, thank you,' Melanie said, taking it from her firmly. 'I don't like anyone doing my hair.' The refusal seemed to please rather than irritate the old woman. As Melanie perfunctorily smoothed her own hair, she went on softly, 'Yes, he worked very hard. Master Roy. He never wasted time. Never wasted *anything*. After school, we moved to Colombo. He was apprenticed. I took in the D.C.'s dhobi. . . .'

'You have been very good to him,' Melanie said with finality and moved two steps towards the door.

But the old woman had not finished with her. 'Bathing pumps!' she cried, 'Did you not bring any? Master Roy always insists. Because of the tiny scorpions in the water, you understand? No, don't worry. There are several pairs always here in the cupboard.'

She is deliberately delaying me, Melanie thought, with an overwhelming feeling of claustrophobia. And then dismissed the idea as unjust. A garrulous pitiful old woman, no more, clinging to anyone who would listen to her. 'I take size four, if you have them. But really, anything will do.'

'There, I have some. Please sit down.' She knelt on the floor in front of Melanie. 'Oh no! Too large. Don't worry, please. There are many more.'

She laid the discarded shoes on the floor and picked up another pump. 'Now he has achieved much. Yet not so much, so his horoscope says, as he will achieve.' She made a business of trying to push Melanie's foot into a manifestly too small slipper.

'I feel like Cinderella,' Melanie smiled to hide her irritation.

'Who, please?'

'Cinderella. She was a poor girl in a western fairy story who married a prince. But first she had to get her foot into a glass slipper.'

The idea seemed to entrance Ayah. She slipped Melanie's foot into a third shoe, grudgingly admitted that it would do, and then sprang to her feet agilely, her strange eyes shining. 'That is what Master Roy one day will be. A ruler. A most powerful man. A kind of prince.'

'But I . . .' Melanie stood up and smiled. She began to say something about her not being his princess, thought better of it, and simply shrugged and walked to the door.

Yet Ayah seemed to finish her sentence for her. On the pretext of opening the door for Melanie she kept her little hand hard on the handle for the necessary moment. 'That, too, was in his horoscope.'

She opened the door. Like a prisoner released, Melanie felt the hot sunlight strike her face. Roy was sitting on the edge of the pool, his feet dangling in the water. Without turning his head, he shouted, 'Ayah, you old witch! You've been at it again! Telling your tales!' Normality, momentarily lost, returned.

He waited till the bearer had set little frosted bowls of paw-paw cubes decorated with acanthus leaves in front of them, and withdrawn before he spoke. Then smiling, 'So now, Melanie, you know all there is to know about me.'

Beguiled by a sense of well-being—the effect of the swim in the pool, lying in the sun to dry afterwards, iced drinks on the terrace, and now lunch tête-à-tête in the cool flower-scented dining room, she said lazily. 'No. Now I know a lot of facts about you. But I don't really know *you*.'

For a moment he said nothing. Spoon still poised, he sat staring at the cut-glass bowl in front of him. A sensation of something, disappointment, dismay, irritation, communicated itself to her as certainly as if he had spoken. Immediately she was concerned.

'And now I've hurt you?'

'Certainly not.' He lifted his eyes to her and smiled. 'I was simply thinking how extraordinarily hungry that swim made me. And wondering when on earth you were going to begin.'

59

'I'm sorry.' She picked up her spoon and swallowed a mouthful. 'I don't know why I said that.'

He ate his paw-paw, dabbed his lips and said, 'But I do.'

'Then tell me, please.'

'Because you are a very truthful person. And what you said was true. I am not easy to know. I have few real friends.' He spoke slowly and softly and yet with a dignity that was curiously moving. 'I walk alone.'

'And now I feel I do know you.'

He stretched his hand across the polished mahogany table. She put out hers. He touched her fingertips, still staring at her. His eyes glowed. Though they were cool grey eyes, unmistakably western, momentarily they seemed to acquire some of the lambent quality of Ayah's.

'Thank you for that.' He withdrew his hand. 'Sometimes it takes time. One's personality is overlaid. And now finish your paw-paw quickly. Soon you will be wanting me to take you back. And you have told me nothing about yourself.'

'There's nothing much to tell.' As she put down her spoon, he lifted a small silver bell and shook it.

'Is that because you are not so old as I?'

'No—just that it's all rather dull.'

'Tell me just the same. Nothing about you could be dull.' He smiled, and then as if on sudden inspiration, 'Or better still, shall I first tell you a little about yourself?'

'Go ahead. If you can.'

He paused while the bearer brought in a large silver tureen which he ceremoniously set in front of his master, and then put smaller dishes filled with brightly coloured titbits all round the table.

'First thing about you,' he rested a finger on the ornamental lid of the tureen, 'you are quite sure you are not going to enjoy this cranky native concoction. Even though,' he lifted the lid with a magician's flourish, releasing a heavily spicy aroma, 'it smells so good. But like a good little girl you're resolved to eat it up and say it's delicious.'

'I thought you said I was truthful,' Melanie protested, laughing.

'Mm. Yes. And so you are. On things that matter.' Roy served her out a small portion, which the bearer took from him and carried over to her. 'Now put a bit of everything from those dishes on top. That's the way.' He watched her benignly. 'Now taste. Well?'

'Delicious.'

He raised one eyebrow and sighed.

'Truly. As-on-things-that-matter delicious.'

'Good. I'm pleased. Mind, had you not said that, I would have had the *apu* thrashed. Not to mention this chap here. Is that not so?'

'Yessah.' The bearer nodded vehemently, smiling broadly.

'Michael is his name. I have given all my servants English names. And now, Michael . . . bring in the coffee and fruit and put them on the sideboard. Then leave us in peace.' Roy turned back to Melanie. 'So I was right about the first, wasn't I?'

'Perfectly. But that was easy. I'm not impressed.'

'All right. Let me see how I *can* impress you. Age, twenty-two. Single. Only child, as I am. Your father is a professional man. A doctor. No, on second thoughts, a lawyer.'

'Solicitor actually.'

'Same thing. In a small country town, not too far from London.'

'Can't you name it?' She made spectacles of her thumbs and forefinger. 'Or is your ESP a bit blurred on the map?'

He didn't laugh. 'ESP?'

'Extra-sensory perception.'

He remained quite serious. 'No. Here, I am unsure. I have never been to England.'

'Hindhead.'

'About thirty miles, is it?'

'Near enough.' She finished her last forkful of the savoury concoction, and smiled. 'I'm giving you full marks so far.'

'You went to a convent school. You thought you might go to university. You were rather good at English Literature. But even in this day and age, convents like their girls to be ladies. So . . .' he spread his hands like Ayah.

61

'Heavens! Am I as crystal-clear and square as that?' She drank some water thoughtfully.

'So instead you went into nursing. Yes?'

'Yes, damn it. Right again.' She pretended to frown. 'I shall believe in a moment that Ayah has been having *my* horoscope cast, too.'

'But of course.' He laughed as if it were a joke, but the laugh didn't reach up to his eyes. 'Then you found you couldn't rationalize suffering.' His voice lost its bantering tone. 'You can't yet as a matter of fact. You must. But that is by the way. So you joined British Oriental Airways. To see the world.'

'This,' she raised her glass mockingly 'is your life, Melanie Grey.'

'Ah, but it isn't! That's the point. Life for you is just beginning.'

He got up, walked over to the sideboard, and brought over the basket of fruit. Then, as he poured coffee, he asked lightly, 'Don't you ever get tired of being a human shuttlecock?'

'No. I love it.'

'Ah, but how d'you know you're *always* going to?' He put a cup in front of her, and then sat opposite her, elbow on the table, chin cupped in his hands, staring.

'I don't. But I love it *now*.'

'And that's enough?'

'I think so.' She stirred the coffee. 'After all, that's what we live in. The present.'

Softly he said, 'This narrow isthmus twixt two boundless seas . . . ?'

She finished for him, 'The past, the future, two eternities.'

He smiled. 'Eng. Lit. I was right, wasn't I?'

'Completely.'

'And there you have your answer. The past and the future are here *now*. But don't get me on to that. We're talking about you.' He pushed a dish of marzipan confections across to her. Don't you ever want to marry and settle down?'

'Of course.' Uncomfortably aware of the intensity of his stare, she said in a deliberately off-putting tone, 'When I meet the right man.'

'Ayah, the old witch, tells me you have already met him.'
Melanie raised her brows, drained her cup and put it down.
'Yesterday.'

His tone, his stare, the heavy scent of the table flowers, the
feeling of containment from the world outside, induced in her
an uncomfortable sensation. Her chest felt tight, the blood
seemed to beat in her head. She felt as if she were trying to hold
a foothold against the sweep of some powerful inexorable tide.

'I met a lot of people yesterday.' She spoke as lightly as she
could. 'I went down to the town. I played tennis. I met my
captain and crew. The Ops room people. Catering. My
passengers. . . .'

'For the *first time* yesterday.'

'That narrows the field of course.' She smiled determinedly.
'After the rains came.'

'Oh.'

Then suddenly he laughed, a lazy throaty sound. He put his
hand across the table and patted hers. 'And now you're
blushing. You are setting your mouth very stubbornly. You
are going to tell me that even so, you met many people for
the first time after the rains came. That charming Chinese
gentleman, the taxi driver, the man with the sad hound eyes,
what was his name? The accident investigator? All these and
many more besides me.' He laughed.

It was all a joke then. The world, slightly tilted, righted
itself again.

'How do you know all this?' She laughed with relief. 'Does
Ayah tell you?'

'Many people tell me many things.'

'But why about me?'

'Because you concern me.'

'But we've only just met.'

He sighed, and spread his hands. 'Have we? I wonder! Tell
me,' he leaned forward, 'haven't you ever felt that you've
been to a place before, even though in fact you haven't?'

'Occasionally.'

'Or met someone for the first time, and recognized that you
knew them.'

63

'Yes.' She smiled. 'Are you going to tell me why?'

'No.' He shook his head. 'All I can say is that time is a strange dimension. It's not an ever-rolling stream. We come and go within it.'

'Reincarnation?'

He nodded, without looking at her.

'Don't you, in that case, wonder who you were before?'

He said either 'I know,' or 'No,' she didn't hear which.

Then he sighed and stood up. He looked across at her, smiling. 'In a moment you will tell me that no matter how strange a dimension time is, you, dear girl, have to abide by it.'

She looked at her wrist watch. 'Heavens, yes. How long will it take us to get back?'

'An hour and a half.'

She smiled. 'Can't you slow up time?'

He replied quite seriously. 'I can't. Some Hindus believe they can.'

'Very useful. Especially in the airline business.'

A shadow crossed his face. 'Ah, we're back to that again.'

He came round the table, pulled out her chair for her, and dropped his hand on her shoulder. 'Shall you come again?'

'Yes, of course.'

'When are you off? Did you say tomorrow? Not a Hong Kong flight, I hope?'

'A 577 service. Colombo–Beirut–London.'

Still with his hand on her shoulder, he walked her across the hall on to the verandah. 'Can you try to keep off Hong Kong flights?'

'Why?'

He just shrugged his shoulders.

'Don't tell me Ayah knows something about those, too.'

'No. Nothing to do with Ayah.' He ran his free hand through his hair. He somehow looked very boyish. 'Now I'm just being the engineer, the British engineer. I don't trust the Chinese. There! Say it!' He gave her shoulders an affectionate squeeze as they went down the steps to the waiting car. 'That's where all my Eastern philosophizing falls down!'

64

He settled her comfortably in the seat and closed the door. 'Anyway, will you try?'

'I can't.'

He started the engine, and pulled the car round the sweep, accelerating smoothly up the drive. 'Well, will you tell me when you are going on one?' He touched her hand. 'Then I can light a candle or pick a temple flower or buy a charm?'

'It won't happen again,' she said, resting her head back and closing her eyes. 'I'm just thinking of the law of averages. Nothing complicated about time and coming in and out of it.'

She felt relaxed now and overpoweringly sleepy. She was acutely aware now that she had hardly slept last night. The last thing she remembered was the gates of the bungalow opening and shutting behind them. Then she must have dozed off. She was dreaming that she was walking through the grounds with Ayah and Roy. The grounds looked exactly the same, but everywhere they went the three of them cast a double shadow. That, Roy was explaining to her, was their past and their future fastened on their backs like the wings of an albatross.

She didn't wake till they reached the Mount Lavinia Hotel, and then only when Roy gently shook her shoulder.

'Was that awfully rude of me?' she asked apologetically, as they walked up the hotel steps.

'No. Very therapeutic.'

'I was dreaming,' she sighed. 'It was all your talk of time. . . .'

Smiling, she pushed open the glass doors of the hotel.

And then it seemed as if in fact she had slipped through some crack in time, back to the morning again. For there was Mr Hannaker, the eternal passenger in transit, standing exactly as she had left him eight hours ago, one arm on the counter of the Oriental Airways desk, holding a flimsy that looked like a ticket in the other hand.

He misread her expression as she and Roy Laughton advanced across the foyer.

He waved the flimsy. 'I've just had a cable. I'm to stay

where I am and investigate the crash.' He gave a funny apologetic smile at them both. ' 'Fraid you're not getting rid of me as easily as all that.'

The cable simply said *Stay put and solve. Logan.*

The Head of the Accidents Investigation Department had an office on the eighth floor and an almost aerial panoramic view of the Thames and southern London. John Logan had a complete disrespect of holidays and leave periods, combined with an unassailable belief in the capacity of his subordinates to come up with the right answer. That there would be other investigators coming to Ceylon—from the airline, the aircraft company, and possibly from the pilots' union—Logan was perfectly well aware, but such experts other than his own he would classify, along with foreign air-crash detectives, as well below the salt.

There could be no qualification and no argument. Hannaker had sent back the one letter *R*, and had then turned his mind on to making his professional plans.

The first thing he did next morning was to go down to the ILS hut directly in line with Runway 28, and speak to the officer in charge. No, there had been no evidence of malfunction either in the localizer or the glide path signals during the night of the crash. Twelve aircraft had landed before the incident, including Captain Dewhurst, and no one had complained. Immediately it was known the aircraft had crashed, the signals had again been tested. They had been perfectly normal—one of the technicians switched on while Hannaker was in the hut for him to be given full visual evidence—just like *that*. No, there had been no repairs, alterations or replacements of parts. Could the heavy rain have had an effect on the ILS signal? There had been stories that this could happen —the officer shrugged his shoulders—but he had never had actual experience of it. And why should it happen simply that one time?

After two hours' intensive scrutiny of the transmitter, Hannaker could find no evidence of malfunction, past or present, and he went along to the Meteorological Office to speak to the taciturn Canadian in charge.

He studied the landing forecasts given to Coates before his take-off from Kai Tak airport, Hong Kong: *wind south-west, eighteen knots, gusting twenty-five, visibility one mile in heavy monsoon rain, altimeter setting 998.* He then compared it with the actual weather conditions, measured ten minutes before the crash: *wind south-west twenty, visibility one mile in rain, altimeter 994.*

'Pretty well the same,' he commented. 'Coates knew what weather to expect.'

'Everyone knows what to expect in the monsoon period.' The Canadian shrugged. 'Especially just round here. Real catchment area . . . Tallaputiya. Annual rainfall more than a hundred and thirty inches.'

'What about down-currents in the storm?'

'With the wind coming in from the sea? No . . . definitely no.'

During the afternoon, he tackled the engineers. Whisky Echo had had its last eighty-hour check the day before it left London outbound. It had come through Tallaputiya the day before the crash on its way to Hong Kong. Nothing had been reported unserviceable, and it had simply been refuelled and had taken off. Hannaker looked through copies of service-ability sheets and work done on Whisky Echo at Tallaputiya during the previous three months. An artificial horizon had been changed in January. There had been a six-hour delay in February for a Number Three engine change. A tyre change, and two brake-drum changes—'Easy to burn up the brakes on this short runway,' the Chief Engineer had said—completed the mechanical incidents to the 707 over the period. There was no evidence at all of any repetitive fault occurring and recurring, which was what Hannaker had been looking for.

Hannaker spent the next morning trying to get access to the scene of the crash. He took the same old taxi. This time, the driver in the daylight had no difficulty finding the lane which Hannaker recognized more from the bangs and bumps than any familiar landmark. For in the bright sunshine every-

67

thing looked different. The rhododendrons were stunted and dusty, and as they reached the top of the hill the temple looked shabby and very ordinary—the white paint peeling off the walls, the stone steps up to the courtyard stained red with the spitty stars of betel juice.

Only the temple tree remained the same, its waxy white and yellow flowers unwilting in the sun.

Everything had changed so much that the dizzy thought came into his head that the night before last had never happened. The huge silver butterfly had vanished. From the open window he could see nothing but long tendrils of curving convolvulus, the green camouflage of creeper and bamboo bushes—till suddenly the fantasy exploded in a blaze of sunlight reflecting from the tilted starboard wing.

A shadow fell across his line of sight. 'It is forbidden.'

'That's all right,' Hannaker said, getting out of the taxi and handing the policeman his Board of Trade card.

'It is forbidden.'

Hannaker tried again, this time with his passport. 'I'm to help the authorities with the investigation.'

'It is forbidden.'

'What's all this in aid of anyway?' Hannaker pointed at the khaki-uniformed activity round the crash. He was accustomed to a police guard—a couple of good-natured bobbies or a fidgety gendarme or two keeping away the inevitable souvenir-hunters, who could strip a crashed aircraft to a skeleton quicker than white ants—but all this palaver was ridiculous. There must have been nearly a hundred police in their Australian-type slouch hats completely circling not only the temple and the crashed aircraft, but also a slimy ten-acre lake that lay a couple of hundred yards east, almost hidden by cedar and mahogany trees. Half the police appeared to be on guard, half were methodically moving through the forest undergrowth.

'What are they looking for?'

Clearly the policeman did not understand. He called over a sergeant, and there was a long exchange in Sinhalese, till the sergeant confirmed, 'It is forbidden.'

Hannaker produced the cable he had received from London. The only difference this made was the suggestion that he should contact Mr Seneratne of the Ceylon Air Safety Bureau who was in charge of the investigation.

Hannaker went back to the hotel, and telephoned the ASB at Colombo. There was no reply. He tried again ten minutes later. Mr Seneratne was out. Eventually he managed to contact Mr Seneratne's secretary, explained his business, and was told that Mr Seneratne was busy with urgent appointments for the rest of the day. Would Mr Hannaker come at nine o'clock tomorrow morning? Punctual, please?

Hannaker went straight from the telephone to the doorway marked *Cocktail*. He felt in need of a long cool drink. Miss Grey was perched up on a red leather stool at the bar, and beside her, standing, a man Hannaker would describe as young-middle-aged. One of the pilots, he would suppose. A little overweight, balding, small carefully-trimmed moustache, an altogether very tended neat appearance. They weren't talking. They were both of them staring at the mirror-backed rows of bottles behind the cocktail bar, as if engrossed in their own thoughts. Miss Grey's profile had a sad composed purity about it. Then she caught sight of Hannaker and lifted her hand.

'Hello, Mr Hannaker.' Up went the smile. 'Come and join us.'

Hannaker walked over, and rested a foot on the brass floor rail of the bar, beside the man.

'What are you both drinking?'

'Orange juice, Mr Hannaker. But no more for me, thank you.'

'Nor me either.' (A slight Geordie accent trimmed to a neat standard English.) 'There's a limit to the citrus that my stomach can take.'

'Have something stronger?'

'Sorry. No can do. Flying later.'

'Oh, may I introduce you.' Melanie Grey leaned forward. 'Mr Hannaker, this is Captain Dewhurst, the Flight Captain here.'

69

'Just the man I wanted to see.' Hannaker ordered himself a lager, and felt in his pocket for some loose change. He was aware that a pair of protuberant green eyes were regarding him coolly and unblinkingly.

'Mr Hannaker is . . .' the girl began to say when the Flight Captain said brusquely:

'We've been put in the picture about you.'

'In that case,' Miss Grey finished her drink, picked a crystallized cherry from the bottom of her glass and crunched it as she slid off the high stool, 'I'll leave you both to it.'

'You're leaving tonight, aren't you?' Hannaker asked.

She nodded. 'Twenty thirty. UK flight.'

'Have a good trip,' Captain Dewhurst spoke mechanically. Hannaker wanted to say, 'Take care of yourself,' decided they would regard it as the most banal sentimentality, so murmured instead, 'Be seeing you. Give my regards to London.'

'Will do.' And then misconstruing his expression, 'Can I phone anyone for you? Mrs Hannaker . . . ?' Her voice trailed uncertainly.

'No, thanks. I'm not married.'

They both stood for a moment watching her lilting walk across the cocktail bar till she disappeared into the main corridor.

'Good thing,' Dewhurst said, '*not* to be married in your line.' He said the last three words coldly.

He downed a mouthful of orange juice. The distasteful expression on his face was not just for the citrus juice. Pilots, no matter how conscientious, regarded accident investigators as bank clerks regard Head Office auditors. Hannaker sighed.

'How about in *your* line, Captain Dewhurst?'

'I'm married.' The protuberant eyes softened as if a warm breath had momentarily misted up a pair of large marbles. 'Three kiddies. Wife's back in England with them. School, you know. Roll on retirement, she says!'

'How about Captain Coates? He was older than you, surely? Was he looking forward to retirement?'

'That I wouldn't know. He wasn't far off retirement. Fifty-four. But a young fifty-four, you know. Otherwise,' the marbles

70

fixed meaningfully on Hannaker's face, 'we wouldn't have let him fly.'

No blame was to be tipped here, Hannaker thought, wryly. Dewhurst was a pilot, sure, but a management pilot, mindful of territory of his own to be protected from mud-slinging.

'Had he any family?'

'Wife. No family.'

'Is she out here?'

'No. There's something about an elderly relative. Her mother, I think. Couldn't be left. So Ron was here on his own for the six-months slip.'

'How many crews d'you keep out here at a time?'

'Three.'

'Consisting of . . . ?'

'Two pilots and an engineer. Also a chief steward and a chief stewardess. The rest of the cabin staff are local recruits. Sinhalese or Chinese.'

'I see.' Hannaker made a mental note to check up on how they got their local recruits. Could a local recruit be planted to find out . . . but what?

'Works very well, you know,' Dewhurst said as if Hannaker's silence were some veiled criticism.

'I imagine it does. Now tell me, Captain, the night before last, you landed at Tallaputiya about an hour before the crash.'

'Yes. Eastbound from London.'

'And the visibility was poor?'

'Sheeting down.'

'You came in on the beam of the ILS?'

'That's right.'

'Did you have any trouble?'

'None.'

The bartender, Siamese or Chinese by the look of him, came over and took Hannaker's glass, 'Sem again, yes, please?'

Hannaker nodded, 'Can I twist your arm, Captain?'

'No, thank you.'

'The ILS was working well?'

'Spot on.'

'You don't think the rain might affect the beam?'

'It certainly didn't with me.'

'Then what do you think happened?'

'It could have been a number of things.' Captain Dewhurst drained his glass and groomed the little toothbrush moustache with a quick teasing movement of his forefinger.

He was right of course. It could. It could be sabotage, as the *Ceylon Daily News* would have it. Sabotage was always a favourite, since it absolved everyone except the manifest villain of the piece. It might be mechanical—engine trouble, controls sticking, flap malfunction. But occurring in those last few seconds? Unlikely.

Which brought one back to the low visibility. And the man.

'Why didn't he divert?'

'It's always a bit dodgy on these special Hong Kong flights. . . .'

'What's special about them?'

Captain Dewhurst pushed his empty glass away across the bar and looked at his watch. 'In any case, the visibility was above company limits.'

'And *you* managed all right?' Hannaker stared into his lager musingly. 'Was he less experienced than you, Captain?'

'More, if anything.'

'Not likely then to make an elementary mistake on an instrument approach?'

'Unlikely, perhaps. But it's happened before.' The marble eyes blinked for the first time. Reluctantly, Captain Dewhurst said, 'You'll know that better than me.'

In spite of the glide-path needle on the ILS dial clearly indicating that they were undershooting in front of their eyes on the instrument panel, nevertheless pilots unaccountably undershot the runway coming in to land by twelve miles, six miles, two miles or just a few hundred yards. On the other hand, pilots, especially management pilots, were pretty damned quick to blame their colleagues. Working on the philosophy that I'd-never-do-a-damned-silly-thing-like-that-so-I'm-all-right, Jack. So one thing tended to balance another.

'Why does it happen? This undershooting, Captain?'

'Well, I do have my own pet idea, you know.' The marbles gleamed. 'Instrument flying is such concentrated work for the average pilot that he leaves it for visual flying the moment he can see anything. As soon as he sees a light ahead, he takes his eyes off the needle, and goes well below the glide path.'

'I think you're right,' Hannaker said. 'It must feel like tearing off a blindfold.'

'Exactly! But of course it isn't. It's like tearing out your eyes.'

'And you think this is what Captain Coates did?'

'Well,' Dewhurst hesitated. 'He's done it before.'

'When?'

'On flight checks. Here, see for yourself.' Dewhurst leaned down to the brief-case by his chair, and taking out a neat file, tossed it into Hannaker's lap. 'His personal record came this morning.'

Hannaker picked it up—a neat collection of papers containing the essence of a man's professional life. A sad bundle of documents—flight check reports, simulator reports, reports on courses taken, standards reached in examinations. He had had his six-monthly medical in March, and everything was perfectly normal. His Air Line Transport Licence was endorsed to fly Comet IV and 707 aircraft. Total number of hours 16,700, of which 403 were on 707s.

'You see he failed the 707 Technical exam twice before passing.'

'So have a number of other captains,' Hannaker said brusquely. He always had a feeling of prying when looking into these personal files, studying the critical comments of one human being on another. Coates had learned to fly in the RAF, and had flown an impressive number of piston-engined and turbo-prop aircraft.

'Jet experience comparatively limited,' Dewhurst said.

'But still a competent pilot.' Hannaker had been studying the flight check records, some of which contained an *above average* assessment.

'You saw those two comments on erratic glide-path flying?'

Hannaker nodded.

73

'You saw on his last check he went well below the glide path?'

Again Hannaker nodded. 'And you think that's what happened on Saturday?'

'Off the record, yes, I might as well say so now. I'm bound to say it at the Inquiry. Open-and-shut case.' And when Hannaker said nothing, 'Isn't that your theory, too?'

'I have no theory. I've only just begun the investigation.'

'Well, if it wasn't pilot error, what was it?'

'I can't even say what it could have been till I've examined the crash. It could have been the beam, of course.'

'I've told you. I found the ILS perfect.'

'It might have gone wrong later.'

'In an hour?'

'It's possible.'

'It's also possible he dropped dead in the last second.' The marble eyes glazed with indignation. Being always right was obviously of great importance to Dewhurst. He was obviously also annoyed at being lured into a theory which couldn't be immediately proved correct, and about which lesser men might argue.

'Anyway,' Hannaker said doggedly, 'I'd like to have it flight-checked. Before they find something the matter and repair it themselves.'

'They wouldn't do that.' Dewhurst sounded genuinely shocked.

'I've known it happen. Everyone tries to cover up after an accident.'

'You surprise me.'

'In this business,' Hannaker said slowly, 'nothing surprises me. Everything's possible.'

'Well, I can assure you that the ILS being out isn't!' The marbles glittered. 'And what's more, I can *show* you it isn't. I've got to do an air test in an hour. If you'd like to come up on it, I'll give the beam a thorough check for you.'

'Thank you,' Hannaker said equably, 'that would be very useful.'

An hour later to the minute—the efficiency of the Flight

Captain in getting things moving in spite of the local inertia was certainly not in doubt—they were again sitting together, this time in the cockpit of a 707 flying over Colombo at three thousand feet.

From his position on the jump-seat, Hannaker could see the blue curve of the harbour, the green lawn in front of the Galle Face Hotel, the flat roofs of high modern blocks contrasting with old red tiles, coconut thatch and corrugated iron, while beyond were the emerald squares of the paddy-fields, the neat coconut and banana plantations. He had heard Ceylon called the Garden of Eden. From up here, certainly, you could see the reason why.

'Coming up to Tallaputiya beacon now.' The view from the window was clearly to Dewhurst of no consequence. 'Here we go!' The pilot punched the stop clock as the radio compass turned abruptly 180 degrees. 'We go out on a course of 100 degrees for two minutes.' He pointed to the round dial of the ILS cut exactly in two halves—one orange and one blue—by the localizer needle. 'Dead on the beam outbound.'

Far down below, Hannaker could see the two runways of Tallaputiya, looking like a piece of sticking plaster stuck on a green skin. The 707's four jets whistled softly to each other in the bright blue cloudless air.

'Two minutes,' the First Officer said. 'Procedure turn.'

Dewhurst tilted up the port wings to alter course forty-five degrees to the right, and started to descend. Just below Hannaker could see foothills now, forerunners of Adam's Peak and the other high mountains in the centre of the island, as gracefully the huge aircraft executed a pear-shaped manoeuvre back towards the beam.

Dewhurst put the wheels down and called for the landing check. As the First Officer and the Engineer droned through the items Hannaker kept his eyes on the needles on the ILS—the localizer at full travel over in the orange sector, the glide path tucked up at the top of the instrument, both showing the aircraft had not yet started to cut the beams.

Then very gradually, the localizer needle started to move, and at exactly the same time, Dewhurst slightly increased the left bank. Imperceptibly the 707 slid into the beam on to a heading of 280 degrees. The needle on the radio compass now indicated the Tallaputiya outer marker beacon dead ahead and nine miles away, exactly in line with their course. Hannaker could see the runway threshold.

From the top of the ILS, now like a long-legged spider, the glide path needle began slowly to descend, till it cut the round face of the instrument horizontally across.

'On glide path.' Dewhurst was keeping his eyes rigidly on his instruments. 'Descending at five hundred feet a minute.'

Watching the Flight Captain's hands, the pale spatulate fingers gripping the control column, Hannaker was struck by the delicacy of their tiny movements. Airspeed 140 knots, altimeter unwinding methodically. Every instrument read exactly right as though they were under Dewhurst's command and he was drilling them. The two needles—localizer and glidepath—made a cross exactly in the centre of the ILS dial.

'The glide path is three degrees.' Dewhurst said. 'Watch and you'll see there's bags of ground clearance.'

They were flying at eighteen hundred feet now, and below the aircraft Hannaker could see the foothills melting away. A small village, a road, jungle giving way to green fields—certainly they all seemed Lilliputian from here.

'Outer marker,' said Dewhurst. 'And exactly on the glide path.'

The ground was coming closer and closer now, but there was still adequate safe clearance, even though just here it was beginning to rise again.

And then suddenly, Hannaker saw three headless trees, the temple on the rock, then the stretch of brown lake water, and afterwards a great swathe cut through the forest, ending in a scattering of silver debris in the middle of which lay the wrecked 707 glittering in the afternoon sun.

Dewhurst had seen it, too. 'Still exactly on the glide path . . . and we cleared that hill by three hundred feet, wouldn't you say?'

'Yes. The needle would have immediately registered if we'd been any lower.'

They might have easily cleared the hill, but they had trouble with the runway. The aircraft touched down smoothly enough, and at exactly the right speed. But even with full reverse thrust and very heavy braking, the pilot only managed to stop it just before the end.

'As you saw for yourself,' Dewhurst said as they taxied to the ramp, 'nothing wrong with the ILS beam.'

'As you say, nothing at all.' Hannaker paused, 'Isn't the runway a bit downhill?'

'Very slightly.'

'Seems rather short, too.' What with the closeness of those hills and mountains, Tallaputiya seemed not the best place for an airport. 'Could increase the tendency to under-shoot, couldn't it?'

Captain Dewhurst turned, brows raised in polite query. But the marble eyes were icy.

'Are you a pilot?'

'No.'

Not a pilot, not a member of the fraternity—just an engineer, low-caste, uninitiated into the mysteries. Dewhurst did not trouble to speak till he had shut down the engines and was climbing out of the seat. Then he said, 'In any case, I hear they got the Flight Recorder.'

'Yes.'

'That'll tell them. . . .'

The words *what I told you* did not need to be spoken.

For an hour in the morning and for the hours after work in the evening, George Seneratne resumed the role of his ancestors in the quietness of his own home.

A dhoti round his waist, his feet bare, he would pay his respects to his household gods—though he was a Buddhist, he attended Hindu festivals and his belief was pantheistic—before walking in the early sunshine over the thick dew on the grass of his tiny garden, breathing in deep the dust-sweet smell of the rain-soaked earth. And at night after the curry and rice meal which his wife had prepared, again dressed only in a

77

white cloth, relaxed and still, he would sit on the verandah at the back of the bungalow, staring up at the diamond-bright stars that seemed so low he could almost touch them, thinking over the day.

At all other times, he was quite different. Dressed in a smart white European suit, horn-rimmed spectacles framing his liquid brown eyes, he was the perfect bustling go-ahead executive.

By his own drive and initiative, he had built up the Ceylon Air Safety Bureau from nothing. While politicians and civil servants dragged their feet in the years following independence, indicating the smallness of Ceylonese civil aviation, then almost entirely dependent on expatriates, and pointing out that Britain through the regulations of the International Civil Aviation Organization could be asked to investigate any air accident that took place on the island, he had pressed forward in spite of discouragement and parsimonious finance. After taking a degree in mechanics at the University of Ceylon, he had learned to fly and had then spent a year in the United States, studying the methods of the Civil Aviation Board and the Air Investigation Bureau, before returning to Ceylon to head his new department.

Intensely nationalistic, it was right that he should recruit his own race for his staff. Even though privately he deplored— after seeing the efficiency of the USA—their slowness and complete lack of a sense of time, he preferred them infinitely to expatriates. Though he had no feeling against the British, he had resented their universality in most of the top and difficult jobs and had naturally welcomed their gradual disappearance—together with the Burghers of Dutch-Sinhalese descent—and their replacement by Ceylon nationals. In his department everybody spoke Sinhalese, and his own English (in contrast to his father who had been at a mission school and spoke it perfectly) was sometimes a little strange and singsong, particularly as there was behind it more than a hint of a New York accent.

While he had kept his staff busy, the Department's work over the years had so far not been great. The Department had advised on the safety side of the new airport at Tallaputiya. But as far as aircraft accidents were concerned, there had only been one, two years ago now, when two light aircraft had collided over Trincomalee.

The 707's crash at the Bharratu shrine was not only the justification for all his efforts and the considerable government expense, it was his great chance.

As his car took him—immaculately Western—on the Tuesday after the accident through the honking streets of the Fort to his office near Galle Face, he was examining in his mind the plans and strategy that he had formulated that morning in the peace of his Eastern meditations.

As was to be expected, there had of course been complications. The Prime Minister's office had rung up anxiously—a statement would be necessary. The Civil Aviation Department had been jittery about possible repercussions over Tallaputiya. The Legal Department was concerned. There had as always been expatriates, European and American, who had come forward to press upon Ceylon their expert advice—as if it had not got an Air Safety Bureau of its own. The Boeing representative had flown in from Madras yesterday, but on having a look at the wreckage and hearing his ideas on the cause of the crash had reported himself to be 'quite happy' to leave it to him. British Oriental Airways, through Reeves their representative, had suggested they send an officer, but he had prevailed upon them that it was at present unnecessary.

And then late last night, when everything was proceeding very smoothly, he had heard that a man called Hannaker had been deputed by the British government under Section Thirteen of the new ICAO Agreement to assist in the investigation.

Furthermore, this man had more or less invited himself round to the Air Safety Bureau this morning at nine o'clock for what he called 'a chat'.

Ahead of the car, bullock carts and taxis were jamming the road. The sweep second hand on Seneratne's watch tapped the minutes in the traffic block. Despite voluble and earnest entreaties, it was already ten minutes past the hour when the

Sinhalese reached Galle Face, and he was displeased to find the Englishman already sitting in his office.

'Good morning.' The over-friendly tone of the man's voice as he got up from the chair seemed to Seneratne a reproach for his lateness, hinted at Eastern inefficiency. 'I'm Hannaker, James Hannaker. Aviation section of the British Board of Trade.'

'Yes, yes.'

The hand-shake between them was rapid.

'As I said on the telephone,' Hannaker went on, still standing, 'they want me to——'

'Yes, yes, yes.'

'If there's anything I can do to help,' Hannaker indicated the faded green canvas bag lying at his feet, 'I've got tools in there that might be useful.'

'We have our own tools.'

'Of course . . . but these are rather special ones.' He gave a crooked smile. 'Born from bitter experience.'

'We have our experience, too.'

'Of course . . . but I have been involved one way or another in several 707 crashes, and I thought——'

'We are very grateful for your offer of expertise, Mr . . . ?'

'Hannaker.'

'Sit down, please.'

There was a short silence punctuated by the slowly rotating fan on the ceiling as Hannaker sat down and Seneratne assumed his rightful position behind his desk.

'As you will suppose, Mr Hannaker,' Seneratne tapped the tips of his fingers together, 'we have made our own modest start on the investigation.'

'Oh, I know,' Hannaker said. 'I was up at the crash site yesterday. Couldn't get near, there were so many policemen'.

'We must take strict precautions against pilfering.'

'Very wise! But I did see a bullock cart going off with what looked like the port wing tip.'

Seneratne bridled. 'It's not that we haven't got tractors, Mr Hannaker. In that marshy ground, bullock carts are better.'

'I believe you, Mr Seneratne. But I would have liked to have had a look at the position of the ailerons.'

'They were neutral.'

'So he wasn't turning?'

'No.'

'What else have you taken away from the crash?'

'Part of the nose cone . . . some fragmented fuselage skin . . . the starboard navigation light. . . .'

'I must say, Mr Seneratne . . . in my view it's essential to leave everything untouched . . . like the scene of a murder . . . till a thorough investigation has been done *in situ*.'

'Mr Hannaker, please believe that a thorough investigation . . . very thorough investigation . . . of the wreckage has been done. I have done it *myself*.'

'Yes, I'm sure, Mr Seneratne.'

'And the cause of the crash was written all over it.'

'There I'm not so sure, Mr Seneratne.'

'But you haven't seen it yet!'

'All the same——'

'Wait till you see it, and then you'll agree with me.'

'I'm very anxious to see it as soon as I'm allowed to.'

'Of course.' The Sinhalese rose from his seat. 'You may wish to start by seeing the pieces we have here.'

'If it's not too much trouble.'

'Nothing is too much trouble, sir. Now if you would kindly come this way. . . .'

Hannaker followed the Sinhalese inspector out of the office, down a corridor and into a large hall which had been equipped as a sort of laboratory, with microscopes and X-ray apparatus. Laid out on long tables were the pieces taken from the crashed 707.

Hannaker went over and had a look at them. On the surface, all seemed perfectly normal. The only thing that was puzzling was why they had been removed.

'And over here,' Seneratne indicated triumphantly what looked like a roll of thin crinkly aluminium foil, 'the most important piece we recovered. The Flight Recorder.'

'I heard you had it.' Hannaker walked across to inspect the

foil recorder cassette, its red protective outer casing removed and lying beside it.

'It will confirm our views.'

'You seem very certain, Mr Seneratne.'

'It will give us all the evidence we want.'

'You'll have to send it back to England for the read-out?'

'Not at all!'

'You can do it here?'

The surprise on the Englishman's face was satisfying. It justified all the fight and effort he had had to get the money out of the government to buy expensive apparatus, and train him to interpret the minute stylus marks, six hundred to each inch of foil.

'We can do it here,' the Sinhalese mimicked back at him.

'At least, let me help you with the read-out?'

'I would not wish to impose upon your time.'

'No trouble.'

'The British are always so kind. . . .'

'I've got a good deal of experience in read-outs.'

'I'm sure, Mr Hannaker.'

'They can be complicated. Ghosting problems, multiple images.'

'We will be able to manage with our microscope.'

Aware of the antagonism just beneath the bland politeness, Hannaker hesitated. 'Well,' he said relunctantly at last, 'you'll let me see what comes out?'

'Naturally.'

'And now, I'd like to have my own look round the crash, if you'd give me a chit or something.'

'Delighted.' From his top coat pocket Seneratne produced a rectangular visiting card, on the back of which he wrote a careful series of Sinhalese hieroglyphics, and handed it over to Hannaker.

'Give that to the policeman and he will let you see inside.'

If anything, there were more policemen than ever. The same sergeant came up to the open window of the taxi, dubiously examined George Seneratne's visiting card, and grudgingly allowed Hannaker through the cordon.

Around the lake and the temple the constables were still looking for something, thrashing down the undergrowth with small black sticks.

Hannaker joined them in their search, going way into the forest. He found a wheel in the undergrowth, then the whole port undercarriage assembly. Lifting his eyes, he studied the lopped-off trees on the near and far side of the lake. The line of the fractured branches was parallel with the ground, showing the aircraft was flying practically straight and level when it hit. There had been no sudden dive to the ground, and the fact that the wreckage was contained in a small area indicated that the speed of impact was comparatively slow—probably not very much more than the normal approach speed of 140 knots.

Unzipping his bag, he took out his camera and photographed the swathe which the 707 had cut through the forest. Then he turned his attention to the hot silver skin of the fuselage and the wings.

Watched by a curious Sinhalese policeman, he worked slowly and methodically, making a sketch map of the wreckage distribution, using a tape to measure distances, drawing in score marks on the ground and matching them with scratches on the fuselage. Then he searched for signs of fire—shadows on the after side of rivets, melted metal spattered on the tail. He peered inside the engines, looking for carbon deposits and scorching. Possibly there had been some break-up in the air, and now he looked for irregular paint smears that might indicate a fracture before impact.

The fuselage had split in two places, and close to the tail there was a gaping hole on the underside—but such damage was perfectly consistent with hitting the trees and the ground. The only thing on the outside of the fuselage that he thought worth photographing was the position of the elevators—full travel upwards.

Then he put his camera back in his bag, and walked towards the main door.

83

It was strange, jumping up into the aircraft from thick jungle grass. Inside, it was cool and shadowy after the fierce afternoon heat. Row upon row of empty seats lay in unbroken ranks slanted over to the left. The rear galley door was open, and Hannaker could see plastic cups still hanging on hooks, trays stacked in position, cans of fruit on the shelves, and a girl's white overall lying on the work counter.

There was nobody else in the cabin. It was very quiet, ghostly even, in spite of the bright daylight outside. There was the usual aircraft smell of metal, kerosene, expensive upholstery and the last faint antiseptic tinges of aerosol bomb. The pink carpet was thick with mud and marked with many footprints, and because of the angle Hannaker had difficulty walking, making his way aft almost like a rock climber, using his right hand to grasp the ledges of the seats, humping his tool bag in his left.

Six of the portholes beyond the main door were shattered, and then there was a jagged hole where the pressurized hull had split. Spilled all over were the remnants of baggage, giving the appearance of a looted house: a high-heeled shoe hung on a curtain rail, a brown teddy bear upside down on the luggage rack. A tortoiseshell-backed hairbrush, a man's sports coat, a red bathing-costume, a cine camera, a green silk dress, a tartan sponge bag, toothbrushes and pyjamas lay all over the place, mixed up with letters and parcels, radio spares and pieces of ship's machinery from the cracked-open cargo compartments.

Slowly he moved down the rows of seats, his eyes examining the red and white upholstery for burn stains, sniffing the air for the least scent of nitrate. He paused at the main fuselage split, ran his fingers along the jagged metal. He looked in the toilets, through the coats still stacked in the vestibule. He took out his magnifying glass, and, pulling back the carpet, patiently examined the door to the cargo compartment before opening it up and jumping inside.

Here it was darker, and he had to use his torch. He examined hydraulic pipe lines, control cables, electric wiring, fuel lines and non-return valves. Some of these had been undoubtedly

84

damaged from the *inside*—but the cargo had broken loose and was all over the place and this was clearly what had caused the damage. It was possible that some of the freight had actually fallen out of the aircraft after it had been holed by the first impact with the trees, for there were skids and score marks on the floor—particularly in the aft locker which was completely empty.

Coming back up into the cabin, now he started looking at the heating pipes, the oxygen masks and outlets. Then he examined the refrigerator and the electric stove in the forward galley, before turning sideways to squeeze through the crumpled door to the flight deck.

There he began checking the engineers' switches and levers, noticed the neutral position of all fire extinguishers, and then moved over to the captain's seat and cautiously lowered himself into it.

In front of him, the instrument panel was a mass of broken glass and twisted metal—but nevertheless it immediately produced for him invaluable information: the hands of the clock stopped at fourteen hours, thirteen minutes and twenty seconds precisely, the altimeter needle registering the exact height of this hill at 195 feet, the compass needle parallel between the lubber lines on the runway heading of 280 degrees, the airspeed indicator still registering 140 knots.

As at Pompeii when the lava poured over the inhabitants, this was the state of living at the moment of death. The operational route books lying open at the Hong Kong–Colombo sector, the pictorial instrument landing let-down plate into Tallaputiya on the throttle box, a scribbled note of a routine weather forecast *wind south-west ten knots at 18,000 feet, usual monsoon rainstorm over Tallaputiya* on the ledge of the windscreen. And incongruously in all that chaos, an unbroken cup with coffee dregs still in it and the remnants of cigarette ash still in the saucer wedged against the side of the fuselage and the smashed first officer's seat. On the console, the flap lever was three-quarters down—the correct position for this period of the approach. The undercarriage lever was down. The engine instruments had all been smashed, but all switches appeared to be in the right position, and the VHF was on the Talla-putiya Tower frequency. The artificial horizons were crumpled. The VOR and the radio compass were shattered and unread-able, and the needle was missing on both the captain's and first officer's rate of descent indicator.

For three hours, Hannaker sat in the captain's seat, methodi-cally making notes of everything he saw. Already in his mind he had eradicated a number of potential killers. There was not the slightest sign of a bomb explosion on board. Nor were there any indications of sabotage. There was no sign of engine failure, control trouble or electrical or hydraulic problems. There had been no fire, either in the engines or the fuselage. The aircraft had not broken up before impact, and there was not a single sign of metal fatigue. The 707 had not been shot down—Hannaker had known that happen—nor had it been struck by lightning.

Every indication pointed to the fact that the 707 was per-fectly serviceable down to the smallest detail when it first hit the trees.

Uneasily Hannaker shifted himself in the seat. He had taken a marked dislike to Dewhurst. Seneratne had clearly taken a marked dislike to him. Being different from people, disliking them, were very bad reasons for rejecting their theories, but it was surprising how often they came into this business. Not being on the same wavelength interfered with communica-tions, bent the beam of truth. Even in himself Hannaker had found it difficult to agree with some people—particularly those who jumped to conclusions, used such phrases as *open-and-shut case* and *the wreckage has the cause of the accident written all over it.*

Yet such people had an annoying habit of being right.

Was Dewhurst right? Was Seneratne right?

Hannaker looked up from his notes at the instruments and the throttle box. Throughout his careful searchings he had been looking for the unusual, the outcast, the atypical, the odd man out. In all his investigation, he had only found three: the elevators fully up, the throttles fully open, and the control column full travel back—and they were all connected.

Just before he died, Captain Coates *knew*. Through the

blinding rain he must suddenly have seen the hillock and the tops of trees. Too late he had tried to climb.

But *why* had he been so low?

The Captain must have been aware he was too low. Staring him full in the face, just as it now stared mutely at Hannaker, was the glide path needle on the round face of the Instrument Landing System—petrified intact at full travel upwards. That proved the instrument must have indicated correctly that the aircraft was three hundred feet *below* the beam when it struck. And because of the almost horizontal attitude when it hit the ground, for minutes before the disaster, that glide path needle must have pointed at *danger*.

Yet Coates had done nothing about it until it was too late.

Why?

Hannaker took photographs of the instrument readings and the positions of the throttles and controls. Then for another hour, he went on sitting in the cockpit, trying to piece together a reason for the Captain's reaction. Sudden illness? Some other distraction? Or just the human desire to get down quickly safe on the ground?

There were no answers to these questions here. Beyond the windscreen now, the setting sun traced in silver the battlements of cumulo-nimbus cloud. A bell started ringing in the temple, and Hannaker saw the Brahmin come out into the courtyard and stand in an attitude of prayer.

He put his notebook and camera back into his bag, zipped it up and got out of the seat. Down here on the equator there was practically no twilight, and now the day was rapidly turning into night.

He had worked his way back into the main cabin, when he heard below him the sound of two people talking.

He stopped. Clearly the voices were coming from the cargo compartment. He went on to the rear of the aircraft, pulled up the trapdoor, and let himself down into the darkness.

He was just reaching for his torch when he saw suddenly a flashlight go on. Two men were actually inside the small aft freight locker, one of them holding a torch, the other one down on his knees examining the same scratches and scoremarks on the metal floor that Hannaker had noticed.

The torch carrier heard footsteps and swung the beam round. There was a strong scent of what Hannaker thought was peppermint toothpaste.

'Hannaker . . . what are you doing here?'

In the side glow from the torch was illuminated the oval pink face of the Station Manager. Hannaker produced the Open Sesame of Seneratne's visiting card.

Reeves appeared to understand the Sinhalese hieroglyphics.

'Mr Fonseca . . . this is Hannaker from the British Board of Trade who is helping Seneratne with the accident investigation.'

The face that turned itself up towards Hannaker and smiled was dark brown and very handsome, clearly of Tamil ancestry. Black hair was brushed neatly down over a wide brow.

'Mr Fonseca is Head of Ceylon Criminal Investigation Department.'

Hannaker put out his right hand. 'How do you do?'

'Delighted to meet you, Mr Hannaker.' Fonseca spoke very correct, rather old-fashioned English with a sing-song intonation.

It seemed to Hannaker as they shook hands that this was altogether a very strange meeting-place—all hunched up under the light of a torch in this duralumin compartment.

'Like me,' he said, 'you appear to be looking for something.'

'Oh, we're looking for something all right, Mr Hannaker.'

'But it's not what *you're* looking for,' Reeves interposed quickly. 'When this aircraft left Hong Kong there was a ton of gold in this locker, and now it has all disappeared. We're trying to work out what the devil could have happened to it.'

In all the newspapers throughout the world, the air disaster at Tallaputiya had flared furiously over the headlines and then had as abruptly been extinguished by the greater pressure of news of wars, strikes, riots, fashion, political elections, murders

and student unrest. Only the *Ceylon Daily News* kept up the
story of the crash on its doorstep, still sticking to its original
theory of sabotage. Mention was made of the tight security
guard round the crash, but rather to underline the newspaper's
cleverness in procuring three aerial photographs—one clearly
taken at lower than tree-top level—which showed, as well as
the policemen, the swathe cut through the forest, the lake, the
temple and the wreckage of the airliner in excellent grisly
detail.

'In London,' Melanie Grey said, coming up behind Hannaker in the foyer as he studied the newspaper, 'the headline's
cricket.'

'You do surprise me.' Hannaker grinned faintly and stood
up. 'Won't you sit down a while? Have a coffee? I didn't know
you were back.'

'Last night, as a matter of fact. Shows your mind was on
other things. No, I won't have a coffee, thanks.' She perched
herself on the edge of a basket chair. She indicated her
towelling bag. 'We're off for a swim. The rest of the crew
and me.'

'Not with the prosperous gentleman from t'other end. What's
his name? Laughton?'

She coloured slightly. There had been a note from Roy
waiting for her when she got back last night. *Hope you had
a good trip. When you've had a chance to rest up, I'll call round for you
at the hotel. Maybe we could go sightseeing. You seem to have been a
very long time away.*

'No. Not this time.'

'Enjoy it before?'

'Very much.'

Hannaker nodded sagely but said nothing.

After a moment she said, 'Can I tempt you to come along
with us? For a swim?'

'You could. But you mustn't. I'm waiting for a car and an
interpreter to take me round the villages.' He looked at his
watch.

'Eye-witnesses?'

'You never know.'

Softly: 'How's it coming along?'

'Slowly.' He paused. 'You did one of these bullion flights from Hong Kong, didn't you?'

She drew in her breath sharply at the question, her eyes darkening. 'Yes. Three weeks ago.'

'What was the procedure?'

'Well, not very different really from any other precious cargo carrying. A bit more not-so-secret secrecy.' She smiled faintly, 'if you know what I mean.'

Hannaker nodded. 'Tell me about it.'

'Well,' she spread her hands on her lap and looked at her finger-nails, sighing not for the chore of answering but for the associations it conjured up, 'just before we left the ramp . . . when all the passengers were strapped in . . . an armoured car drove up to the steps.'

'With guards?'

'Yes.'

'In uniform?'

'Yes.'

'How many?'

'Three. And the driver. Two of them brought on the boxes and stowed them in the precious cargo compartment. The other one supervised.'

'The driver stayed with the van?'

'Yes.'

'How long did it take?'

'That time, about three-quarters of an hour. There was a lot of to-ing and fro-ing and argument.'

'Were you late leaving?'

'Nearly an hour.'

'Did the passengers grumble?'

'A bit.'

'None of them knew what the cargo was? Or the cause of the delay?'

'No.'

'But the crew did?'

'Yes.'

'And at this end? At Tallaputiya?'

'Nothing very much. Two plain-clothes detectives came on board as soon as the passenger door was opened. They stayed till everyone was off.'

'Including the catering crew?'

'Yes.' She paused and raised her brows at Hannaker, 'Is that any help?'

'Every fact helps.'

She looked at her watch.

'Don't let me hold you up.'

'You're not. The boys are trying to lay their hands on a *ghari*. And Gemma . . . she's the other stewardess . . . doesn't appear to have surfaced yet.'

'Oh.' He smiled shyly. 'Where did you think of going?'

'There's a beach about five miles south. Lovely little bay. The water's marvellous.'

'I envy . . .' he was going to say you but without meaning to said '. . . them.'

A mistake which Miss Grey did not appear to notice, except by a faint colouring in her cheeks. 'Ah! Eureka! Success at last! There they are now!'

She stood up. A group of four men had just pushed their way through the swing doors and were beckoning frantically. At the same time a striking-looking pale-faced dark-haired girl came running down the staircase to join them. They all made a pretty picture of youth and gaiety. Why did he, Hannaker, feel so suddenly protective? And why did he feel such an immediate urgency to solve this particular case—as if they were all at terrible risk?

The tour round the thatched mud hut villages proved lengthy and interesting, but from Hannaker's point of view unrewarding. Much gesticulating, hands clapped over ears and much indication by heads buried in folded arms, that always there was noise. Much noise. Too much noise. But no eye witnesses. Hardly surprising on a night like that.

Hannaker went back again to the temple. He stood in the temple courtyard. Only the shadows had changed since last time, and some petals had fallen off the blossoms of the temple tree. A thin elderly priest with a hump back and milky-rimmed dark eyes told him in a mixture of Tamil and bad English that the Brahmin was not available. But Hannaker was invited inside the temple.

The same place in the afternoon light looked airy and cool. Even the paintings on the wall had lost their life and power. But faintly, insidiously, the smell remained. As if, like Lady Macbeth's hands, all the scrubbings and the whitening and the prayers could not quite sweeten . . .

Or was it only Hannaker's imagination? Was it not just the very sweetness itself? The sweet scent of temple flowers drawn out by the sun came drifting through the open door behind him.

'Pray you, may I help you, yes, please?' The priest bowed his hunched shoulders lower.

Hannaker began again as he'd done all afternoon. 'Did anyone here actually see the aircraft crash?'

Haltingly and with mime, the priest told him that, no, no one had seen the crash itself, though the Brahmin had seen it many times before. But with the eyes of the mind, did he understand, not with his mortal, fleshly ones. At the time of the crash a devotion was going on. Even so, they had heard this great noise. Once again, hands, this time thin ascetic hands, were clapped over ears.

'And what did you do?'

'Naturally we finish our prayers.'

'Naturally,' Hannaker echoed softly, coldly. 'Then? After your prayers were finished?'

'We go there and help.'

'By that time,' Hannaker tried to keep the bitter note out of his voice, 'help had already arrived?'

'Oh, yes certainly! Much help.' The priest spread his hands. Ambulances, many ambulances, fire engines, lorries, cars. He himself had not been one chosen to go into the aeroplane. But many had helped to bring out the people. The Brahmin had allowed them—clearly it was a privilege—to bring the bodies into the temple and out of the rain.

But before the aircraft crashed, or at the time of the crash no one had seen anything.

The next day they had continued to pray, the monk told him, peering up into Hannaker's tired face. They had said many prayers. Pressing his thin old hands together, he followed Hannaker back into the courtyard. In the light of day, of course, he added, blinking his milky-rimmed eyes against this present glare. No one had gone down. They had stood here in the courtyard and the Brahmin had brought out his prayer wheel and again many prayers. And below them was just the silver aeroplane and a how-you-say-it . . .

He waved his hands to indicate a swarm. Of butterflies. Many, many butterflies of many different colours. He nodded several times. It seemed to Hannaker that his crumpled face bore an expression of exaggerated piety. What the old chap was giving him to understand, he didn't quite know.

Perhaps that the swarm of butterflies were the now happy souls of the departed. If so, he had no convert in Hannaker. Hannaker had seen them before in the jungle. Not over an aeroplane, but once when he was on an investigation in India. A gauzy trail of delicate butterflies swirling like a white scarf. . . . Over a deer slaughtered by lion. Over a kill.

A gauzy square of winged insects—dead, these ones—lay every morning on the floor of Reeves's office in front of the electric air cleaner, until the Tamil bearer saw fit to come and sweep them up.

It was Thursday. Disaster day plus eight, as Reeves privately referred to it. Fonseca had called early. And the bearer was taking his time with the dustpan and brush, no doubt hoping to overhear something interesting which Inspector Fonseca was obviously about to impart.

'Do you mind if I smoke, yes? Please?' Inspector Kishti Fonseca settled himself more comfortably in the Station Manager's VIP chair and held aloft a thin black cheroot.

'Of course not. Go ahead. I like the smell. Even though cigars don't like me.'

Reeves slid his desk lighter across to the police inspector, and to be sociable unwrapped the waxy paper of a Digestif Rennie.

'You look tired, man.' Fonseca surveyed Reeves through the flame. 'And not to be surprised too much at, eh man?' With a wide sweep of his quick brown hands he indicated Reeves's piled desk, the new emergency charts on the wall.

'I am a little.'

Since the disaster Reeves had hardly slept. At his desk by six in the morning, he rarely left it before midnight. Besides running the schedules as if nothing had happened, there was so much to arrange—the baggage disposal, the insurance, the burials, the legal problems. In times like these the manual of the Management Course, his Bible, no less, told him to delegate. But to whom it did not say. In the still hours of the first late night Reeves had made himself two large charts—one of every item on the freight and baggage manifest, and the other of jobs to be done. Filling in on the first each item as it was found. Striking each one off the job list as it was accomplished.

Yesterday he had been able to strike off funerals. They had been carried out during the afternoon in the various religions and denominations with dignity and decorum. They had all been attended either by the High Commissioner himself or a suitable representative. Even now there reposed on Reeves's desk, just by the bumph that had come in for Hannaker, a copy of this morning's *Times of Ceylon*, neatly folded to show a photograph. Sir Arthur Atcherly in plumed hat and full uniform leaving the church of St Stephen the Martyr in Colombo after the joint funeral of Episcopalians and Free Church. Just as there had been one the day before of Sir Arthur calling on the Minister of Aviation. And another two days previously of his official call on the Prime Minister himself to express the condolences of Her Majesty's government.

Of course there were other less reassuring items inside the paper which his secretary so discreetly folded—the flaring up of the old argument about Tallaputiya itself. Why was a new aerodrome for Jumbo Jets considered necessary? Why were not Ratmalana or Katanayaka simply lengthened? Why was this particular site chosen? Why had the objections of the Hindus not been taken more into consideration? The flaring up of the old jealousies too. Why were big licences such as these given to foreign operators?

But discounting what one might for factions and jealousies, the unfortunate fact remained that the disaster had blotted the escutcheon of the new airfield at a very early stage. Particularly when it had also resulted in the temporary loss of the gold. No wonder Reeves was tired. When he dared to let himself think about it, this was the kind of ultimate of station managers' nightmares.

Fortunately the accident and the gold were clearly two separate issues. And at least in all confidence Reeves could delegate there. He himself was no expert in accident investigation or detection. He had found out that under Section Thirteen of the ICAO Agreement, Hannaker's appointment by the British Board of Trade could not be opposed, and a special memo from the Department had highly commended his services. Seneratne and Fonseca were highly respected in their separate fields. Indeed the happenings of the last five days had drawn him closer to the little Police Inspector than he would have hitherto thought possible. Was not Fonseca the one who had reminded him of the gold?

'It does not seem so very much time since we arranged all the security, eh man?' Fonseca said, as if reading Reeves's thoughts, when the bearer reluctantly departed. 'Very fortunate as it turned out that we were so very careful.'

When the Ceylonese government had bought these bargain tons of gold, and the contract had been given—not without some political heartsearchings—to Oriental Airways, the main Hong Kong–Tallaputiya operator, Reeves and Fonseca had personally in this same office arranged its security.

'Four weeks ago.' Reeves sighed.

The gold would be sent in six batches. The dates of the consignments would be selected by computer in a Hong Kong bank, and no one, literally no one knew whether any flight was a gold carrier until four hours before take-off. The news would be flashed to Reeves at Tallaputiya hidden in the departure

95

signal that warned him of the crew, the passengers and the rest of the freight by simply using the word *metal* as a code. On receipt Reeves would then telephone Fonseca apparently about nothing—but two detectives would nevertheless appear to supervise the unloading to the main bonded store, or would stand guard there until an armoured vehicle arrived to transport it to the Colombo bank. The arrangements had worked very successfully and without hitch for three such flights. Until the day the fateful signal came through the ticker tape . . .

BA 708/13 *Crew: Coates, Smith, Barrett, Morrison, Tamplin, Pallitt, Wickeremsinghe, Jaywaseera. Colombo Pax 25 M, 11 F, 6 C. London Pax 17 N, 10 F, 4 C Colombo cargo kilogrammes ship's spares 3000, metal 1000, radio parts 3000, mail 1000, manufactured goods 1800.*

'Much water has flowed under the bridge since then as you say, man.' Fonseca blew a cloud of aromatic smoke up to the ceiling.

'Most of it pretty muddy.'

'Beg pardon?'

'Oh nothing. Just my way of saying it has been a difficult time.'

'Difficult? Oh certainly so. But the water as you would say is getting clearer. We are making great progress.'

'You've found the gold?'

'Not quite, man. But we know where it is.'

'That's very good news. Very good news indeed.'

Reeves sat back, folded his arms over his stomach and prepared to listen.

Like all raconteurs Fonseca was prepared to take his time. 'Now we've examined together the big hole below the cargo locker, haven't we, man?'

'We have.'

'And we've looked at the scores made on the duralumin floor made very clearly by sliding many wooden boxes?'

'Yes.'

'And we know that there were generous-sized holes all over the fuselage?'

'Sieved like a colander.'

96

'And that a very great deal of the rest of the baggage and cargo fell out. Many many pieces of which are still missing?'

Reeves glanced at his manifest chart on the wall, where engine spares, ships' parts, manufacturers' crates still remained unaccounted for, and nodded ruefully.

'So it is a fair assumption that the gold also fell out?'

'That seems to be the generally held theory.'

'But you and I, man, are puzzled because none of it has been found? After all, there were one thousand kilo bars.'

'Completely baffled.'

'Do you guess, man, *why* none has been found?'

'No. But I'd be very glad if you could see fit to enlighten me.'

Fonseca leaned right forward in his chair and tapped his cigar slowly and impressively. 'None has been found because the gold fell in the lake itself.'

'All of it?'

Fonseca nodded. 'All of it.' He paused. 'And do you know why I know that, man? Because we have done some very careful and difficult mathematical calculations. Height of aircraft, weight of boxes, speed, location.' He got up, walked over to the plan on the wall and stabbed his cigar towards the blank ellipse of the marshy lake. 'All calculations bring us to an answer within fifty yards of *that*.'

'So you'll never get it back?' Reeves reached for a Rennie.

'Oh, that is not to say so. But it helps to know where it is, does it not?'

'If you're sure?'

'Of course we're sure. My colleague, Mr Seneratne, confirms my observations that there was *no sabotage*. The boxes did not have wings to fly away. Or legs. There were no unauthorized vehicles or people to carry it away. We are still diligently searching the forest just in case. But if not there, where else could it be, man?'

Reeves was unable to answer his question, and putting his cigar back with a flourish into his mouth, in silence Fonseca went on smoking with evident satisfaction.

It was into this comfortable atmosphere that Hannaker broke a few seconds later. Engine and airframe log books, crew training particulars, medical and competence certificates had been flown out from England the day before, and Reeves had promised to give Hannaker a chance to look at them before forwarding them on to Seneratne for the official inquiry. There they were, in a pile on his desk, and as soon as the investigator's head came round the door, the manager held them up aloft for him to take hold of and be off.

But Fonseca, perhaps prompted by his own success, asked Hannaker genially, 'And how is the accident investigation coming alone?'

'Slowly.' On the point of going out of the office, Hannaker paused. 'What about the cargo?'

'Not so slowly, man. We know where it is.'

'Do you, b'Jove! So you've recovered it?'

'We have not recovered it *yet*. That will take time.'

'Why?'

'In Ceylon very unfortunately, man, we do not have a big enough dredger.'

'A *dredger*? Whatever for?'

'To drain the lake. The lake by the temple.'

'You mean the gold's in there?'

'It is.'

'*All* of it?'

'All of it.'

'Well,' Hannaker said slowly, 'that's convenient.'

Sensing a disruptive influence, Reeves said hastily as a cue for Hannaker's exit, 'You'll want to be reading through those reports now. I can't let you have them too long.' But Fonseca had already forestalled him and brought the investigator into the conversation, as he asked, slightly nettled, 'What do you mean by that, Mr Hannaker?'

'Just that it seems a bit too good to be true.'

Hannaker left the door and advanced into the room. He went over to the window and leaned on the sill.

'What are you trying to say, man?'

'Too neat. Falls into shape too prettily. Accidents aren't like that. They're untidy, messy things. D'you know what I mean?'

'No, man.'

'Besides, you won't know for months if you're right. You may *never* know.'

'But if it is not in the lake, man, where is it?'

'The forest? It's a big place.'

'That is being diligently searched, man.'

'Every yard?'

'Every *inch*, man.'

'Then of course,' Hannaker thrust out his lower lip, 'someone might have gone off with it.'

'*Stolen* it.' Mr Fonseca swivelled himself round the better to stare at Hannaker? 'But *who* would steal it, Mr Hannaker?'

'I don't know. That's not my department.'

'It is not indeed, man. But that is not my theory either. So *who* does your theory say *might* have taken it?'

'Someone who knew there was gold coming in.'

Fonseca made an impatient hissing noise. 'Only a few government and bank officials knew. Very high up. Very honourable. And they would not know it was coming *that day*.'

'Reeves here knew. And you knew. Others might have known. Seized the opportunity when the aircraft crashed. What is a stronger possibility is that someone came across it accidentally.'

'Such as?'

'Well, apart from someone being near the scene coincidentally, there were the fire and ambulance crews.'

Just to one side of him, Reeves let out a little exclamation of protest. Hannaker heard the crackly sound of a Rennie being hastily unwrapped.

'All the drivers and crews of the Safety Services have been interrogated. Their movements have been rigidly checked. All are in the clearest. And may I say, man, that Mr Reeves here and I myself have officially paid tribute to the magnificence of their behaviour on that night.'

'That is so,' Reeves nodded, his mouth full of crunched-up peppermint stuff.

'Then there were Seneratne's men. *They* went right over

the wreck very soon after. They removed pieces of it too. *Before I was able to examine it in situ.*'

'All have been rigidly investigated.'

'Mr Reeves told me the shock of the accident drove the gold right out of his mind. It was you and your detectives who remembered.'

'That is so,' Fonseca nodded graciously.

'So that the aircraft was unguarded for several hours.'

'There were two policemen. After that a large cordon.'

'Then,' Hannaker said doggedly, 'there's *your men*.'

'Goodness gracious, man, you are surely not suggesting . . . ?'

'I'm not suggesting anything. I'm going over possibilities.'

'All my men are of the highest integrity,' Fonseca said, sharply drawing in his breath.

'There might be one rotten apple.'

'Beg pardon, man?'

'One of them might have found some of the boxes, hidden them, and said nothing.'

'Look man, they didn't know what they were looking for.'

'They would if the boxes were splintered.' And before Fonseca had time to interrupt, 'In any case there must be some rum customers on the island.'

'Some what?'

'Dishonest persons, *he* means,' Reeves said. 'Criminals.'

'I mean people that might be worth checking up on. In Britain for instance, if there's a gold snatch or a jewellery theft, they know roughly who might have done it.'

'In Ceylon people in general very honest.'

'You go on like that, you'll be talking yourself out of a job.'

Hannaker smiled but the CID chief did not smile back. 'You know what I mean. You're close to India. You must have some types known to be or have been in the gold racket. Smuggling. That sort of thing.'

'But, man, it is all too circumstantial. It does not stand up to hold water. You mean a gold smuggler might by coincidence be passing through the forest. On a night like that? When behold . . .'

'There's Gunn,' Reeves swallowed and said suddenly.

'Gunn,' Hannaker asked. 'Who's he?'

'A very poor-quality American,' Fonseca said. 'A pilot. He sells sightseeing trips.'

'Does he indeed!' Hannaker said thoughtfully.

'Takes aerial photographs for some of the newspapers.'

'Go on.'

'Does survey work occasionally.'

Hannaker slid off the sill. 'Why d'you say he's a poor type?'

'Information about him is very scarce. But he has a shadowy past,' Fonseca said. 'I understand he was once a Pan American pilot.'

'They gave him the bullet,' Reeves said.

'Why?'

'I haven't seen fit to ask him. He's not a man you'd chat up. Smuggling, I think. Since then, he's taken the downward path. Bums around.'

'Could he have had anything to do with it?'

'To do with *what*?'

'Moving the gold?'

'Certainly not,' Fonseca said. 'Number one, he would not know of it. Number two, he was not near the place. Number three, he would have no organizing ability whatsoever to dispose of it. The gentleman is, as Mr Reeves said, a bum. Just a bum.'

'Where does he live?'

'In the Pettah. That will tell you the sort of gentleman he has got into.' Fonseca rose.

'Have you questioned him?'

'I do not make a jester of myself.' And nodding to Hannaker, the Tamil Inspector said good day to Reeves and walked with great dignity to the door. More in sorrow than in anger he said, 'It is always the same with westerners. You bring wrong eyes to this eastern scene. Here we do not think, read, watch big crimes all the time. You may not think very much good to my theory, Mr Hannaker.' He opened the door and stood, a dramatic little figure declaiming his curtain line, 'But yours is, as you say, straight out of the story book for the marines.'

'Truth is stranger than fiction,' Hannaker called after him. But the door had closed behind Fonseca. His brisk angry footsteps retreated down the corridor.

'Now you've gone and upset *him*.' Reeves accented the final word as if Fonseca was the last on a long list. There was, now he came to think of it, quite a list—Mr Seneratne, Captain Dewhurst, himself—

'I don't see why.'

'Because you're an accident investigator, Mr Hannaker.'

'I'm always upsetting people because I'm an accident investigator?'

'That's not *quite* what I meant. You've upset him because this isn't your line of country. The *accident* is *yours*. The gold search is *his*. I have already had difficulty stopping too many well-meaning people putting their noses in. They are very fussy about spheres of influence out here.'

'And you don't think the two are connected?'

'I am perfectly certain they are not.' He paused. 'So is every other reasonable person.'

Hannaker raised his brows at Reeves's barb, but did not take issue with him. 'This man, Gunn, have you got his address?'

'No.'

'Never mind.' He stood up. 'I expect I could find him.'

Reeves pursed his lips but said nothing. He watched Hannaker walk to the door. For the first time he looked closely at Hannaker's face. Perhaps it was after staring so long at Inspector Fonseca's glowing nutty brown skin, but Hannaker seemed inordinately pale, his mouth set a trifle too strained and grim. For the first time then it dawned on Reeves that Hannaker was going to be a real problem and not the splendid help he had been cracked up to be.

The Pettah, Reeves had said. That was where this American Gunn lived. This pilot who'd had some shady connections with gold in the past, but who was considered by both Reeves and Fonseca to have no connection with this gold of the present.

The telephone book told him exactly *where* in the Pettah. There was only one Gunn in the Pettah telephone exchange and just to make it easier still, after the name was added, *Gunn's Airways Inc.* The address was 37 Kalatura Street.

It proved to be an insanitary place. An area behind the rocks and round the port, full of the smell of fish and decaying vegetables, and the honking of horns and the grunting of bullocks. Hannaker set off for it after early breakfast the next morning. He took the train along the coast to Colombo Pettah station. Then purposely took neither taxi nor rickshaw, but went exploring round the area. He was, he knew, probably wasting his time. But maybe not. He had learned from bitter experience that phrases like, 'you won't find anything *there*,' or 'no need to check that,' were signals to investigate those things. After an aircraft accident, there was a tremendous urge to explain it immediately, as though the world had toppled. And an almost audible sigh of relief when the cause was found. He stood for a moment, watching on the other side of the crowd-filled street, a hawker with a barrow of mangoes. The shaft of a bullock cart had tipped the whole lot over. There was a great shouting and execration until other street traders and friends and relatives scooped it up into a golden pyramid again. Not unlike an aircraft accident, Hannaker thought wryly, pushing his way forward, peering at the painted street signs, trying to avoid broken-down lorries laden with crates, and the droppings of the bullocks, and ant-scoured husks of rotten fruit.

37 Kalatura Street, when he finally found it, turned out to be a two-storey building of mud and brick, covered with peeling orange paint. At the entrance a group of children were playing with a fat dusty brown Abyssinian cat. The name 'Gunn' appeared to mean nothing to them. But Hannaker's query brought forth a waterfall of giggles. He produced a handful of rupees and asked the biggest one his name but he didn't seem to understand that either. Hannaker picked his way in.

Inside, the place appeared to be divided into a series of flats. Downstairs was clearly occupied by two large Sinhalese families that overflowed from the doorways, so Hannaker climbed up the concrete steps to the second storey.

Up here it was quieter and totally deserted. There were no doors to knock on. To the left, a bright bead curtain hung down over an entrance. Through it Hannaker could see a sparsely furnished living room covered in rice matting. The only visible seat was an old Victorian-style chaise-longue, lumpy and in disrepair, untidy with books and papers. There were the remains of a meal on a low table. Distantly beyond the room itself Hannaker heard the sound of splashing water.

'Mr Gunn?' Hannaker called hopefully.

There was no reply. Only the cat which had escaped the children came unhurriedly up the stairs and rubbed itself against his legs.

'Mr Gunn?' Hannaker bent to scratch the cat's head. As he did so, still peering through the bead curtain for any sign of life, something caught his eye on the window ledge at the far side of the room.

It was a very ordinary wooden box, but its shape and size were what interested Hannaker. Rectangular, about five inches long, its shallow sides appeared to have been scored by wire. The idea it conjured up in his mind made Hannaker lift the bead curtain. The cat fled. On his rubber-soled shoes he walked carefully across the room. He reached the window sill. There was still no one around. Hannaker stood for a moment in front of the box, frowning. Then he stretched out a hand to pick it up.

'For God's sake, mister,' the slow lazy voice caught Hannaker on the hop with his fingers poised over the box. 'Don't be bashful. Be my guest. If you want a smoke, help yourself.'

Spinning round, Hannaker saw a thick-set shadow emerge from a passage leading off the room.

'Mr Gunn?'

The shadow materialized as a man of about thirty-two or three. Broad-shouldered, narrow-hipped, slightly bow-legged, and an inch or so shorter than Hannaker himself. His face was on the small side for his body and square—all the lines going somehow straight across—straight thick brows, narrowed eyes, short upper lip, square jaw. An ugly aggressive face. His soaked hair was slicked down over his forehead as if he'd just come from under a shower. He advanced with a deliberate sideways rolling gait, which combined with the fact that he was stark naked to give him a pugnacious simian appearance.

'That's me, mister.'

He stuck out his jaw, stared for a moment at Hannaker's hand now outstretched towards him, then reluctantly transferred a bar of yellow soap he was carrying from his right to his left hand.

'My name's Hannaker,' as they shook hands. 'Jamie Hannaker.'

'Well what d'you know?' Gunn dropped Hannaker's hand, lifted the wooden box which had so engaged Hannaker's attention, and flipped it open. Inside were two neat rows of cigarettes. 'Go on. Have one. You didn't come all the way up here to tell me your name was . . . what was it now . . . Hannaker? Mighty interesting though that fact is, mister.'

'No thanks,' Hannaker said, 'I don't smoke.'

Gunn scratched his backside thoughtfully with the bar of soap, his eyes fixed on Hannaker. They were lively hazel brown, with laughter lines at the corners. Those laughter lines were not in use at the moment.

'No bad habits eh, mister?'

'None at all,' Hannaker grinned.

The other man didn't smile back.

'So you didn't want a smoke, mister.' He narrowed his eyes. He snapped his fingers. 'So I know who you are.'

'I doubt if you do.'

'You're a collar.'

'Certainly not.'

'You got it diestamped on you, mister. F and B bloody I. Or the Limey equivalent. Your skin.' He extended his own mahogany-brown arm and admired it. 'You're just out from London, England, mister. That lightweight suit. No Colombo tailor ever stitched that. Those big feet. That hangdog face. You seen all the seamy side, ain't you, mister. It hurts you-all worse than it hurts us, I shouldn't wonder.'

'I can see,' Hannaker said coldly, 'once you've made up your mind, that's it.'

'And I know why you're here.' Gunn slid his hand through his wet hair so that it stood up in spikes. Underneath was a wide intelligent forehead. Not all brute strength and ignorance by any means, Hannaker remembered thinking.

'Why you took such a fancy to that cute li'l ole box my granny gave me?' He dropped into a southern impudent exaggerated drawl. Then savagely, sharply. 'Well then, mister, if that's what you figure, why don't you search the place? Go on. What're you waiting for?'

Now it was Hannaker's turn to eye the other thoughtfully and unsmilingly. 'All right. If you insist.'

Leaving wet Man Friday footprints over the matting, Gunn walked, with a fine show of injured innocence, over to a chest of drawers. He pulled them open, disclosing an untidy mass of papers and books. He flung open the door of an old cupboard set into the wall. A couple of pairs of soiled dungarees hung on nails. A pair of gum boots stood on a shelf beside a stack of cat food, and a tin of biscuits. Hannaker walked over, peered in the cupboard, lifted a can of the food and tossed it in his hand, as if to see if it weighed more than it ought.

'No gold in there, mister. Me, I'm just fond of animals.'

He jerked his head and beckoned Hannaker into the dusky corridor from which he had appeared. He kicked open a door.

'Bath . . . cum . . . kitchen. . . . I'll jest pull the plug out . . . you kinda interrupted my ablutions.'

'I'm sorry.'

Gunn leaned over the bath. Soapy water gurgled noisily away. 'Now you know there's nothing stuffed down the spout?'

'Down *that* one, anyway.'

'Oh, and there's my van parked outside. If you'd like to look it over?'

'Presently,' Hannaker said equably, unmoved by Gunn's indignation. Just for a second he saw a tiny flicker of something like warmth touch the hazel eyes, and then as quickly be extinguished.

'First, I'd like to know one thing.' Hannaker sauntered

back into the living room, and picked up the wooden box. 'How did you know the gold was missing?'

'I get around, mister. I hear things. But you're barking up the wrong tree now, mister.' He neatly took the box from Hannaker and put it back where it belonged, 'Certainly this old friend here once carried packaging and a one-kilo gold bar. But that's ancient history, mister. There's a new bloody administration in at Gunn Airways Inc. Jest coffin nails, that's all the old box carries now.'

'*Did* you deal in gold? *Once?*'

'Sure.'

'Why did you give it up?'

'Let's say I saw the light, mister. Or I didn't see the light for too bloody long. Or I got my finger ends singed. Or mind your own bloody business. That's all you have to know. I'm *not in the racket now*, mister, so don't jump to any of your off-the-peg straight out the Snout's Book conclusions.'

Hannaker drew in his breath slowly and said, 'Look here, Gunn. I wish you'd get it into your head, I'm *not* a detective.' All the same he had an uneasy feeling he'd been acting like one. Perhaps, as Reeves had said, he should stick to his own profession. For in spite of his hostility, he warmed to Gunn. He knew that, handled properly, Gunn might be a useful source of inside information. In an attempt to pour oil on troubled waters he added, 'I'm an aircraft accident investigator.'

'And the best of British luck to you, mister.' Just for a second a more bitter, more personal animosity touched the ugly square face. The eyes narrowed. But behind there was a curious look, not anger, but pain. There had been, Hannaker was sure, some accident in Gunn's past. One perhaps for which he had been blamed. But maybe he was mistaken. The voice was still the same—drawling and insolent. 'Now me, mister, I'm allergic to investigators. *All* kinds of investigators. Real allergic.' He rubbed his arm thoughtfully with the soap. 'Bring me all out in a rash.' He stared down at the dark-skinned hairy arm as if he expected to see an immediate reaction. 'Know what I mean, mister?'

'Yes,' Hannaker said sharply, 'I know what you mean.'

He stared levelly at Gunn, forcing the other man to look straight back at him. 'I *also* have an allergy. To accidents, Gunn. To avoidable accidents.'

Gunn said nothing for a long time. Hannaker was acutely aware of the shouts and screams of the families on the ground floor, the cries of the street traders below the windows. Yet the room seemed very quiet. In that quiet, Gunn, he knew, was coming to some sort of decision. Even the sound of the same fat cat pushing aside the bead curtains and padding into the room sounded loud, made Hannaker turn. The spell of quiet broke. Gunn suddenly blinked his eyes and looked down at his left hand as if astonished to find himself still holding the soap.

'And you reckon this 707 do at Tallaputiya was avoidable.' He tossed the bar of soap on to the table.

'Most accidents,' Hannaker spoke slowly, treading carefully, 'are avoidable.'

'Most.' Gunn snatched up the word as if he might tear it apart, shrugged, letting it go and asked, sticking his hands on his hips, tilting his head on one side, 'So the pilot's the fall guy again, is he? That what you're trying to pin on him? Pilot error.'

'Not if it wasn't so.'

'But that's the way the cookie's gonna crumble, eh? Under-shoot?'

'On the surface perhaps.'

'Then what about the rain?'

'His visibility was very poor. But that, surely, would tend to *support* the pilot error theory.'

Gunn advanced a pace. 'What about the airport itself, mister?'

'Tallaputiya? Yes, that's something I wanted to ask you about. You're a pilot. What's your opinion of it?'

'D'you really want to know?' Gunn narrowed his eyes, but the hostility had diminished. 'Then sit down.' He swept the books and papers off the sofa, waved Hannaker to it with an inviting lordly gesture. Then he brought up a hard-backed kitchen chair and sat on it, opposite Hannaker. The cat jumped on to his knee. He stroked it absent-mindedly, eyes fixed on Hannaker. 'I'll tell you. It's such a place, I wouldn't even keep my Cessna on it.'

'I noticed myself that the main runway was downhill.'

'And too short.'

'I would have thought perhaps so.'

'Those hills—they crowd you.'

Hannaker nodded.

'Well, there you got it, mister. My opinion of Tallaputiya.' He went on stroking the cat.

'I'm inclined to agree with you.'

For the first time Gunn almost smiled.

'Why did they build it there?' Hannaker asked.

Gunn laughed shortly and without humour. 'You just come from London, England? Well, mister, what about your third airport row? Same here, only eastern setting.'

'I follow you.' Hannaker smiled faintly and nodded.

'An' a sight more freer-flowing oil as well,' Gunn stroked the palm of one hand with the fingers of the other.

'What were the alternatives to Tallaputiya?'

'Negombo. That was odds-on favourite. Flat. Close to the sea. But close to Colombo too, so the land cost a bomb. They tried to winkle a loan out of the British government. But they wouldn't play ball. Election year, I reckon it was.'

'Where else?'

'Ratmalana. That's military. An' they wouldn't let their clammy hands off it.' Gunn shrugged his shoulders. He set the cat carefully on the floor and stood up. 'It's getting kinda hot in here. How about,' he suddenly mimicked an English voice, 'some of the wine of the country? A drop of jungle juice?'

'Thank you,' Hannaker nodded.

Gunn disappeared into the bathroom-cum-kitchen. The cat jumped up on to Hannaker's lap, kneaded itself comfortable and curled up. From the passageway came the sound of glasses on a tin tray.

'So in the end it was Tallaputiya?' Hannaker called to Gunn.

'Yep' he shouted back. 'A couple big wheels in the Senate

109

owned land thereabouts. They wanted it. An' there was a lot of Sinhalese Buddhists in the government.'

'So?'

'So the Bharratu shrine wasn't sacred to them. Some ways, it was one in the eye for the Tamil Hindus. A squit bang on their doorstep. Have you talked to the Brahmin there? Holy Mother of God, did he have the gift of tongues!' He put his head round the doorway lest Hannaker had not understood. 'Prophecy.'

'What did he prophesy?'

'Jest that, mister. Jest like what happened.' The head disappeared again. 'That his gods would get real mean, an' smack 'em down.' There were more sounds of preparation from the kitchen. Hannaker looked at his watch and sighed. His eyes travelled round the room, came to rest on the untidy table where Gunn had finally relinquished his soap.

When Gunn reappeared he was wearing a tight-fitting pair of white cotton ducks, and he carried a tin tray on which were two tall glasses three-quarters full of steaming brown liquid.

'Superstitious lot, of course, the Sinhalese.' Gunn swept to one side the remnants of the meal and set the tray on the table. There was a saucer filled with thin slices of lemon. Hannaker smelled the fragrance of tea.

'The wine of the country,' he grinned as Gunn handed him a glass. He helped himself to a slice of lemon. 'What better!'

'I kicked the hard liquor,' Gunn said not looking at him, 'along with the gold.'

'Ah, yes, the gold,' Hannaker said casually as if it had slipped his mind. He drank gratefully. 'Sounds like a story, Care to tell me?'

'One day maybe, mister. Not now.' He sat himself in the chair. For the first time Gunn noticed the cat asleep in Hannaker's lap.

'Not often she does that, mister.'

'Perceptive animals, cats,' Hannaker grinned.

'Bad sign that if they take to you. Dogs, yes. Cat's, no.'

'Means she trusts me, though,' Hannaker said.

'Yep, I'll give you that. She trusts you.' Gunn drained his glass. 'Now me—that's more than I do. Have a refill?'

'No thanks. I must get going.' Hannaker lifted the cat gently and set it on the floor beside his feet.

As he bent down, for the second time that day his eye caught something. Shoved under the Victorian chaise-longue was a pair of shoes. Very dirty shoes. Covered right above the lace holes with once liquid, but now solidified, mud. Dark grey-green, the same distinctive colour as the mud around the crash lake.

Hannaker straightened, and got to his feet.

'Well,' he said lazily, 'you might say that goes for both of us. The trusting bit.'

'Then we're quits, mister.' Gunn gave him a mock farewell salute. 'Come again.'

'Will do.'

Hannaker sauntered out and down the stairs. The information about Tallaputiya, the muddy shoes. Mentally, he sorted through his haul as he went along. But that wasn't all he'd noticed. Gunn himself, for all his insolent couldn't-care-less manner, had been under considerable stress. That bar of soap carried like a badge of his insolence and innocence, a badge to show a man more interested in his bath than his visitor. When he'd finally tossed it aside, it was squeezed hard, waisted in the middle with the marks of Gunn's thick strong fingers printed on it, and the cracks where his nails had dug in.

The Air Safety Bureau laboratory faced due south, and cheerfully and cruelly the morning sun poured in. The place was like a hothouse, and the air was far too warm to breathe. Standing beside Hannaker, Seneratne's face was glistening with sweat. And the shirt of his assistant was clearly wringing wet.

Seneratne's excuses of being too busy to see him had suddenly given way to a pressing invitation to the Ministry. Hannaker had guessed the reason for putting him off, and though he had been impatient, he had not been unsympathetic. A lone worker himself, he understood the desire to work alone and in peace and not to have a tentative vision of truth rudely shattered by the observations, doubts and misgivings of others. Groping for solutions was a tenuous and delicate job. One plucked ideas out of the air and tried to work on them. The whole business was like stitching bubbles together. Sometimes a team could do it, working together with understanding, giving each other belief. Sometimes it was better to work out your own answers. Perhaps because he resented Hannaker's far wider experience, perhaps because he wanted all the credit for himself, perhaps because there were other things involved, Seneratne probably preferred the latter course.

'We have now checked everything,' Seneratne said. 'We have found no indication of engine or airframe failure. Have you?'

'Not yet,' Hannaker said.

'Have you found any evidence of sabotage?'

'None.'

'Have you any theory of what might have been the cause?'

'No.'

'Well, we have,' Seneratne said with satisfaction.

'But you've seen the Flight Recorder readings.'

'Exactly, Mr Hannaker. And we have interpreted them. Come over here, sir.' Seneratne led the way to the other end of the laboratory. 'Now I shall re-create for you exactly what happened on the night of the crash.'

Years ago, Hannaker had read *The Time Machine*. Of course H. G. Wells knew a thing or two about time, how it operated on different planes. But here, in this stifling Ceylonese glass-house, Seneratne had done much the same. With the flight recorder from the crashed 707 and the tape recording from Tallaputiya Tower, he had reconstructed the last few minutes in the mortal lives of eighty-one souls.

There were graphs, flight recorder read-out readings on airspeed, height, course, pitch, altitude and acceleration, together with photographs and instruments recovered from the crash. But most graphic of all was an actual model of the aircraft's instrument descent on the ILS.

The whole thing had been done to scale, with minute attention to detail. Hills, roads, streams, trees—even the outer marker beacon—had been reconstructed perfectly from wood and plasticine, and painted. There was the swathe through the forest, the lake, the hillock, the white-painted buildings of the Bharratu shrine—then further to the left and waiting, the lead-in lights on their matchstick stalks, the ILS hut and the long grey stretch of Runway 28. From the ceiling on strings hung miniature 707s, culminating in an exact reproduction of the wreck. The flight of the aircraft down the ILS glide path was represented by green string for normal, red string for atypical and dangerous.

Seneratne turned to his assistant and nodded.

There was the click of a tape-recorder switch. Immediately they were back eleven days in time. Captain Coates's voice, tetchy and sounding tired, fourteen minutes and fifty-one seconds exactly before the crash, now echoed round this hot bright-painted room: 'Hey—this thing's deteriorating, isn't it? Coming down in buckets up here. What's the latest visibility?'

'Latest visibility . . . ?' The controller's voice hesitating, trailing away.

'Hell . . . d'you think I'm at a bus stop? I want the visibility *now*!'

Hannaker was conscious of Seneratne watching his face. As though excusing Coates, the Ceylonese said softly, 'He was a man of fifty-four . . . in bad-weather night conditions . . . about to land on instruments at the end of a tiring flight. So naturally——'

Coates's voice, booming out crossly, interrupted him. 'Haven't you got that visibility *yet*?'

'Visibility . . . one mile. In heavy rain.'

'You can say that again!'

'Captain Dewhurst landed an hour ago.'

'What was the visibility then?'

'Same, sir. And above your Company limits.'

'I know. . . . I know!'

'Captain Dewhurst reported seeing the lead-in lights further than a mile.'

More cheerfully: 'We'll come down and have a look-see.' And one minute later, 'On procedure turn!'

Now Seneratne pointed at the green string drawn tight above the model. 'He goes out forty seconds . . . instead of forty-five . . . and turns on to the runway heading of 280 magnetic. He overshoots the ILS beam, and immediately brackets back. The flight recorder readings show rough flying.'

'It would be very bumpy,' Hannaker pointed out.

Coates's voice again, 'Procedure turn complete. Height twenty-five hundred.'

'It was, in fact,' Seneratne said, 'twenty-three hundred.'

'But he soon corrected.' Hannaker ran his fingers down the green string. 'Here he is . . . dead in line with the runway, descending at five hundred feet a minute exactly on the ILS glide path, ten miles from the threshold at his correct altitude of two thousand feet.'

'Over the outer marker at fifteen hundred feet,' Coates's voice now sounded quite jaunty. 'On the glide path.'

Hannaker looked at the flight recorder readings attached to the long pin that indicated the outer marker. 'He *was* at his correct altitude of fifteen hundred feet. He *had* been descending correctly on the three degrees ILS glide path. His air speed was 140 knots . . . quite correct. He *was* on the ILS localizer beam on a course of 280 degrees . . . also quite correct. Three minutes before the accident . . . we have the proof here . . . everything was perfectly normal. And then——'

'Exactly, man! Suddenly, he puts the nose down. Instead of descending at the five hundred feet a minute of the ILS glide path, he comes down steeply . . . averaging six hundred and fifty feet a minute.' Seneratne grasped the red string that ran from the outer marker pin straight down over the little grey glass lake to the green plasticine hillock and the scattered silver pieces of model aeroplane. 'Why, man . . . why?'

Hannaker said nothing.

'D'you know what I think?'

Hannaker still said nothing.

'Over the outer marker, through the heavy rain either the Captain or the First Officer caught a momentary glimpse of a lead-in light. Instrument flying is very fatiguing,' Seneratne shrugged his shoulders. 'Captain Coates was tired. He abandoned his instruments to fly visually, pushing the nose down to get underneath the cloud. Five miles out, instead of being at a thousand feet, he was at eight-fifty. And two and a half miles out, instead of being at five hundred feet, he crashed into a two-hundred-foot hill.'

'In other words, he got hooked on a disappearing light.'

'It's happened before . . . hasn't it?'

'Many times.'

'That's it then?' Seneratne said.

'I agree it's a possible theory.'

'It's the *only* theory, man. Pilot error! Giving up an instrument approach for visual!'

Hannaker hesitated. 'It's all just a bit too simple.'

'But why look for complications?'

'I can't see a captain of Coates's experience doing a silly thing like that.'

'Well, then! Well, then!' Impatiently the Sinhalese pointed to the angle in the string, the fatal bend downwards of the refracted glide path. 'How d'you explain this? What other explanation is there, man?'

'Whisky Echo,' the Controller's voice boomed out at them from the tape recorder, 'Clear to land.'

The three of them stood there in the heat and the sunshine, saying nothing.

'Whisky Echo . . .' The placid hum of the tape recorder was the only sound. 'Whisky Echo . . . report please.'

Still just the noise of the machine.

'Whisky Echo . . . are you receiving me?' The voice of the Controller had gone higher. 'Do you hear?'

No reply.

'Whisky Echo . . . are you overshooting? Are you diverting? I do not hear your engines.'

A minute went by. 'Whisky Echo . . . do you hear?'

Still nothing.

Then a torrent of Sinhalese. Two voices, three voices, all chattering together. Sounds of movement, echoes. And then suddenly interrupting, the same voice in English, 'Oh my God! What to do? *What to do?*'

This, then, was all that was left of the British Empire in Ceylon: this unimpressive building on the road to a suburb of Colombo. Just a dozen offices, and a reception annexe furnished with the *Illustrated London News* and the *Ladies Home Journal*—indistinguishable from a dentist's waiting room except for two large coloured photographs, one of the Queen and the other of the Duke staring at each other questioningly as if asking themselves where the hell it had all gone.

For gone was the Governor's residence with the guards at the gate, the ceremonial carriage and the cavalry escort. Gone was the pomp and circumstance, the power and the glory. These three thousand square feet remained the sovereign territory of the British High Commission. And the man behind the desk of the largest office, dressed in a plain grey lightweight suit, was Sir Arthur Atcherly, the British High Commissioner.

He was a slim man, freckled, with sandy hair and a small sandy moustache. He had looked much more impressive in his white-plumed hat, with a sword at his side. But these accoutrements were tucked away in an *almirah* in his residence, and almost never worn. Never was there mention of the considerable past achievements for the benefit of this island. When the Buddhists took over the missionary schools, no protest crossed his lips. When Sinhalese was declared the number one language to be taught instead of English, only a murmur about the commercial disadvantages had issued. At Rotary Club Meetings, Trade Fairs, and business lunches, the High Commissioner could always be heard expounding on the quality of British tractors, British radio equipment. British bridges, and British mini-skirts. Where else in the world today to wave the Union Jack except on a plump and pretty British bottom? Atcherley had, reluctantly at first but whole-heartedly now, espoused the New Look in British diplomacy—his mission to turn colonies into customers.

And customers had to be right.

And the policy too was right. Peace followed prosperity. Communism followed chaos. It was over twenty years since the British government had granted independence to Ceylon, and after a difficult and bloodthirsty start, things were beginning to improve. The fighting between Sinhalese and Tamil that had gone on for two thousand years was over. And though in Sir Arthur's opinion the animosity had taken on a more underground form, on the surface all seemed well. Poverty there still was of course. Rationalization had not made the progress it might have done. But that was largely the Sinhalese temperament.

If he had been allowed one wish for this beautiful little island, he would have given them a strong and (low be it spoken) if necessary a dictatorial government. Ceylon cried out for a leader. A lion. The trouble was there were no lions in Ceylon—neither animal nor human. Atcherley had a very fatherly affection for the people, but a less lion-like race it would be difficult to imagine. He had often remarked, where it was discreet to make such remarks, on the irony of their calling themselves after Sinha.

Yet for all their absence, lions were woven into the destiny of Ceylon—in their drawings, their paintings, their statues, their literature. And it was no coincidence that the only real peace the island had known, had come from the Pax Britannica. From the British lion. But Sir Arthur could not remind them of it.

In all circumstances he knew his role was to walk a tightrope. It did not make his job any easier when a British aircraft crashed on approach to a new Ceylonese airport killing eighty-one people, many of them Ceylonese nationals. He and his staff had worked unceasingly—both publicly at the funerals and privately with the government—to smooth over a potentially explosive situation.

At that particular moment, just after twelve on Saturday morning, he was dictating for his masters in Whitehall an account of the action he had taken, together with his forecast of the probable consequences, to his Sinhalese confidential secretary in her British blue cotton frock. The Diplomatic Bag left for London at two o'clock and though the letter was long he intended to catch it.

'. . . the newspapers are less vociferous now. The police are satisfied that they know where the gold cargo is, and we have offered assistance in procuring suitable dredging equipment. This is the first major crash to be investigated by the Ceylon Accident Investigation Department but they appear to be putting up a very creditable show. Therefore . . .'

The telephone on the desk interrupted him in full flow, and he was frowning as his secretary picked up the receiver. She listened for a moment and then covered up the mouthpiece, 'It's a Mr Hannaker, sir. He would like to see you. It's about the accident investigation. . . .'

'Oh, yes. Hannaker.'

The name rang a bell. The man accredited, tactlessly in Sir Arthur's opinion, from Whitehall. The very fact of their doing so had caused a quiver on the tightrope which Sir Arthur could well have done without.

'Tell him to make an appointment for tomorrow. No, on second thoughts, tell him all right, but for a very few minutes only.'

He immediately dismissed the girl, rose from his chair and the moment Hannaker came through the door their hands connected.

'Do sit down. That's quite a comfortable chair.' His small pebbly grey eyes assessed Hannaker swiftly. 'We don't run to air conditioning. But it's not too bad, is it?' Having done the man-to-man stuff, he sat down, put his elbows on the desk and the tips of his freckly fingers together, and said, 'It's about the accident, I take it?'

'Yes.'

'Regrettable business.'

'Very.'

'But you're getting results?'

'Largely negative.'

'I thought they had more or less arrived at their conclusion.'

'By they,' Hannaker said dryly, 'you mean the Ceylon Air Safety Bureau?'

'Of course. And the police too. I understand that they know where the gold is. But that's not strictly your pigeon.'

Hannaker inclined his head but said nothing.

'Now tell me, Hannaker, by negative evidence, you mean that certain possible causes have been eliminated?'

'That is so. More or less eliminated. There appears for instance to have been no mechanical failure.'

'Good, good!'

'Captain Dewhurst and I tested the ILS beam. That seems to have been working properly.'

Sir Arthur nodded.

'What about sabotage? Hong Kong's thick with Communist agents. I have never felt that that eventuality could be completely ruled out. Very clever with these timing devices, you know.'

'There is no sign of any bomb on board.'

'Pity!'

Sir Arthur pushed his left wrist forward, looked at his watch and raised his sandy brows at the lateness of the hour. 'Which brings us to the British pilot, I suppose. A great pity. But everyone makes mistakes.'

'Oh, there are many other factors to be considered as well. Tallaputiya itself. That's why I wanted to see you. I understand there was a great deal of dissension about the building of it.'

'My dear fellow, when *isn't* there dissension about the building of anything?'

'But in this case rather more.'

'I wonder.'

'The Hindus at the Bharratu shrine for instance.'

'Yes, that was unfortunate. But if it hadn't been *that* shrine it would have been some other. The whole island's thick with them.'

'I understand too there was a great deal of political lobbying. Bribery. That sort of thing.'

'Well, my dear chap, you seem to know far more about it than I do.'

'The runway, for one thing,' Hannaker said doggedly, aware

that His Excellency was fast losing patience with him, 'is too short for big jets.'

'You surprise me.'

'And there's no Ground Controlled Radar Approach.'

'This is all rather too technical for me. Have another chat with Seneratne. Excellent chap. Their ways may be different from ours, but they're basically sound. Don't try to rush them.'

'That's the opposite of what I'm trying to do. I think *they're* going far too fast.'

Sir Arthur sighed. Throughout his twenty-five years in the Diplomatic Service, his own countrymen had been both a blessing and bane to him. They worked hard. They had integrity. But many of them wore a pair of British-made spectacles—and spectacles were among the few British products he did not plug. They saw things in faraway places exactly the way they saw them in Twickenham and Berwick-on-Tweed. If something differed from British customs, it must be bad.

'I don't quite understand,' Sir Arthur said, understanding perfectly.

'The Ceylon authorities are jumping to conclusions.'

An Oxford man himself, the High Commissioner had immediately identified Hannaker as a good earnest technical type, and now he smiled in a fatherly way. 'I think we all, Hannaker, have a tendency to underestimate people in developing countries. Did you know that two thousand five hundred years ago the Ceylonese were building cities, painting pictures, making irrigation schemes while our ancestors hadn't got around to discovering woad?'

'But we have a lead, admittedly somewhat shorter than the one you mention, in aircraft accident investigation.'

'Even so, they're a clever people. Take a day off. Go up to the ruined cities. Stand still and marvel! You'll get it all in a better perspective.'

He slid his wrist round again.

'I haven't the time at present,' Hannaker said coldly. 'There's a great deal of ground still to be covered. One thing

I want to avoid is the Air Safety Bureau here rushing ahead and setting a date for the official Inquiry.'

'Oh, didn't you know?' Sir Arthur's hands flew apart. He picked up the memo pad on his right, thumbed over a page. 'I had a message an hour ago from George Seneratne. The Inquiry has just been fixed. For June 26th. And in private.'

Three days later, Hannaker walked empty-handed again out of yet another government building. This time the Ministry of Public Health.

Though unlike George Seneratne and the Sinhalese operations office in charge of the ILS hut, Dr da Silva had been only too enchanted to come to meet Hannaker at the department, and put before him any help that it might be his honour to give, the help was in fact of the negative variety.

Dr da Silva had performed the autopsy on Captain Coates and the other crew members. There was, he seemed genuinely regretful, no evidence that Captain Coates had suffered cardiac infraction. No cerebral thrombosis nor haemorrhage. Nothing that might in his opinion result in sudden loss of consciousness.

Yes, in answer to Hannaker's question, the contents of the stomach had been analysed. Captain Coates had taken no alcohol or drugs. He had not been overcome by any gastric infection or sickness. Nor had he suffered from food or any other type of poisoning.

But . . . Captain Coates was fifty-four. Physically a very young fifty-four. But, how could he best put it? It was not just the elasticity of the arteries that was entirely important. Every year one's reactions got a little slower. He himself at forty-two was well aware that he was nowhere near so quick as twenty-four.

'And you, my dear sir, at how old? Thirty-eight? Nine?'

'Thirty-six in fact.'

'You are not quite so quickly reactive as ten, five even, years ago?'

'Maybe you're right.'

'Also, we get very immovable in our ways. We get like the

work elephant,' he shaded his eyes. 'Blinkers. We see what is just in front of us. What we think we ought to see.'

'We develop a set, as they say in aviation psychology.'

'Exactly, my dear sir. We see what we expect to see.'

Hannaker pondered the doctor's remarks, as he walked hands in his pockets down the stone steps of the Ministry building. He tried to sift through them along with the other negative evidence he had dredged up over the last eleven days. Counting over the bits that looked more solid than the rest. Yet each point seemed to have its counterpoint.

A slightly older pilot. But a healthy one.

A badly sited airfield, its main runway too short and with insufficient aids. But one where there had not till now been any accident, and about which the pilots, though grumbling, had not officially complained.

Bad weather. But weather in which other pilots had landed safely.

Low visibility. But the airfield was equipped with a serviceable Instrument Landing System.

Hannaker could have named a possible explanation for almost every step he descended. Or, while he was thinking on those lines, was it not like most accidents, a combination of several causes, not just one on its own? Each leading into the other as these steps were part of a flight.

Half-way down the steps there was a stone landing. Hannaker stopped and wiped his forehead. Then of course there was the gold. Somehow he could not get the coincidence of that out of his mind.

But even if it hadn't been for the disappearance of the gold, would he have been content to let the cause go as pilot error?

Wasn't he basically, he accused himself, resuming his descent of the steps, simply following a hunch? Listening not so much to the voice of science and reason as his own intuition. In its way it was just as unscientific as the superstitions that befogged this island—the horoscope-casting, the devil-dancing and self-hypnotism. Or was he being, as Margaret used to say, simply cussed? Faced with Seneratne's determination to blind the aviation world with the speed of his newly acquired science, with Fonseca's amiable illogicality, with Reeves's snout in the sand attitude, was he not merely asserting his own true British scepticism?

Still undecided about his own motives, Hannaker stepped on to the pavement.

Over the city, there was a peculiar white explosive quality of sunlight after yet another night's torrential rain. Moisture still hung in the air, heightening the smell of tarred rope, diesel oil and vegetables, vivifying the bitter green and the orange of the flame trees, the red geraniums in the hanging baskets, the coloured *tats* or blinds over the windows and the saris and the faces which now filled the pavement and spilled on to the road in front of the slow bullock-carts and honking cars. It was all such a mixture—oriental shops beside modern stores. Ivories, silks, Chinese carpets, Kandyan silver, amethysts and aqua-marines for sale side by side with refrigerators, English fashions, Scotch whisky, car accessories. Here was a shop selling neat-sized transistor radios that announced itself as one of the Sinha Radio chain—no doubt part of Laughton's empire. Beggars came up, holding out their hands for a *santosam*. Boys on bicycles wobbled past—and here twisting its way through this Eastern-Western scene, familiar yet alien, a red London double-decker bus.

Hannaker, about to turn right with the main stream of the crowds towards the market, saw it and paused for a moment. Its destination was some unpronounceable name for some unknown place, but its number was 22. Hannaker was pierced with a sudden feeling of homesickness. Not for the London of now, but ten years ago. Margaret and he in the early days just before they bought the fatal cottage in the country. Catching the 22 bus from outside the Ministry to World's End—which was then just a few barrows and one decent pub. Getting off the bus there, Saturday noon, to meet Margaret and do the week-end shopping, and have a beer and a cheese-sandwich lunch. Margaret standing on the pavement waiting, basket empty, hand upraised to shield her eyes from the spring sun. Daffodils and tulips in the barrows and pyramids of polished apples, and the smoke of coal barges and the smell of the river.

Hannaker blinked his eyes. The red bus drew in to the kerb with much necessary sounding of horn. A coolie whipped his cart away literally from under the tyres. The conductor gabbled and gesticulated, needlessly urging his passengers to disembark. A strange-looking crowd for a London bus dragged their baskets and boxes and children behind them and alighted. They were followed, strangest of all, by Miss Grey, dressed in a crisp white cotton dress, nipped in at the waist by a gold leather belt, and carrying a large empty shopping-basket. A kind of mirror vision, past and present, dazzled him.

She began to smile when she saw him, and took a couple of steps forward. Then something in his expression must have disturbed her, for she hesitated and looked as if she might have hurried past him, had not the crowd on the pavement made that impossible.

'Hello, Mr Hannaker. I haven't seen you for days. Are they making you comfortable in the hotel?'

'Very, thank you.' And in a gentle parody of her professional politeness, 'And how about you? Are they working you hard?'

She smiled and shook her head. 'I've had nearly a week's stand-off. I'm on a Hong Kong trip tonight.'

'First time I've seen an English girl on a Colombo bus.'

'Well, they're English after all.' She smiled, 'And they're better than the taxis.'

'You might just have a point.'

'Two points in fact.'

They stood for a moment, smiling shyly. He tried to think of something to say to detain her. But they were being jostled from behind by the people anxious to get past them. She took a step sideways. She seemed about to say goodbye, when he asked hastily, 'Are you going to the market?'

'Yes.'

'I was going that way myself. Well worth seeing, they tell me. Mind if I come along with you?'

'Not at all.' She smiled politely, but as he fell into step beside her she shot him a quick puzzled glance.

'Why d'you look so surprised? Men like to shop sometimes, you know.'

124

'I did know.' She laughed. 'It wasn't that.' She moved ahead of him past a street vendor selling silver images, 'It was just,' she said as he came level with her again, 'that I thought you were waiting for someone. Someone you expected to get off that bus.'

'No.' It took him a few seconds to get that single syllable out. She noticed the pause. Perhaps she even sensed the reason for it. But she said nothing. Either Oriental Airways trained their stewardesses brilliantly well, or she possessed a rare intuitive sympathy.

All the way along the street she seemed to stitch over his silence with a quick thread of local interest, pointing out the new skyscraper buildings, the Dutch clock tower, the entrance to the ornamental gardens.

When they came to the wide street that led down to the port, there was a traffic-duty policeman perched in a tall blue and white painted box. 'Don't try to cross till he tells you. Otherwise it's a traffic offence. We don't want to land up in gaol.'

'It might have its compensations,' he said, smiling gently, taking her arm as the point-duty policeman blew his whistle and beckoned imperiously to the crowd.

On the other side of the road, there was the market for her to chat about. It began with barrels of salted fish, some open stalls selling squids and shell fish, and what looked like red mullet. Then the narrow street opened out and there were rows and rows of shops that were no more than concrete boxes, filled with love-loves, red rambutans, custard apples and pot chatties. Boutiques, Miss Grey said they were called.

'I suppose that's where all these trendy shops get their name from. Boutiques?'

'The King's Road type? Yes, I think so.'

'I once lived not far from the King's Road. We had a flat in a place called World's End.' They had stopped outside a fruit-seller's boutique. A wizened old Tamil in a white loin-cloth squatted between twin pyramids of purple mangosteens and paw-paws. Not so bright as the polished mangoes. But sweet-smelling. 'When we were first married.'

Hannaker paused. He hadn't offered that information to

anyone before. That moment in front of the fruit-seller's stall, he recognized as memorable.

Miss Grey said nothing. But he felt her silence as something warm and comforting. He turned and walked on. He couldn't remember what the next stall was. Baskets, perhaps. All sorts and sizes, with strings of brown beads made of polished coconut wood. 'Margaret, my wife, was killed in a car accident.'

'I'm sorry.' Two small conventional words, but spoken with real and unconventional compassion.

'It was a long time ago.' For the first time Hannaker recognized that as true. He also recognized something else. An easing of a pain that had once seemed irremediable.

They sauntered on through the main part of the market. From all sides now street vendors pressed their wares. A dark hand opened, disclosing a fistful of coloured crystal, a thin arm waved, jangling its dozens of gold and silver bracelets. Mysterious white packets were thrust under their noses. Amulets on gold and silver chains swung hypnotically. The air was thick with the smell of rotting fruit, spices, incense, leather and bullock dung.

They passed a horoscope-caster's boutique, another doing brisk business telling the future from different-sized sticks. 'They probably do just as well,' Hannaker remarked softly.

'As *you*, do you mean?'

'In my weaker moments, yes, that's what I mean.' He took her hand.

'And in the rest of the moments?'

'Then I know better,' he grinned.

'Good.' She still held on to his hand.

Struggling free of the forward-moving crowd, they walked down a side alley to the left. Along here some of the concrete boutiques were untenanted, and the crowd less dense. They picked their way over the filthy baked earth littered with fruit skins and fish heads and rotting vegetables.

In the far corner in the gauzy shade of a strange-looking tree—rather like a giant pink dandelion puff—a gypsy squatted between two flat straw baskets.

'A snake-charmer,' Miss Grey whispered. 'D'you want to watch?'

'Why not?'

At first the gypsy sat cross-legged and unmoving. Then as a few more people gathered, he picked up a long thin pipe from the dusty earth in front of him and began to play.

Quivers of music, thin head wavering as heat shimmers rose in the heavy air. Slowly a few more people gathered. Hannaker kept his eyes on the baskets.

At first nothing happened.

Then slowly, almost in unison, out of each one appeared a dark flattened cobra head, rising in a swirling uncoiling movement against the background of the strange tree trunk. Intermittent shafts of sunlight penetrating the light gauzy shade struck a muffled gleam from the thick mottled skins. Between the great extended ruffs the eyes gleamed brightly.

'They don't look drugged,' Hannaker said.

She shook her head. Now that the show had begun, the crowd was thickening. People pushed up close behind. There was an overpowering smell of sweat and betel leaf and stale spices.

With a slight shiver, Hannaker watched the gypsy pick up a cobra, force open its jaws, push back the lips and show the poison fangs still intact.

'How does he protect himself then?' Hannaker asked her. 'Does he fill himself up with serum first?'

'I don't think so. I've heard they have a snake stone just in case, but they just don't seem to get bitten.'

Now the snake-charmer picked up the other snake and demonstrated its fangs with the quick confident throw-away gesture of a conjurer showing the empty top hat. That done he placed a cobra on either side of his knees, squatted back on the earth again, picked up his pipe and resumed his music. The crowd watched and listened entranced. Up again from their coils came the cobra heads, swaying. Behind and around, very slightly the crowd swayed too. No one spoke. Occasionally, absent mindedly, someone spat out a squirt of blood-red betel juice.

'Why don't they bite?' Hannaker whispered. 'It's not just the music, is it?'

'No.' She frowned. 'No one really knows. It's the way he handles them, too. He's got confidence. He doesn't expect them to bite.'

The cobras had reached up now to the snake-charmer's arms. They were twining themselves round, in a slow smooth somehow unstoppable way. The crowd still swayed in unison. They even seemed to chew in unison. The only sound was the working of their jaws, the soft slither of the snakes' bodies, and that high music which prickled the skin.

Now they had reached up to the gypsy's shoulders. Slowly their heads pulled back so that they were straight and level with the gypsy's eyes. Hannaker studied the man's eyes. They had a steady unblinking luminous quality. The little bright eyes of the snakes seemed held by them. The whole scene reminded Hannaker of something, but he couldn't think what.

'They do what he expects them to do, is that it?' Hannaker asked her. 'I heard something like that earlier on today.' He remembered Dr da Silva's words. 'They see what they expect to see.'

Only a different context. Or was it?

His eyes returned to the snake-charmer. Suddenly he knew what each flattened head reminded him of. A shadowy aircraft, flaps down on the approach just coming in to land.

'It's stifling here,' he said, suddenly aware of the crush, the smell of bodies and dried fish and fruit and oil and animals, the splashes of betel-leaf spit. He felt oppressed by the trans-fixed faces all around him, jaws working, eyes glazed, waiting perhaps for the odd time that disaster might happen. 'Let's go.'

She didn't protest that they hadn't done any shopping. She followed him meekly as he elbowed his way through the onlookers, let him take her hand and pull her down the crowded aisles between the boutiques, till they were out on the wide street that led to the harbour again.

A light breeze from the Indian Ocean cooled his face, and gently lifted the swinging curtain of Miss Grey's hair.

'Do *you* believe in the power of thought?' he demanded of her suddenly.

She turned, smiled slightly at the roughness of his tone. 'Obviously *you* don't,' she said gently. 'But yes, I think I do. Sometimes. And in some things. In personal things. Not the move mountain variety. I think perhaps it works on living things. You think of someone, and suddenly you have a letter or a phone call from them. Or they appear.' She smiled up at him. The sun, the sea and something else illuminated the blue of her eyes. 'Do you know what I mean?'

'Very well.'

In a quick surge of affection for her, he wondered if he should tell her that just an hour ago, outside the Ministry building, he had been thinking about her, when suddenly she appeared. And then with dismay he remembered that it was not of Melanie Grey that he had been thinking, but of his wife.

'Yes. I heard you had an audience with His Excellency,' Reeves said, packing the papers on his desk into neat piles, one eye on the wall clock, which said seven-thirty, already half an hour after the time Mrs Reeves liked him in the bungalow for dinner. 'How did he receive you?'

'Cordially and cautiously.' Hannaker also glanced at the clock. Like Reeves he didn't want this session to spin itself out too long. In another two hours Miss Grey's flight would be taking off for Hong Kong. If, presently, he took a stroll towards Catering he might conceivably run into her.

'He'll have heard about you, of course.' Reeves pursed his lips.

'Yes.'

'His Excellency has a very difficult job,' Reeves said severely. 'Walking a diplomatic tightrope.'

'So he told me.' Hannaker paused. 'He told me something else. That the date has been fixed for the Inquiry. The twenty-sixth of June.'

'I did hear something of the sort.'

'And *I* told *him*,' Hannaker got up from his chair, 'that I want to be in on it.'

'Oh, that wouldn't do at all. To push yourself in. Yours is only a watching brief.' Reeves began to search hastily under the tidy paper piles for the pink and white box.

'In the top drawer,' Hannaker drawled. 'I saw you put them in there.'

'So I did.' Thankfully Reeves pulled it open, fumbled in the box, and unwrapped a Rennie. '*You* must know,' he crunched rapidly, 'that if the Sinhalese authorities don't see fit to ask you, I think it would be very undiplomatic of you to demand it of them.'

'That's why,' Hannaker said equably, 'I'm telling everyone in good time.'

Time. That word again. Hannaker looked at the clock. Since he had come in here to discuss the last few days' work with Reeves, three aircraft had taken off and two had landed. The stars had shifted by a thousandth of a degree in the heavens. The moon had imperceptibly changed its face. Soon it would be time for the voice of Oriental Airways to summon its passengers for the scheduled flight to Hong Kong to the departure gate.

Hannaker walked to the door, and put his hand on the knob. It was time for today to stop banging his head against a peppermint wall.

'We'll talk about it again,' he said, bidding Reeves goodnight. Then he walked quickly down the corridor, out for a moment into the moist night air, and then up the ramp to the new concrete building of the Catering Department.

Melanie Grey was standing just inside by the departure blackboard. She turned her head as the door opened behind her.

Hannaker stopped and smiled apologetically. 'Fancy running into you here!'

'Of all places,' Miss Grey finished for him.

Hannaker lifted the corner of a white cloth covering a food tray and murmured, 'Mmm, smells good!'

'It smells awful.'

'Then I take it the crew eat something different?'

'What's this?' she asked. 'An official inquiry?'

'Of course,' he said, leaning an elbow on the counter and watching the assistants fill up the food trays, which the stewardess carefully checked against her list, and then nodded to the loaders to slide them over to the trolleys. Melanie Grey had a rather endearing habit of moving her lips soundlessly as she counted and checked.

The Sinhalese Catering Officer bowed slightly. 'All c'rect then, miss?'

'Yes, thank you.' Melanie signed the indent and handed it back with a smile.

'Here, let me.' Hannaker stretched a hand forward as she started to lift a polythene bag full of toys and magazines and games and comics. 'I'll carry those.'

'That's all right. The loader will take them, come to that. Anyway, you're not allowed on the aeroplane.'

'Of course I am.' He tapped the breast pocket of his jacket. 'Pass from your Station Manager. Very Important Person.'

She laughed and handed him the bag.

'Anyway, I'd like to take a look round.'

'Is that why you came?'

'That and to see Reeves, yes. Why?'

'I thought there might have been another reason.'

'There was. But we won't go into that now.'

He held the door open for her. 'Cheeri-cheerio,' the Sinhalese said. 'Have a very fine trip, Miss Grey.'

'I wondered perhaps'—she smiled with lowered eyes—'if you wanted me to take anything back for you?'

She preceded Hannaker down the step and on to the path. She walked very straight and stiff, the little cap perched on top of her scooped up hair.

'I'd like you to take *me* back with you. No, that's not true,' as she turned and glanced at him, surprised. 'I'm stuck into this now. I wouldn't want to leave.'

'Nothing else? No message for your girl friend?'

'Other than to tell them all to be patient . . . nothing.'

He walked in step with her on to the tarmac, the bagful of

amenities bumping against his leg as they went. It was total night now and all the lamps were lit. Yellow runway lights, white perimeter and apron lights, distant lead-ins, red obstruction lamps, blue lights from the hangars, golden blobs on the top of marshalling vehicles—all forming a terrifying pattern of vast and inhuman complication. Miss Grey seemed unfairly diminished by such illumination. She was nothing now but a pale profile walking beside him on whom the wheeling lights flickered over, lit up and threw away again. A painful anxiety stirred.

'Where is she?' he asked.

'The aircraft?' Echo Echo. Just over here.'

She pointed a little to the left, where a 707 was parked, its steps lowered and a yellow lit fuelling tanker in position beside her.

'Been through Customs?'

She nodded and held up a small overnight bag to show the chalk mark. Then she looked at her wrist-watch. 'Time I got a move on.' Briskly she quickened her pace, till they got to the passenger steps. 'D'you really want to come up?' she asked turning.

'Of course.'

'What do you hope to find?' she asked him as she stepped in over the threshold.

'Nothing,' he said with a kind of desperate fervour which she didn't notice.

She began walking down the aisle, the exact replica of the one he had examined for the tenth time that afternoon. The painful anxiety deepened. He had the feeling he wanted to shout to her, 'Don't go!'

He put his hand on one of the seat backs.

'Hey! I've just straightened that,' she said turning suddenly and smiling severely.

'Sorry.'

He found himself looking on the luggage racks, and under the row after row of empty seats. 'I'm supposed to do that,' she said, her smile tensing at the corners of her mouth. She finished her walk up to the front, turned.

'I'll take a look up front,' Hannaker said, and pushed open the door to the flight deck. From out of the shadows a white figure glided forward, an overalled figure, carrying something in its hand.

Dark eyes rolled, a white smile flashed on, the arm was thrust forward to show a homely dustpan and brush. 'Cleaner, sah! Little behind schedule, sah. Sometimes very dirty round the crew seats. Not possible to get out properly with the vacuum cleaner.' And smiling, past Hannaker to Miss Grey, 'Everything satisfactory . . . yes, miss?'

'So far, yes thank you.'

'We have finished now, miss. That was last job. I like to see to it myself. So no complaints, you understand.'

Coming forward into the beam of light from the passenger cabin, Hannaker saw the man had a foreman's badge on the pocket of his overall. 'Have very fine trip, Miss.'

Hannaker heard the flight-deck door shut behind him. He stood for a moment blinking his eyes to get used to the darkness. Then he turned and felt his way forward. The backs of the two pilots' seats were silhouetted against the light-pricked windscreen, as he sat himself down in the left-hand one.

Memories of sitting in the same seat in that other aeroplane this afternoon made his spine tingle with apprehension. He stared at identical instruments, except that here they were all of a piece, no glass broken, no needles bent. For the hundredth time, Hannaker asked himself how a man could make a mistake such as Seneratne said. Simple fatigue? A sudden loss of concentration or confidence? Just plain being in a hurry?

He raised his eyes to the windscreen. From the vantage-point of the nose cone the aerodrome spread out round him. The huge circle of the perimeter track, criss-crossed with runways, a cobweb bedewed with glittering lights. And the aeroplane in it, caught like some tiny fly.

Hannaker frowned. An uneasy sensation that he was on the verge of some discovery irritated his mind like a forgotten name. Outside the tanker had finished refuelling. The hose was withdrawn. The vehicle began slowly to move round the nose of the aeroplane, its golden roof light flickering, casting as it went a vanishing spatter of yellow light in the cockpit, leaving it darker than before. Like the light, the sensation had gone too. Impatient with himself, Hannaker got up, walked through to the passenger compartment, and back to the rear galley. Melanie Grey was finishing off her check of the switches. She stopped, smiled briefly, and then went on with what she was doing. Hannaker watched her thoughtfully. Water tank, water pressure. Everything seemed normal and satisfactory. She began stowing the stuff from the trays into the refrigerator and the cupboards. Hannaker bent down, craned his neck to make sure there was nothing already in the cupboards.

'Do you know something you haven't told me?' Miss Grey demanded suddenly, her eyes very dark and intent.

Hannaker shrugged. 'There's lots I haven't told you.'

'Yes, of course. But you know what I mean. Something that might concern me.'

Hannaker thought for a moment, then he said truthfully, 'Yes.'

'Me and the aeroplane?' Her eyes travelled round the tiny galley. She shivered slightly.

'No.'

'Then you don't think someone's likely to put a bomb on board?'

He shook his head. 'No.'

'You were acting as if you did.'

'So I was. But I don't really. That's just me being super-cautious.'

'But why?'

He shrugged. 'I can't go into all that now. I thought maybe you might have guessed.'

She stared back at him solemnly. She neither nodded nor shook her head. But the colour suddenly came up under her fine smooth skin.

'Take care of yourself, that's all,' he said softly.

He stepped back to the head of the stairs.

'I will.' She just touched her lips with her two fingers. 'You do too.'

That was all. But that was everything.

134

FULL MOON

Pasalosswaka

THE FESTIVAL OF WESAK burst over Ceylon in a silver sky waterfall of fireworks and celebrations. The full moon at Wesak is the forerunner of growth and abundance, heralding success and prosperity, and despite the steady thrash of the rain, up went the stars and the rockets and the chrysanthemum bursts. The pools on the terrace and the streets reflected their fall.

Hannaker watched the display from his bedroom window, wondering if he should turn his silver over in his pocket as Margaret had always said he must, when they first heard the cuckoo at home in May.

Just for luck. He needed luck. He needed the May moon goddess's success. More than luck, perhaps, he needed time.

He sat up into the early hours, meticulously going through every report and every test. He studied the flight-deck crew's confidential reports. The first officer had applied for leave to get married next month. Deliberately Hannaker dragged his mind back from the sympathetic vision this conjured up. The fiancée's name was Monica Tamplin. Where had he seen that name before? Of course. The chief stewardess on the flight. Could that fact have any possible bearing on the crash? There used to be an old superstition amongst air crews that a pilot was most likely to have a crash about the time he got married. It wasn't altogether superstition.

Hannaker read on. Outside, the fireworks died away. There was nothing but the rain. He took up Captain Coates's file. There were the two flight checks mentioned by Captain Dewhurst, when Captain Coates had gone visual and come down under the beam.

He went through all the flight-check reports again—but they told him nothing new. Captain Coates was clearly a competent pilot, with no previous accident in thirty years' flying. Of course he could still make a mistake, but there was no real evidence that he was prone to error. Hannaker sat for a long time, hands in his pockets, lower lip thrust out, thinking. He opened Coates's medical file. An item caught his eye. Just over a year ago, Captain Coates had been worried about his vision. He had been sent to an optician in Colombo. There was the report. Nothing wrong with his eyes. But did that mean that about this time of year, when monsoons were on and visibility bad, that Captain Coates *mistrusted* his eyes? That might be almost as dangerous as impaired vision. Hannaker made an entry under the heading *pilot performance*, and, just as a flamboyant dawn was breaking, went to bed.

He woke very late to another bright morning and, impatient with himself for losing valuable time, hired a private car to take him up to the wall of the temple, and then picked his way across to the crash site. These days he had no trouble getting through Fonseca's men. Only two police stood guard on the aircraft itself, and they, staring enviously at their comrades unhurriedly thrashing in amongst the undergrowth, seemed only too eager for any break in the monotony.

'Good morning, sah.' They waved him inside, not bothering to examine his pass. One of those stepping forward, perhaps to practise his English, asked him, 'What you hope to find this day, sah?' With emphasis on *this*, and a wave of his hands above him as if to indicate that *this* day of all days he might indeed be lucky enough to find it.

'I don't really know,' Hannaker said, smiling wryly. And to himself more than to the policeman, 'The truth, I suppose.'

More smiles and nods. A flood of Tamil, and Hannaker clambered up into the aircraft.

Today, ominously, it was empty. Nobody now from the ASB troubled to work on the crash. The ASB had arrived at their theory, and did not want it upset. Hannaker walked thoughtfully up and down the aisle. The carpet was already mildewed and live with white ants. So were the rows and rows of seats. They could tell him nothing. At the rear, the door of the galley, half off its hinges, still stood ajar. The fractured mirrors in the

Ladies' Powder Room still reflected the pink plastic-quilted walls, now peeling with the monsoon rains.

Hannaker walked up to the nose. In some sad macabre way it was like playing Hunt the Thimble. But without the chorus of childish voices. No one shrieked *You're getting warmer! Warmer! Boiling hot! No, cooler, colder! Cold! Icy cold!*

Hannaker knelt on the sloping floor to go over the inside workings of the artificial horizon again. He shivered. Outside, the voices he could hear spoke in Tamil. There was nothing but the threshing of the undergrowth, the buzzing of flies and insects and the occasional piercing squawk of a bird.

He must have worked on the instruments for a couple of hours when he heard a shout go up. The sun was just past its peak and it was baking hot in the cockpit. There was sweat running down his back and he felt dizzy with the glare. When he heard the noise he peered out, and there was a little knot of policemen, gathered round Fonseca, talking rapidly in Tamil, and gesticulating excitedly. The Inspector then waved them forward and they began to move off into the forest. As they went, other policemen tossed aside their sticks, and Pied-Piper-like followed on. Hannaker jumped down through the hole on the nose cone, and went after them.

Turning round to dismiss the unwanted followers, Fonseca spotted him. 'Ah, Mr Hannaker. Come along. It seems my men have found something.'

He waited for Hannaker to come bounding up. Sunlight dappling through the trees lit his smiling eager face.

'The gold d'you reckon?'

'Perhaps some of it. I do not know yet. A wooden box, my sergeant says.' He shooed the men ahead of him, 'Let us go and see to believe, as you say in the West.'

Picking his way carefully through the muddy jungle track, holding back branches politely to assist Hannaker, he said earnestly, 'Let us hope that it is, eh, man? Then all can be,' he wound one hand rapidly round the other, 'tied up.'

'Yes.'

'And you can go, with relief, home to your leave.'

'Who told you about that?'

137

'Mr Reeves. He was much concerned, man, about your leave.'

'I see. Kind of him.'

'He is a very kind gentleman, Mr Reeves.'

'Yes,' Hannaker sighed. 'It's getting very wet underfoot. Have they found what they have found in the lake?'

'Very close, man, very close.'

Ahead of them, the men had stopped and gathered together. Here, about twenty yards from the edge of the lake, the branches and shrubs had been cut down, and the men were pointing at the corner of a box just visible through the marshy ground.

'Well, it's certainly something,' Hannaker said. 'Too big for a gold box though.'

'We shall see.'

Two policemen had come forward with spades, and snapping his fingers impatiently Fonseca waved them to begin.

'Tell them to dig wide in case it's a part of the aircraft itself.'

'Of course.'

Another flood of Tamil. Then smiling shyly, 'But I don't think it is, man. Today is the day of success. What we find today, man, will be the gold.'

Hannaker smiled wryly, and shrugged. He brought out his notepad and made a sketch of the position of the small corner visible. He watched the men draw out a long rectangle with the corner of their spades.

'Like digging a grave, is it not, man?' Fonseca said.

'What I was thinking,' Hannaker said. 'Or opening one up.'

He stepped forward and squatted on his haunches to make sure that the spades came in contact with nothing that they might damage. Now the forest was silent except for the sound of the digging.

One of the men stopped suddenly and spoke to Fonseca.

'They are touching something, man.'

'Could they clear it now manually?'

'I will tell them.'

The policemen put down their spades, and scooped the greeny-black oozy soil away with their cupped hands.

138

'Too big for a gold box,' Hannaker said softly.

'Wait and see, man. There is not enough visible to judge.'

'Too black.'

'This soil stains all things very rapidly.'

'That's leather.' Hannaker reached a finger down and touched the corner of the box. Dark brown leather dyed black with the ooze. A handle now was visible at the side. Initials that had once been picked out in gold. A small overnight bag, or a lady's make-up case.

Fonseca's dejection had not yet conveyed itself to his men. Excitedly they lifted it out and brought it to him. While he examined it, Hannaker walked over to the hole they had dug out. He knelt down and measured how deep the case had sunk.

When he turned round Fonseca had the bag open. 'Powders and unguents, that is all,' he said, shrugging his shoulders.

Hannaker nodded but said nothing. He always disliked this uncovering of personal effects. He hoped Fonseca would not make any comment on the transitoriness of human vanity. But the detective was too busy with his own disappointment. He walked beside Hannaker back to the aircraft.

'Mind you,' Hannaker said judiciously before he clambered back into the wreckage, 'everything that is uncovered is a clue in its own way.'

'That is so, man, that is so.'

'How heavy would you say that case was?'

'We will find out exactly of course. But at a hazard, one, two pounds?'

'When dry?'

'When dry I am estimating.'

'So for its weight it sank fairly deep.'

'And the gold for its weight would sink much deeper, man! That is what you say. You agree with me now, yes?'

'No, I neither agree nor disagree. I simply want to learn whatever we can from anything.'

'Then like you say, good hunting, man.' Fonseca lifted his hand as Hannaker eased himself up through the hole in the duralumin.

'And to you.' For a moment he watched the little Tamil,

head sunk thoughtfully on his chest, walk back slowly to the edge of the forest. Then he returned to his solitary task. He worked on the instruments for as long as there was sufficient light to see by. The net result was what he called negative confirmation. At the time of the accident every instrument appeared to be working perfectly.

He squatted on the floor for a moment, elbows on his knees, chin cupped in his hands. It was almost nightfall. The insects and flies which had pestered him all day had given way to the continuous electric whirring of crickets and the crack of fire-flies. The police had stopped their beating of the undergrowth. There was no sound now from the forest except the occasional clop-clop of the jungle fowl. And now incongruously, with the heavy smell of the dank lake and the perfume of jacaranda and the temple flowers, came the hot spicy aroma of curry as the men retired to cook their evening meal over a charcoal stove in the shelter of the temple wall.

Hannaker stood up. The full moon had risen, and held briefly the centre of a small stage of sky, curtained on either side by billowy gathering clouds. Its radiance filtered through the holes and tears in the airframe, to produce an eerie cobwebbing of fragile light.

Mindful of the night's downpour to come, Hannaker gathered together his tools, packed them in his bag. He was about to scramble through the hole in the fuselage when he heard the sound of the temple bell.

Peering around, he saw no sign of a devotion. No wor-shippers. No monks. No sign of anyone. Just the slow tolling of the bell and the yellow glow of a few small candles that had been lit round the courtyard parapet. And then, as he watched, he saw, high above him, a tall figure come out into the court-yard, and stand right up at the parapet, looking down at the wrecked aircraft. Quite clearly in the moonlight, he recognized the thin bony face of the Brahmin.

Hannaker jumped down from the 707, and walked over the trampled grass to the temple rock. He stood staring up at the Brahmin, but though he must have been clearly visible there was no sign that the high priest had noticed his movements.

Candlelight flickered over a face already paled by moonlight, and still as a wax effigy. The chilling thought came into Hannaker's mind that the priest was in some sort of trance. Odd fragments of his wide but none too deep reading came into his mind. Perhaps the priest was engaged in some sort of astral levitation. Perhaps his mind or soul had left his body. Then he remembered an account of the Druids, how the High Priest in moments of ecstasy actually grew physically taller. And now in the weird mixture of tossing candles and blanching moonlight the man above him seemed to tower unnaturally tall.

'Father?' Unsure how to address him, doubting whether in any case he would understand English, Hannaker's voice came out harsh and loud.

The face above him remained totally empty, the eyes half closed.

'Yes, my son?' The soft voice, the perfectly formed English were more startling than a shout.

'Am I interrupting your prayers?'

'No, my son.'

'Then may I come up and speak to you?'

The bell had stopped tolling now and there was complete silence. A long silence, until reluctantly from the figure above came the words, 'If you wish, my son.'

Hannaker hurried up the steps. The figure at the parapet did not turn as he came into the courtyard. 'Come over here, my son.'

There was a light shawl over the Brahmin's shoulders, but under his dhoti his feet were bare. He kept the long fingers of his hands together in an attitude of devotion—exactly as Hannaker had seen him on the night of the crash. He had a high forehead domed to the centre of a skull thinly covered in white hair.

'What is it you wish to speak with me about, my son?'

Close to, his skin was aged to a pale brown, the colour of a Victorian daguerreotype. A colour of universality. An old man anywhere might have looked like him.

'About the crash,' Hannaker said, standing beside him and pointing.

141

'Yes, my son. But what in particular about it?'

'I am trying to find the cause.'

The Brahmin said nothing. He turned slightly round to gaze fixedly at Hannaker. A curious luminous expression touched his face. A smile, in that it lit his face. And yet not a smile. The lips did not move, and the emotion that lit his face was one not of humour, but of pity. 'The cause,' he repeated softly, giving the word a different weightier, almost metaphysical meaning.

'Yes,' Hannaker said doggedly.

The Brahmin bowed his head. Then, 'You and I have seen each other before, have we not, my son?'

'That is so. I came here shortly after all this happened. I was on my way home. I was going to catch this same aircraft. When I came here before it was just by chance.'

'Chance.'

Again the soft elevation of the word to a different dimension of meaning.

'Yes. But since then, I've been told to help investigate it.'

'Without success, my son?'

'I haven't solved the problem.'

'You have found nothing to explain this? Nothing that you can accept?'

A faint but audible emphasis on the one word 'you'.

'Nothing positive. So far.'

'What are you searching for so often down there?'

'A clue. A fragment of truth.'

This time, the Brahmin did not repeat the last word in his odd soft voice, but it seemed to echo around the courtyard. The unsmiling smile was back on the old man's face. But he said nothing till in a different tone of voice he asked crisply, 'And what exactly do you wish to know from me?'

Slightly off balance by the altered tone, by the whole interview in fact, without time to prepare for a steady lead-up of questions, Hannaker found himself saying, 'I believe you prophesied that this would happen?'

The Brahmin unlatched his fingers from their attitude of devotion, thrust them instead up the sleeves of his dhoti, and bowing his head, said humbly, 'My son, I have not the gift of prophecy.'

'Many people have told me you did.'

Again what might have been a smile. 'A tale, my son, in any language is always magnified in the telling.'

'But you opposed the building of Tallaputiya.'

'Yes, my son.'

'Why?'

He spread his hands. 'For two thousand years, men have worshipped here. As Adam's Peak is sacred to the Buddhists, so is this shrine to the Hindus. Here men have found serenity, Jnana. Oneness with God. Not only Hindus. But all men. For it is a man's dharma that is important, not his religion. As the Mahimna-Stotva says "All these paths O Lord, Veda, Sankhya, Yoga, Pasupata, Vaishnava, lead but to Thee, like the winding river that at last merges into the Sea".'

'And when they built it?'

'*Then* we endeavoured to free ourself from its distraction. To,' this time there was a smile, bleak and unused, 'rise above it, as you might say, my son.'

'And you never said this might happen?'

'That, my son, is different from prophecy.' Back went the fingers to their stations of devotion, the lids of the eyes half closed. Choosing his words carefully, the Brahmin said, apparently going off in a different direction, 'Some of us believe that the world itself was created by sound waves. There is no cause to look so startled, my son,' the Brahmin chided without glancing at Hannaker. 'You have perhaps seen a glass shattered by a certain note in a voice?'

'True,' Hannaker said. He had a strange feeling—very hard to describe, to identify—that there was something he ought to remember. Yet perhaps because of the impending storm, his mind didn't seem to be functioning properly, and anyway the Brahmin was going on in his sing-song, curiously hypnotic voice.

'There are many kinds of waves, as you know. Sound, light, thought waves. The most powerful of these are thought, my son. And this sacred place,' his hands freed themselves, and cast around to encompass the courtyard, the monastery, the rock on which the temple stood, 'was a beacon, a lighthouse, for good. The coming of the airfield brought distraction. Harmful vibrations. And evil.'

'How?'

'Exactly how,' the Brahmin's fingers homed together again, 'I do not know.'

'Because it was evil?' Hannaker persisted.

'There was evil associated with it—yes.' Then quietly 'It was an English poet who wrote "And evil on itself shall back recoil".'

'Have you tried to get the airport closed?'

'We do not pray for such tangible things as you in the West.'

'Then you just prayed?'

'Just?' The un-smile, the elevated word.

'I mean you didn't do anything positive about it?'

'There is nothing more positive than meditation and prayer, my son.' He pressed his fingers against his own temples and closed his eyes.

'Perhaps not,' Hannaker said softly. 'But my problem still remains.' He folded his arms and stared down at the remains of the aircraft. From here he could see the marram grass and the creeper already beginning to come up over it, as if under his eyes it were being made ready to float away down some long green river of time. Out of reach of Hannaker's fingers, before he could snatch its secrets away.

'You have spent too long,' the Brahmin suddenly said with sharpness as if he had read Hannaker's mind, 'searching down there. You must raise yourself. Project your mind out towards truth. You will not find truth down there.' He gesticulated downwards dismissingly and then drew himself up. 'You will find it,' he said, putting his thin hand on Hannaker's temples, the fingers pressed gently like cold smooth electrodes, 'in your mind. You have the answer. But you do not yet know it.'

A curious feeling, elusive and yet absolutely convincing, grew in Hannaker's mind that he did in fact almost know. That the truth was only a finger's reach away.

Then the Brahmin dropped his hands. A warm luminous

expression touched his face. The dark eyes glowed with something like affection. He put his hand on Hannaker's shoulder, gently propelling him forward till they came to the top of the steps.

'I hope that I have helped you, my son.'

A faint wind, prelude to the coming storm, stirred the forest. A few petals from the temple tree drifted to the baked earth of the courtyard floor. The moon shone on a face which, at that moment, Hannaker would swear was pure and guileless, and, yes, holy.

Hannaker nodded his head. 'Yes, thank you.' And then more urgently than he intended, 'One thing I want to prevent is . . . that . . . happening again.'

A brief spasm twisted the Brahmin's hitherto calm face. He bowed his head, sliding his hands inside the wide sleeves of his dhoti.

'Good night, Father.'

'Good night, my son.'

The Brahmin raised his head, and slowly lifted his right hand in farewell. Behind them the clouds had overwhelmed the moon. Only the flickering guttering candles lit the Brahmin's face. They peaked and pointed it as the smoking oil lamp had done that night of the crash. Now all Hannaker saw was a very human face—thin and old, crafty and mean.

Melanie Grey was up front in the cockpit, and clearing away the crew's empty coffee cups from the throttle box, when the weather actual from Tallaputiya came through. She heard the Sinhalese controller, muffled by the rubber round the earpiece of Captain Dewhurst's phones which he always wore right on the back of his head, announce in a sepulchral sing-song psalm: '. . . wind south-west thirty knots, gusting, visibility one mile in heavy rain. . . .'

'As usual.'

Dewhurst listened without any apparent emotion, his half-closed eyes gazing unblinkingly at the sight beyond the windscreen. All the way from Hong Kong there had not been a wisp of cloud. The perfect pearly disc of the full moon had paled the stars, giving the sky that strangely dead and frightening emptiness.

'Exactly as forecast,' said the First Officer cheerfully, 'Roll off the monsoon. I could have told you what that forecast would be.'

'Really?' Dewhurst slid his cold marble eyes round to regard the First Officer, who, oblivious, rubbed an apple he had saved from lunch on his trouser leg, and nodded affirmatively.

'When you're a captain. *When*,' Dewhurst repeated the word ominously, 'You will find out there are worse things to cope with than the monsoon.'

'Oh, yes, sir. I'm sure, sir.' He smacked Melanie playfully as she bent to pick a chocolate wrapper off the floor, 'Stewardesses, sir. In other words, women.'

'No, Mr Mansell. Second pilots who think they know all the answers.'

'Oh, I see, sir. Yes, well, sir.' Mr Mansell wiped the smile off his face.

'And for heaven's sake. You can't be hungry. Get rid of whatever it is you're chewing. Get me the let-down charts. And ask for descent clearance. And Miss Grey, I don't like rubber ham sandwiches.'

'Sorry, sir.'

Melanie paused for a moment after the flight-deck door shut behind her. Captain Dewhurst was edgy. At the best of times he was no one's, except maybe Mrs Dewhurst's, favourite pin-up. But she had never seen him before in such a nit-picking mood. Maybe it was the delay, she thought, bracing her shoulders, preparing a bright smile on her face as she walked down the aisle. More likely, it was the *reason* for the delay. The loading up of another consignment of bullion. Somewhere, just about here, below the pink carpet and the duralumin skin, was what they used in fairy stories to call a king's ransom.

'Yes, a beautiful sight,' she nodded in agreement to an Australian lady sitting just aft of the wing, gazing soulfully at the moon. 'Weather in Ceylon? Oh, a bit drizzly, I expect.'

Maybe Dewhurst was thinking as she was thinking, that the

146

load was the same, the time the same, and now the weather was the same, as . . . she mentally shook herself. She was tired, that was all. She shouldn't have been on this flight at all. She hadn't had her proper stand-off in Hong Kong. But Gemma had gone sick after some party, and so Melanie had been called out.

Down the length of the aisle she walked smiling. The local stewardesses, the Sinhalese and Tamil girls, princess-like in their blue saris, the two Hong Kong girls in satin cheong sams, were deftly collecting the last of the plates and glasses, smiling, and gossiping cheerfully. Melanie felt immediately ashamed of herself.

'Are we on descent?' the Chief Steward asked, as she reached the galley doorway. He didn't look up from his bar books.

'Just about.'

'How much longer?'

'Estimating twenty-eighteen.'

'Less than half an hour. Get those dolly birds cracking on the washing up. Hand out the landing cards. Dewhurst's on the prowl tonight.'

Under their feet the duralumin floor tilted forward. The quiet engine sounds went quieter still. They began descending fast, faster down some invisible slope. As though someone had breathed suddenly on the windscreens, all the stars went out. There was the sound of rain rattling on the duralumin skin. Melanie handed out the last of the landing cards.

Just as the 'Fasten Your Seat Belts' sign glowed red at the far end of the cabin, the flight telephone rang. The Chief Steward answered it with an angry little pout.

'God wants you, dear, so best be quick.'

'Why?'

'Didn't say. Maybe he wants to hold your hand.' He beckoned to the local stewardesses, 'Come along Lotus Leaf, and Jasmine Flower and Inter-Flora whatever your name is, get strapped in. . . .'

'Smack it more likely.' With a backward grin at the Sinhalese and Chinese girls strapped in side by side now like a

147

cage full of bright tropical birds, Melanie walked with some apprehension up front.

Captain Dewhurst turned as the flight-deck door opened. He jerked his head for her to come and stand beside him. Gone was the gritty mood of twenty minutes ago. The Captain was at his most gracious.

'I thought you might like to watch the landing, Miss Grey.'

'Thank you, sir.'

'And thank *you*, Miss Grey, for turning round so quickly in Hong Kong.'

For all his faults Captain Dewhurst tried to be a just man and a successful flight captain. Good behaviour should be rewarded. And it was a well-known fact that Captain Dewhurst regarded watching the master at work as no mean reward.

'Tired?'

'Not specially.'

She stared up at the windscreen cascading water. The dark rain-filled sky reflected back the phosphorescent glimmer of the dials, giving an eerie underwater effect as if they were in a bathysphere diving steeply into the deeps.

Now it was getting bumpier. The 707 began pitching and rolling in the uneven darkness, as carefully Dewhurst came out of the procedure turn and lined the aircraft on the ILS beam.

'Gear down.'

The First Officer leaned forward and selected. There was a clanking noise. Melanie could hear the aircraft slowing.

'Twenty-five hundred feet, sir, on glide path.'

The needles on the instruments jumped up and down like fireflies. In all this bumpiness, Dewhurst was having to almost wrestle with the controls. Under the little toothbrush moustache his lips were buttoned up in concentration, the protuberant eyes fixed on the instrument panel. It must have been like this that night, Melanie thought, turning her head slightly, peering out into the drenching rain for the hope of a light.

'Tallaputiya Tower. Victor Kilo reporting at the Outer Marker at 1500 feet.'

They were descending faster. Rain and darkness still blinded the windscreen.

There was a sudden burst of bright yellow under the wings, as the landing lights came on. And then abruptly, the aircraft seemed to dive into smoother air. The clatter of the rain on the skin stopped. The hem of the cloud swirled and parted.

Looking down, Melanie saw the lights from little huts, the solid black mass of the jungle heads just under the aircraft.

They were very low.

'More power.'

The engine noise increased.

'*More power!*'

Dewhurst was pulling back on the stick. The jets roared. Ahead, Melanie could see everything—the silver arrow-tip of the lead-in lights, the green lights of the threshold, the small pearls on either side of the runway. And just before the runway, caught in the beam of the landing lights, a square white vehicle, an ambulance, stationary on the Colombo road.

Then the landing lights were over it. The vehicle merged into the darkness again. It gave Melanie a momentary shiver as if for a split second time had shimmered backwards. Then she shrugged it away. A local ambulance on its normal duty, or maybe some ground type getting jumpy after all this talk of short runways and unsatisfactory airports.

They were skimming over the threshold. There was a squelch as the rubber tyres connected with the wet runway. Then reverse thrust roared up, and the 707 gradually slowed and swung off the runway on to the taxi track.

The First Officer started the after-landing checks.

'That was a break. The weather clearing just like that.'

'What does that mean, Mr Mansell?'

'Bit low coming in, weren't we, sir?'

'Are you trying to say that I went below the glide path?'

'Oh, no, sir, no, of course not.' The First Officer winked at Melanie. 'All I meant sir, was jolly good landing, sir. After all that bad weather, smooth as silk.'

The crew car took them from Tallaputiya to the hotel, but Melanie felt too tired to join Dewhurst and the others in the traditional after-trip unwinding session in the bar. She went to her room, had a bath and then flopped straightaway into bed.

Immediately, she went into a heavy sleep—but an hour later, she was awake again. Only half-conscious, she lay in a sort of dream state, longing to get back to sleep again and yet being unable to. After the heavy rain, the night was cool, and the sea was only whispering softly against the sand and the rocks of the bay. There was something keeping her awake, a regular beat that drowsily at first she thought was her heart until she heard shouting and singing and realized it was the sound of tom-toms.

Devil-dancers.

She had heard them before, seen them in their huge pop-eyed masks and their long coloured reed skirts, brass bangles and neckbands jangling as barefooted and sweating they danced outside the house of someone stricken by disease or misfortune, gesticulating wildly as though they were catching the devils out of the air and trampling them underfoot. She knew little about their purpose or pageantry, but she did know they kept at it.

Sure enough, all night the tom-toms went on. They were still going strong when she came down to a late breakfast. She went down to the beach, and spent most of the day sunbathing, but behind her eyes she could still actually feel the thumping of the drums. There was a man in the village 'very ill, very ill indeed,' the waiter at dinner told her. And when the monsoon clouds came sweeping in from the sea that evening, the tambourine rattle of the rain just harmonized with the steady beat of the tom-toms.

They seemed even louder as she came out of the restaurant. She was just going into the lounge when through the open door out to the verandah she saw a flash of a wet white bonnet, and then up the steps from the Porsche the hurrying figure of Roy Laughton.

'So there you are!'

He came into the foyer, brushing the rain from his white linen double-breasted jacket and smiling, 'I've just been out to Tallaputiya to meet you.'

'I came in yesterday.'

'So Reeves told me.' His forehead crinkled in genuine concern. 'You shouldn't have done it, you know.'

'The other girl went sick.'

'Even so . . . even so. It's far too tiring. And anyway . . . isn't it against the law?' He stood in front of her, his eyes examining her face quizzically, his whole expression a mixture of worry, amusement and irritation. 'Melanie, you look awfully tired.'

She coloured slightly. 'It isn't so much the trip as those drums.'

'I know one should never tell a lady she looks tired, but I happen to be really rather angry with you.'

'I'm sorry about your trip to the airport, but really I didn't expect——'

'Oh, I don't worry about that! It's *you* I worry about.' He put his hand under her arm and began gently propelling her out on to the back verandah overlooking the terrace and the sea. 'I was going to suggest we went out tonight . . . there's quite a good club in Colombo. But I think it would be far better if you took things quietly.' He pulled out a wicker chaise-longue for her. 'There you are . . . put your feet up. And we'll have a drink.'

For over an hour they sat talking alone together on the deserted verandah, until Dewhurst and the engineer came over and joined them, and afterwards Reeves. Finally, round about ten o'clock, Hannaker came over and sat on Laughton's left.

'I hear you won't be with us much longer, Hannaker.' Laughton picked up his gin and tonic and sipped it. 'Pity . . . I'd have liked you to have come over to look at my factory.'

'Thank you. I might still have time to take you up on that.'

'Good! It was just that I saw Seneratne the other day, and he told me the whole thing was solved.' Laughton paused. 'And on the other business, Fonseca . . . smart man, Fonseca . . . appears to have got that completely buttoned up too.' Then, noticing the look on the accident investigator's face, 'My dear Hannaker . . . don't look so surprised! This gold business is an open secret. *Everybody* knows.'

The conversation then became general, discussing Ceylon

and the elections, the Sri Lanka Freedom Party, and finally, for the tom-toms were still punctuating the conversation, the devil-dancers and what Dewhurst called 'their antics' in Mount Lavinia village.

'It's easy, of course, to despise such ceremonies . . . link them with witchcraft and ju-ju,' Laughton said. 'But it's surprising sometimes what these devil-dancers achieve.'

'You're not going to tell me they actually *cure* people?' Dewhurst asked.

'Oh, yes, I am! Seen it many times. Hopeless cases, too.'

'I suppose,' Hannaker said, 'that miracles . . . Lourdes and so on . . . are not very different.'

Laughton turned and smiled at his new ally. 'Exactly!'

'You surely don't believe in miracles, Hannaker?' Dewhurst asked.

'I don't disbelieve.'

'There's more to it than meets the eye,' Laughton said. 'Not only can these devil-dancers drive evil spirits out. They can drive them in.'

'You mean pins in wax images?' the engineer asked.

Laughton nodded. 'That sort of thing, yes.'

'Well, I wish they'd belt up,' Dewhurst said. 'Last night they disturbed my beauty sleep. So I think,' he got up, 'I'll toddle off to bed now.'

The engineer went with him.

Laughton said to Melanie, 'And you should have an early night!'

The party slowly broke up. Melanie went out back to the foyer and said goodnight to Laughton before going up to her room.

Left on their own in the semi-darkness, Hannaker sat politely with Reeves until he'd finished his drink. Then he accompanied him to the front of the hotel where he had left his car under the portico. The rain was still pouring down, but just before they reached the Station Manager's small Morris Minor, the tom-toms suddenly stopped.

'I'd just got used to them,' Hannaker said. 'What's up? Has the patient died? Or have the devils been driven out?'

Reeves gave a short laugh as he opened the side door and climbed into the driving seat. 'Nothing so melodramatic. The money will have run out. Don't you know you've got to have *money* to drive out devils?'

LAST QUARTER

Awa Attawaka

SHADING HIS EYES against the glare of the sun, Hannaker watched the naked boy shin up the long smooth trunk of the decapitated palm.

This was where the 707 had first struck—a colony of tall trees, their feathery foliaged heads, neatly severed now, resting on the earth below. Just before impact Captain Coates had been pulling the aircraft upwards. That was how the rear fuselage and tail had been ripped to pieces in a desperate attempt to climb, making the aircraft into a crippled cornucopia, scattering cargo over lake and jungle like manna from heaven.

There was no doubt that this had happened. A pathetic pile of evidence—six tartan hold-alls, twenty blue blankets, sixty pairs of ladies' shoes, innumerable cameras and radio spares—had been recovered by the policemen from the undergrowth, together with the toys and plastic cups that had floated on the lake, to prove Fonseca's point. As regards the gold . . . well, being heavy, it had immediately sunk into the slimy depths. The vanity case that had been recovered proved his point. The lake was where the large ship's spares and other heavy items of cargo that were also still missing would be. Fonseca was already beginning negotiations—which were bound to be protracted—to get that dredging machinery.

'Sah!'

The boy had found something. He threw it. There was a soft plop into the sand at Hannaker's feet—a minute piece of jagged duralumin from the rear underside, further unnecessary proof that the aircraft was nose-up when it first struck, that it had been ripped open just forward of the precious cargo compartment, that the gold *could* have ejected.

But *all* those kilo bars? And every one into this ten-acre lake?

Hannaker stared across its black oily surface, and screwed up his nose in disbelief. Thick with black mud into which bubbles came up from beneath to burst, leaving a reek of nauseous gas. No waterlilies, not even waterweeds could grow. He was quite sure that the sewage for centuries from the temple would be collected here.

'Sah.'

The boy had come down from the tree and was standing beside him, holding out his hand. There was no point in further investigations on the forest swathe cut down by the aircraft, and Hannaker handed over five rupees, which gross overpayment made the boy disappear immediately.

Rather more slowly, Hannaker walked round the lake and back to the temple steps, where his hired car and driver were waiting. He stood there for a few moments in the shade of the rock, watching a couple of policemen under the 707's port wing drinking water from their flasks.

They were the last remnants of Fonseca's cohort, and their duty was simply to keep guard. There was no need of a further search, since the jungle floor had been thoroughly combed and no gold found—in itself proof to the Inspector that it could be nowhere but at the bottom of the lake.

There was none of Seneratne's men around the crash. The Air Safety Bureau had also solved its separate problem, and there was no need to explore further the inside and outside of the 707.

At least, Hannaker thought ruefully, he had succeeded where politicians for two thousand five hundred years had failed—he had united Buddhist with Hindu, Sinhalese with Tamil. Both of them shared one view of him. Seneratne certainly regarded him as an interfering pseudo-expert with racist tendencies, trying to whitewash a British pilot's error that was obvious for all to see. Fonseca regarded him more highly, as an amateur detective trying to teach his grandmother to suck eggs. Both were convinced he was treading on *their* territory. He was exploring areas in which he had no right to be, examining things he knew nothing about—and arriving at unfounded conclusions. He was a visitor, here on sufferance.

As such, he should proffer polite advice, and only when asked for. After all, it was only they who knew the context, the full circumstances. He might guess, they *knew*. The cause of the crash and the disappearance of the gold were quite separate. To suggest otherwise was crazy.

Was he crazy? Hannaker leant against the rock face and considered the matter, trying to be dispassionate. In spite of all the science involved, an accident always had heavy emotional overtones. Emotion could bend the truth, distort fact. He was aware now that there was another reason, quite apart from the fact that this was his profession, why he had to solve the cause of this crash—and quickly. If you feared for someone's life, then you saw dangers in everything. Common sense went out of the window. Was the fact that Melanie was regularly flying on this type of aircraft on the same route into this aerodrome the reason why he was flitting from one possible cause to another, each will-o'-the-wisp theory becoming more fantastic than the last? Was it because of his feelings for her that he was so sure there was going to be an identical repetition of the Whisky Echo crash?

Seneratne's pilot-error theory was certainly the most plausible in the circumstances. Fonseca's theory was certainly possible. The two fitted together like left and right hands.

He shifted his shoulder, and began whistling tunelessly and unconsciously. He still went on thinking, trying to reconcile his own position and his own approach.

Around him, the lizards slithered between the mossy rocks and the flies buzzed. The sun beat down on the green jungle around. Now he was turning over in his mind possible trajectory paths of oblong boxes weighing about one kilo from a height of eighty feet.

They would be thrown forward, but how far? Enough to leapfrog over the lake? Hannaker looked across its bland unreflecting surface, hugging its secret—yes or no—to itself.

Hannaker tried doing sums in his head—calculations relative to the distance forward an object weighing one kilo would travel from a height of eighty feet dropping at an angle of ten degrees upward from the horizontal at a speed of one hundred

156

and forty knots. But he knew there were so many variables that Fonseca's arithmetic alone would not produce the answer.

The minutes passed, and he had got no further. He was in the car, half way back to the Mount Lavinia Hotel, when he became conscious of the name of the tune he was still whistling.

It was an old pop number, *Love and Marriage*, that declared they went together like a horse and carriage and you couldn't have one without the other. It suddenly struck him that the same philosophy could well be applied to the two separate theories of Messrs Fonseca and Seneratne.

If he could disprove the Fonseca theory, then the Seneratne theory was undermined. And since science wasn't going to help much on the trajectory problem, the only thing to do was to suck it and see.

He leaned forward in his seat and told the driver to turn off the Mount Lavinia road, and go to the right into Colombo. There he left the driver parked in the Fort, and made his way to the Pettah and Gunn's place.

Gunn was out, but he left a message on the table: *I've borrowed your cigarette case and I'd like to hire you and your Cessna for one hour tomorrow afternoon, confirm with Hannaker, Mount Lavinia Hotel.*

Then he picked up the wooden box and went back to the car, and after climbing into the back asked the driver, 'Can you tell me some place where I can get a good strong box made quickly?'

'Large box, sah?' The expression on the driver's face was a mixture of cupidity and sympathy.

'No, a small box. Lots of small boxes.'

Yes, indeed, the driver knew just such a man, a distant relative in fact, who made beautiful boxes of any size he cared to mention. He would work through the night to oblige a customer.

There was an added advantage in that he lived close. Within minutes Hannaker was inside his workshop. The place was very dark and smelled of sandalwood. The concrete floor was thick with sawdust, which muffled his feet. At first he thought the shop was empty. But from behind a stack of what looked like sailors' ditty-boxes, with stately soundless movements, came a very old man with a wax-coloured face, his hair drawn tightly back from a high forehead, and held by a tortoise-shell comb.

'I want some boxes,' Hannaker said. 'I want them made to exact measurements. And I want them in a hurry.'

'We are accustomed, sah, to making boxes to very exacting measurements in very quick time.'

'I shall want them by tomorrow.'

'Much, sah, will depend on decoration.'

'No decoration. Just twenty boxes.'

A flicker of interest and surprise crossed the man's face, and was quickly snuffed out. He stepped back and reached for an old-fashioned slate and slowly wrote down the measurements.

'Twenty boxes is very great number to make in very short time, sah.'

'But you can do it?'

The old man shrugged. 'Much will depend on the wood that you choose. For what purpose, sah, will you be requiring these boxes?'

Hannaker produced Gunn's box. 'This is what I want. Same measurements, same wood.'

The old man stared at the box for a very long time. He took it and turned it over in his thin hands. He brought it close to his eyes. This time when he looked at Hannaker the flicker of interest was unmistakable. 'This fibre wood, sah.'

'So I believe. Have you got some?'

'Oh, yes, sah. It is much used to make,' he seemed to hesitate, 'shipments.'

'Of what?' Hannaker asked sharply.

'Of many things, sah. Very satisfactory but not cheap. Twenty boxes . . . will be expensive, sah.'

'How much?'

He named a figure, which Hannaker supposed he ought to have argued over, but he didn't. He simply nodded, said, 'All right, so long as you have them ready by twelve o'clock tomorrow.'

Then he made his farewells and went back to the car.

'Everything satisfactory, sah?'

'Yes, thank you.'

'The hotel now?'

Hannaker nodded.

Back at the Mount Lavinia, the desk clerk hailed him as he went over to the lift, and handed over a slip of paper. 'Message for you, sah.'

A note from Gunn—*See you two-thirty tomorrow at Katanayaka. But where to and what for? And why my only cigarette box?*

Why, Hannaker thought, going up in the gold-meshed lift, did everyone ask questions and no one ever adequately answer them? He walked along to his room and lay on the bed, hands behind his head, trying to sort out his own questions and answers.

Though the blinds had been lowered all day, the room held a soft lulling warmth. He must have dozed off to sleep, for he was soon in some strange fragmented dream—sharp, distorted and colourful as pictures in a stained glass window. He was trying to fight his way through the jungle, trees netting over his head, feet being sucked down by the marsh. Then suddenly there was a trumpeting and a rustling, and Reeves came on to the scene in the guise of a wild boar, but still in British Oriental Airways uniform. And then he had fought his way out of the jungle, and was back with the old carpenter in his shop, surrounded by tier after tier of coffins. And here was Fonseca telling him that the old man had made off with the bullion in the coffins he had made for the victims of the crash.

Hannaker awoke with that curious certainty and relief of having solved a problem, only to be brought back out of fantasy into reality again.

He must have slept for quite a time. It was quite dark outside. His room was lit only by the muffled incandescence of the hotel's neon lights on the front façade. He felt stiff and hungry, and he had probably missed dinner. He felt depressed, baffled and lonely.

On a sudden impulse, he lifted the receiver. Immediately after her Hong Kong service, Melanie had gone off on a quick trip to London. He asked Reception whether the slip crew had arrived in from the UK.

'Oh yes, sah. Four hours ago.' The voice sounded slightly shocked. 'Is one o'clock in the morning, sah.'

He was conscious of a feeling of relief that she was back here safe, not far from him in this hotel. But more than that, he was conscious of a desire, haunting as homesickness, to trust someone.

She would be very tired, and it was unheard-of to interrupt aircrew in their first sleep after a trip. All the same, he rang her room, and when she answered simply asked whether she would like to come with him tomorrow on a joy flight.

She didn't ask him why. She simply said rather breathlessly that she would love to.

In the clear light of day he was not sure how far he should trust her, either. Women, with the exception of Margaret, always talked too much. Everybody talked too much. And when people talked too much on an airline, the whisper didn't just go round the village or the High Street, it went round the whole world.

All the same, he was inordinately glad to see her. She came tripping down the hotel steps, as he stood by the taxi, exactly at one thirty. Being security conscious, he had collected the boxes in two suitcases by a taxi shortly after ten, and had done a bit of shopping round Colombo at the same time. Then he had spent the rest of the morning in a secluded corner of the beach, with a shovel and a pair of scales digging in the sand.

Each box now weighed one kilo and ninety grammes (this last being the weight of the box), and all twenty were safely in the suitcases and loaded into the boot of the hired car, which waited, its engine panting and sending off little shimmers of heat, under the hotel portico.

She was wearing orange linen slacks, and a lettuce-green shirt, which for some inexplicable reason, accentuated the blue of her eyes. Her hair was scooped back into a pony-tail. She carried a bright orange scarf, and a pair of giant-sized sun glasses. As she climbed into his hired car she said in that same breathless voice, 'Did you think I was too old to build sand-castles?'

He pulled the door shut behind the two of them.

'No.'

'I thought I'd been invited to the dig.'

The taxi edged out of the hotel grounds and on to the Colombo road. 'Change of plan.'

'You didn't look as though you were enjoying yourself.'

'What d'you mean?'

'I saw you this morning from my room. Oh, don't worry . . . I don't think anyone else saw your return to childhood.'

'Good.' He stared moodily out at the catamarans drawn up under the coconut palms, and trying to rally to her teasing, 'I like to keep that side of my personality quiet.'

'Together with the side that rings girls up in the middle of the night?'

He felt immediately guilty. 'Sorry about that. It was just——'

'No, not to worry, please. I was *glad* you phoned.'

'Wake you?'

'Yes, but I went out like a light straightaway afterwards.'

'Good trip?'

'Very smooth, thank you. It was blowing a gale in London, if that's any consolation.'

'It is.'

'And when I got up,' she went on, smiling gently, 'there you were loping off down the hotel garden with a carrier-bag of wooden boxes.' She half turned, so that her eyes were full on his face, and their expression was sombre. 'For a moment,' she said calmly and very clearly, 'I thought you were off to bury the missing gold.'

She lowered her eyes and looked away. For over a minute the only sound in the taxi was the low hum of the engine and the hiss of the tyres on the hot tarmac. Then Hannaker asked in what he hoped was a casual tone, 'How did you know it was missing?'

She stared down at her clasped hands. 'All the crews knew about the gold on board. And we did think it a bit odd there was no mention in the papers. Then when we got back last night, we heard the whole lot had disappeared.'

'Who's *we*?'

'Captain Carstairs and the slip crew.'

'Who told you?'

'The Customs Officer who checked our baggage.' She gave a quick nervous laugh. 'A loader had told him. Loaders always know almost everything. And what they don't know, the cleaners do. And then Reeves's indigestion was bad and that's always the sign of a crisis. . . .'

Her voice, which had been on a higher-pitched, more nervous key, broke off and trailed away.

'How the hell did they find out?' It was a question to himself rather than to her. In irritation and helplessness, he clenched his right fist and banged it down into the open palm of his left.

'Everyone finds out whatever they want to know in this place,' she said, speaking softly now. 'You'd be surprised.'

'I shouldn't be. But I am.'

'Everyone has a relative in the right place, and they all seem to confide in one another.'

'I know just what you mean.' He was thinking of the driver and the distant cousin who made good strong boxes. Would that piece of information now be dispersed around the island, till it came to the ear that was interested to hear it? Always supposing, of course, that there was such an ear. Hannaker stared in front of him. They had gone through Colombo now, and already were approaching Katanayaka airport on the other side.

'And have the loaders got a clue as to where the gold's got to?' He smiled grimly, 'I'd be glad of a lead.'

'It sank in a marshy lake near the temple . . . that's what the grapevine says. It's a ghastly place. Years ago, a whole bullock cart went down in it. The two animals, driver, everything.'

'Was this the Customs chap again?'

She grinned apologetically. 'Yes.'

'Nothing ever recovered, I take it?'

'Nothing.'

'Convenient sort of disappearing net,' he said as the driver decelerated only slightly to swing through the airport entrance gates. 'I don't believe it.'

'Just as you don't believe the gold bars are in the lake?'

'You're getting as good as your Customs friend at putting two and two together.'

'And making five?'

'No . . . four. But you won't tell him, will you?'

The taxi stopped, and Hannaker paid the driver off. Carrying the suitcases, he kept silent as they went through the main hall and out on to the private aircraft apron. Then he said, 'And you won't tell him or anybody else what we're doing today?'

'Of course I won't.'

'Your remarkable arithmetical prowess has already told you what that is?'

She laughed and nodded. 'Who's doing the flying?'

'Chap called Gunn. Know him?'

'I know *of* him. What's he like?'

'You can see for yourself. There he is now . . . over by the yellow Cessna. Making a big show of looking at his watch. But if he tries to bite your head off, take absolutely no notice. . . .'

'You're five minutes adrift, mister. Time's money.'

'It's my nickel,' Hannaker replied equably, dumping the cases by the aircraft door.

Gunn glanced incuriously at the girl, and then wiped his hands on the sides of his cotton khaki trousers in readiness for the chore of introduction.

"Miss Grey . . . Mr Gunn.'

They both simultaneously smiled at Hannaker's formality, and then as if resentful of the other's amusement, disclaiming any possible alliance between the pair of them, quickly swallowed their smiles again.

'You bumming a ride then, mister?' Gunn addressed his question to the girl.

'I've heard it better put,' she said sweetly. 'But that's the rough idea.'

We don't make a bad trio, Hannaker thought, as Gunn flicked her a sharp-toothed smile of approval. 'Actually that isn't strictly true. I invited her.'

'Be my guest,' Gunn frowned. 'I charge extra for guests.'

'I want her to give me a hand.' Hannaker opened the suit-cases. 'With these.'

Gunn viewed the contents dispassionately. 'Looks like my cigarette box has pupped.'

'Here's yours.' Hannaker lifted up the empty box. 'Thanks for the loan.'

'What you figuring on doing with this lot, mister? We taking them along as well as——' he indicated Miss Grey with a backward jerked thumb.

'Yes.'

'Delivering them some place?'

'You could call it that.' Hannaker paused. 'I want to drop them.'

'Drop them *where*?'

'On the approach to Tallaputiya.'

'It figures,' Gunn said, still staring down in concentration at the boxes.

Suddenly, he stretched out his foot and very gently, like a big cat idly pushing at a dead mouse, he shoved it hard against the nearest case. When it didn't move, a slight derisive smile touched his thin lips.

'One at a time or the whole caboosh?'

'A stick of ten, followed three seconds later by another stick of ten.'

'That's where,' Gunn jerked his thumb at the girl, 'comes in?'

Hannaker nodded.

Gunn frowned at Melanie with an expression of exaggerated doubt. 'Mind you don't fall out too, mister. My insurance is real mean about losing paying guests.'

'I'll try not to.'

Gunn loaded in the cases. 'O.K. Hop in, mister.'

It was not immediately apparent to whom he was referring, but Miss Grey obediently climbed aboard.

'Now your turn, mister.'

Hannaker jumped up, and then Gunn followed suit. It was almost unbearably hot inside the Cessna. The greenhouse heat exaggerated the curious smell, common to all aircraft, of petrol and oil and upholstery. Now mixed in with it was the smell of the new fibre wood, and some perfume Melanie was wearing.

The heat and congestion with the three of them and the cargo at the back seemed to irritate Gunn. He took out an oily handkerchief and flapped it around like a fan.

'Come on, mister! Shift yourself!' He stabbed a finger at the right-hand seat, and the girl who had been hesitating, smiled, coloured slightly and sat herself down. Then Gunn shoved his way into the pilot's seat, and Hannaker, the tallest by far of the three, hastily squatted down on the floor behind them.

Gunn strapped himself in, slid open his window, and drew in great gulps of air with exaggerated gratitude. Then, deftly and rhythmically as a pianist's, the thick fingers flitted over the tiny dashboard, switching on the fuel, putting on the electrical and radio switches, pressing the starter button. The propeller in front of them wheeled round twice, and then burst into life with a puff of smoke.

'Colombo Tower, Delta Lima . . . taxi clearance.'

'Delta Lima cleared to Runway 27.'

The Cessna moved slowly forward, sucking in a cool fresh stream of air through the open window, as Gunn taxied round to the runway.

'Delta Lima, cleared to position. Cleared take-off. VFR climb.'

Stopped on the runway, gently panting, propeller idly chopping the sunshine into rainbow slices, Gunn made meticulous almost caressing movements over the dials and switches—fine pitch, flaps ten degrees, throttle nut tightened—performing his Tom Thumb take-off check as if he were about to yank into the air a Jumbo jet. An odd customer, Hannaker thought tolerantly, eyeing the short-nosed, long-lipped, simian profile, cameoed now against the mingled aquamarines of sky and green palm trees. But how odd? A natural pilot in love, if any man was, with his craft? Yet playing games with this little toy in this little backwater when the skies of the world might be his. The whirring propeller of Hannaker's mind spun his mood through the spectrum from tolerance back to mistrust, as he watched Gunn finish his checks, and then waggle his body like a champion golfer before teeing off into a more comfortable position in his seat.

'And what do you do for a living, mister?'

'I'm a stewardess. With Oriental Airways.'

'And don't they teach you to strap yourself in before take-off?'

Irritably, the square hand flipped two straps from the back of the seat on to the girl's lap. Ignoring her apologetic little smile, Gunn turned to Hannaker, 'And you, brace yourself against that stanchion, mister. We're ready to roll.'

Gunn stretched his hand forward and opened the throttle wide. The Cessna gave a little bark—a child's piping compared to the mammoth howl of the big jets—and began moving forward, faster and faster till with a silky precision and grace it soared up into the sun-filled air.

The runways, the white buildings, the paddy-fields fell away. Up over Colombo, over temples and red roofs and ochre-coloured roads, over leathery banana plantations, over emerald paddy-fields and brown rivers towards the mountains to the east of Tallaputiya.

Now between the two heads in front of him, Hannaker saw coming up into the screen of the window the sinister brown path, like a parting in luxuriant green hair, leading through the black smudge of the lake to the silver ashes of the wreck—the swathe cut by the 707 through the forest. And he found himself once again watching Gunn. The normal frown the American wore seemed to deepen perceptibly. For a moment a strange tension seemed to hold him. Then he drew a deep breath, and turned his head. The bright blue eyes were blank.

'You got permission to drop that stuff, mister?'

166

'No.'

For a second Hannaker thought Gunn was going to stick to the rules and not do it. At the back of his mind, in some odd way he even hoped that he would. He wanted to find some tight hard confines beyond which Gunn wouldn't go. Some area where integrity of living matched the precision of his flying. But Gunn simply shrugged and turned his face forward. His right hand rested on the throttles, gently easing them back. The noise of the engine died to a gentle clop-clop-clop. The nose dipped down as the aircraft descended. With the left wing tilted up in a gentle bank, Gunn circled the swathe, carefully scrutinizing the ground below, clearly looking to see if there was anyone anywhere near the area.

'Heard there were swarms of police here.'

'There were,' Hannaker said. 'But there's only two now. You can see them at the other side of the wreck. We couldn't possibly hit them.'

'You hoping that no one sees the drop?'

'That's the idea.'

'The best of British luck then, mister. You'll need it.' Gunn opened up the throttles and climbed. 'And if there *is* trouble, I know nothing of what you're doing back there, you understand? Otherwise, I'd lose my licence.'

'I understand.'

'Right then. I'll go up and ask for a normal practice ILS to the field. I'll approach real low at 140 knots, and start a ten degree climb at the first impact point. O.K.?'

'O.K.' Hannaker said. 'I'll arrange the boxes in two piles of ten. And can I open the door?'

'You can,' Gunn said. 'And you, mister.' He slapped the girl none too gently on her thigh. 'Go and take up your position aft.'

The girl unstrapped herself and scrambled to the back, while Gunn talked to the Tower, getting permission for his practice approach.

As the aircraft wheeled up into the sky and banked into the direction of the runway, Hannaker felt his mouth go dry, not so much from excitement as from anticipation. The girl stood beside him, her hands already poised on the ten boxes in front of her, staring out at the kaleidoscopic panorama of road, forest, sea, sky that was flickering across the square hole of the open doorway. She was to push her boxes out on Hannaker's signal, just after he had unloaded his own.

Impatiently he began fingering the cool fibre-wood lid of the top box. Gunn was taking his time to line up, doing a long run up, positioning the aircraft with the wings exactly level.

Would he be right? And if he was right, what would it mean?

Then at last, they were descending. Beyond the co-pilot's empty seat, he could see on the instrument panel the altimeter slowly unwinding, and the ILS indicator showing full travel below the glide path.

900-800-700 feet, with the speed building up all the time. Gunn was holding the Cessna beautifully steady.

Six inches away from his face, the slipstream whistled. The girl's fingers tensed on her pile of boxes, as the side of a hill pockmarked with rhododendron bushes came looming up, big and green and bright, and then a waterfall seemingly so close they could reach out and touch it.

'Twenty seconds to go!' Gunn's voice from the front. 'Stand by.'

Now they were right on top of the trees, skating just above the foliage. Twenty feet away, the port wing tip seemed actually to dip below the spreading branches of a breadfruit tree. The Cessna was paralleling the descent of the hill, bumping a little now on the upcurrents from the ground. Hannaker put his hands behind the ten boxes in front of him. Then suddenly, the engines roared, the nose tilted upwards.

'*Now!*'

He pushed. Out through the opening went the pile of boxes, as though a toy-house built of bricks had disintegrated.

Then he touched the girl's arm. 'You now!', and out went her boxes.

Falling, they scattered. Hannaker saw them form in two crazy patterns, each maintaining an odd sort of formation as he followed them down with his eyes—twenty rectangular boxes, spreadeagled in mid-air against a background of green jungle and black lake. For a moment in time, they remained transfixed in his memory, like bombs falling from an aircraft—one of them tilted high at an angle away from the others, six of them almost joined together in a higgledy-piggledy decoration—all the time getting smaller.

He put his head right out of the aircraft, felt the cold force of the slipstream tearing his hair, following them down, down, down.

'Here . . . careful!' He was suddenly aware of the girl's hands hanging on to his shoulder. 'You look pleased. Did we make a hit?'

He brought his head back into the aircraft. He smiled. 'Sort of . . . yes.'

He had watched all twenty land, the slight green flurry as they plummeted into the trees—well to the other side of the lake. Not a single one of them had fallen anywhere near the black greasy water.

Gunn climbed back up into the sky. All he said was, 'That should please you.'

'Yes.'

'Want to land now?'

'Please.'

Gunn motioned the girl to get back into the right-hand seat, told Hannaker to close the door, and banking on his port wing, turned the nose of the aircraft towards Katanayaka airport. Thoughtfully he glanced at Hannaker. The blue eyes which had remained blank and business-like throughout the exercise were narrow and sharp with interest. 'We-ell, mister,' he drawled softly, 'A dollar to a dime, them gold bars ain't all in that there lake.' He gave a short bark of laughter.

Hannaker watched a tiny drift of cloud flurry over the wing and disperse. 'I would say you had the odds almost exactly right.'

'Then where in hell can it be, mister?'

More shortly than he intended Hannaker said, 'You tell me.'

Frowning he gazed down at the many-coloured pattern of the island below him. But he wasn't admiring the beauty. He saw the concealing mat of the jungle, the intricacies of the ruined cities, temples and holy places protected from prying eyes by strict taboo, imposing villa fortresses and official buildings, dry river beds, mountains and crags, and caves. 'It's like looking for a needle in a haystack.'

Gunn shrugged his shoulders, and moved the elevator bar forward gently. Slowly and smoothly, they slipped down through the gin-clear air. The sun caught their shadow, flinging it over the shiny heads of the jungle trees, the water green of the paddy fields. He took up his R/T microphone.

Before he spoke into it, he said to Hannaker with soft and eminent reasonableness, 'Mister, if I was doing such a fool thing as looking for a needle in a haystack, I'd get me a magnet.' Then pleased with himself, speaking chirpily to the Tower. 'Delta Lima . . . landing clearance.'

He listened, head on one side, smiling patiently to the clatter of accented English.

Seeing Melanie smiling slightly too, Hannaker said irritably, 'Unfortunately there is no such thing as a magnet for gold.'

'Runway 27. Roger and out.' Gunn called into the microphone. And then sideways in the same breath, 'Zat so, mister?'

He lowered his brows, stared through the windscreen, apparently intent on making it a smooth soft landing. Without a detectable moment of contact, their wheels glided on to the runway and they were speeding down the long grey strip of concrete. Using the brakes sparingly, Gunn brought the aircraft round to the dispersal, and with finicky concentration completed his miniscule after-landing check. Then he sighed and sat back.

'You're right and wrong, mister. It ain't a magnet, sure. But there *is* a gadget. Works on gamma rays, so'm told. I might jest be able to lay my hands on one for a coupla days.' He flipped open the buckle of his seat belt, turned and smiled with caricatured innocence. 'Cost you more'n a nickel. But what d'you say?'

'How much is more than a nickel?'

'Six hundred rupees.'

'How long for?'

'Jest one day.'

Hannaker whistled. Gunn shrugged his shoulders and got out of his seat.

'Come on, mister,' he said to Melanie, 'Get a move on. Time's money. This is all he paid for.'

As they stepped on to the warm tarmac, the American said with a persistence and intent that might at any other time have made Hannaker more wary, 'Well?'

'All right. Though God knows, I can't search much in a day.'

Gunn laughed, not just his usual derisive bark, but with an exultant note. 'Don't worry, mister. You'll be surprised.' He walked a few paces, 'Same as anything else . . . what you really have to know is where to begin.'

With monotonous inevitability, the rains came again. Melanie lay awake listening to the downpour. She wished she could rid her ears of the sound. It drowned out everything else as if acting like a screen beyond which subtler, more menacing sounds might take place. But *what* sounds she didn't know. The sound perhaps of the jungle draining into the lake, where the gold, Jamie Hannaker said, didn't lie. The sounds of Fonseca and Seneratne, sifting through the clues, or covering them up. The sound of Gunn's light aircraft perhaps, having a look-see around, or flying a load of cheap crap in to southern India— or why not something precious? The sound of the priests at their everlasting prayer.

Or was there really no menace at all? Just the strange time-less ways of the East with which, as Reeves suggested to her, a man like Hannaker simply couldn't cope. 'He's his own worst enemy. Too unbending. Out here you have to compromise a bit. The truth isn't just beam on. It's shades of meaning either side.'

'That's him, though, isn't it?'

'Well, not *just* that. This came at a bad time for him. Just when he'd worn himself out for years. Or so I'm told. Not been the same, they tell me, since his wife was killed. . . .'

The thought of Jamie's fastidious gritty integrity being

nothing more than a neurosis born of that accident was a daunting one—for him, for her, somehow for everyone.

'Trouble with these people who get a bit neurotic,' Reeves had unwrapped a Rennie, 'they tend to be infectious. Other people get smittled.'

She fell asleep thinking about it all. And that last sly remark of Reeves, 'I'm sure if *you* were to take a spot of UK leave, we'd have him home in no time flat.'

She woke to bright sunlight. Everywhere had a clear rinsed look. Behind the hotel gardens Mount Lavinia stood close and sharply defined as if it had stepped a mile or so nearer in the night. She dressed and went downstairs.

The windows were open on to the terrace again. The tiles were dry, the tables set with white cloths and glittering silver. In the far corner, Jamie was drinking a cup of coffee, and reading the morning papers.

'Anything in,' she said, sliding into the chair opposite him, 'about you boys bombing up the jungle?'

He looked up and smiled, with his mouth but not his eyes. The sunlight showed up the lines of fatigue in his face. 'No. Thank God! Not so far.' He folded the paper. 'You're up late.'

'I went to sleep late.'

Suddenly he said 'Why don't you take some leave?'

'Just what I was going to say to you,' she smiled. 'Telepathy.'

'Don't let's start on that again,' he said, his eyes on her face, watching her as she gave her order to the waiter.

'Would you take leave if I did?'

Mournfully but firmly, 'No.'

'At least,' she shook out her napkin, 'you could take today off.'

'Are you free?'

'Yes. Stand-by tomorrow. Out Monday.'

Hannaker frowned.

'Where to?'

'Hong Kong.'

'Back Wednesday?'

'Yes.'

Hannaker's frown deepened.

'Well,' she said, dipping her spoon into the paw-paw, 'Shall you take the day off? Come for a swim? Let's just lie on the beach?'

She had an overpowering desire to reach across the table and smooth the worry lines off his face.

'Sorry,' he said sharply, getting up. 'Not a hope. I'm right in the midst of something. I've got to try to get hold of . . .'

But he didn't say who or what. He just gave her a brief nod as if he hardly saw her, tossed his newspaper on the table, and hurried out. She watched his tall figure shamble through the doorway and disappear into the foyer. When he had gone she shrugged angrily and poured some coffee. Jamie Hannaker, she told herself, drinking the coffee so hot that it brought tears to her eyes, might be clever in his job, but in at least one way he was a fool.

She reached for the paper and put it by her plate, folded where he'd been reading it. There was a column headed, *Tallaputiya Disaster Inquiry*. She read on: *The Inquiry set up to investigate the cause of the accident to aircraft Whisky Echo of British Oriental Airways will convene on June 26th. Our correspondent has been informed that Mr J. Hannaker, who has been kindly assisting on behalf of the British Government, will be returning to London early next week.*

Melanie put down the paper, and sat staring thoughtfully at the patterns on the white damask tablecloth. When the shadow of a man fell on the table at first she thought that Hannaker had returned. A bitter little thought sprang to her mind that if he had, it would simply have been to fetch his paper.

She looked up. Roy Laughton stood beside her. 'They told me at the desk that I'd find you here. Even for a human ping-pong ball you've been remarkably elusive these last few days.' He pulled out a chair, straddling it, and smiling at her quizzically. 'Well, why the frown?'

Unconsciously she glanced at the newspaper.

'Oh, *that*!' He read the column quickly. 'Well, at least it's good they know the answers.'

173

'I'm still not sure.'

He grinned lazily. 'I didn't come to argue.'

'What did you come for?' She smiled over the rim of her cup, found the coffee was now cold and put it down.

'To take you out for the day.'

An hour ago she would probably have refused. 'Where to?'

'Anywhere you like. You name it. I take you to it.'

There was something she thought, getting out of her chair, to be said for lack of grittiness in a man. 'Anywhere,' she said, 'where we can forget about aeroplanes.' But really she meant anywhere, damn him, where I won't think about Hannaker.

'Careful now! Don't hurl yourself over!' Climbing over a ledge, Melanie's left foot in its high-heeled crocodile shoe skidded on the loose scree, and feeling herself slipping, she clutched at the red overhanging rock, as three hundred feet sheer below, the green glaze of the jungle shimmered in the sun. Roy's voice, sharp with concern, sounded behind her. His hand shot out, gripped her arm and steadied her. For a second they stayed joined together, quite still against the granite, as if they too had been carved out of it, like the kings and mistresses and gods and elephants hewn out of the rock over a thousand years before. In that second, something beyond the momentary quick reflex of fear made her wish she hadn't come. Sigiri. The Place in the Sky on the Rock of the Lion. Even the name itself held an indefinable menace.

'Isn't this place supposed to be evil?' She breathed over her shoulder, remembering some of the tourist information in the airline brochures.

'Now who's the superstitious one? People were terrified of the place, that's all.'

'Why?'

'There had been so much bloodshed.'

'I felt . . .' she began to say, and then stopped.

'Besides,' he went on teasingly, 'it all depends on your point of view. My father—he was a devout Baptist—thought the

Vatican was an abode of all evil. Anyway, its just those silly shoes. They're no good for rock climbing.'

'I didn't know we were going rock climbing.'

'Well, you chose Sigiri.'

'Did I? Yes, I suppose I did.' She wiped her forehead with the back of her hand. They had driven along, apparently aimlessly, towards Colombo discussing where they should go, when suddenly he had pointed out the huge rock mass on their right.

'D'you know what that is?' He had stopped the car.

'Sigiri.'

'D'you know anything about it?'

'I know it's a hazard to aircraft. And they can't get an obstruction light on top. But there's a ruined palace, old as the Pharaohs.'

'The jet-age child.' He had sighed and shaken his head, and asked her if now with the sun just at that angle she could see how splendidly it looked like its Sanskrit name, Lion. Sure enough, some quality of the light then had turned the granite a tawny colour, silhouetted and reshaped the rock's huge head, and etched the monsoon weathering lines over the shoulder, till they resembled sinew folds. It had seemed then the obvious thing to say, 'Why not there?'

'I should have known,' Melanie forced a laugh, 'that it would mean a climb.'

'And I should have warned you. Here! Take those shoes off. Let me carry them.'

'But I'll ladder my tights.'

'Nonsense. The rock is smooth. That's why you slide. If you ladder them, I'll buy you a hundred pairs.'

'Thus spake,' she laughed, 'the Sultan of Sigiri,' thinking pityingly that sometimes Roy showed how deeply his child-hood poverty had bitten. She slipped her feet one at a time out of her shoes cautiously so as not to lose her balance. He bent down, retrieved them, and put them into his jacket pockets.

'This place we're standing on, d'you know what it is?'

'A look-out?'

'No.' He held her arm tighter. 'The lion king's execution

platform. That's why it's so narrow. From here, disobedient wives and rebellious subjects were given one push. And off!' He shook her arm playfully, 'Go on! Look down!'

'I don't want to. I don't like heights.'

'Shame on you! I love heights. Brace yourself! I won't let you fall.'

Gingerly, she craned her neck. Far below against the foot of the rock the jungle swayed and swung like the sea. But not an unbroken sea. Just visible above the jungle heads were broken towers, minarets halved like egg-shells, bell-like dagobas, shattered columns, crumbling temples. All the granite and rock and rubble of a huge ruined city, washed now with creepers drowned in foliage like some Atlantis of the jungle.

'Once a metropolis as big as London,' Roy said softly. 'Makes you think.'

'Makes me shiver,' Melanie said.

'Down there was the barrack square where the bodies fell. Some people say they can still mark it out.'

'It gives me a horrible feeling,' Melanie shuddered. 'It's like looking down on water. After a while you feel it drawing you towards it.'

'Then away we must go!' He pulled her back and turned her round with a smile. 'Forward again. Not much more of this difficult bit. Then we'll *really* see something.'

About fifty yards further on, the ledge widened, the gradient slackened and the going became easier. The path wound round, and they were on a more southerly, less sheer face of the rock.

'I still can't see how we get to the top,' Melanie said, shielding her eyes to stare up at the overhang. 'Do we wind round and round like a helter-skelter?'

'No. After a while because of that overhang, the path peters out. That's the clever part of it. There's only one way up. *Or down.* Once they were up at the top, they were safe.'

Now that the path was wider, Roy relaxed his grip of her arm, and rested his hand on her shoulder. On this side of the rock, it was very hot and still. The sounds of the jungle were tightly boxed within the tight foliage. The only noise was the padding of their own feet, and Roy's breathing as he walked protectively close behind her.

Melanie was about to say something just to break the silence, when the path turned another corner and fell back to make a shadowy gallery about sixty feet long and half as wide. It was floored in soft sandy scree into which their feet sank as if in a carpet.

'There!' Roy came up beside her and slipped his arm round her shoulder. 'What did I tell you? They are worth climbing up for, aren't they?'

The gallery was walled on three sides by smooth pale rock on which were life-size paintings of incredible beauty and freshness.

'Beautiful, aren't they?'

She sighed. 'Very beautiful.' And walking further in, 'All women?'

He nodded. 'The ladies of the Lion King's court.'

Some skill of the artist gave the portraits a three-dimensional living quality. The eyes stared directly at the onlooker. The expression varied from glowing face to face. The postures, natural and relaxed, different and yet related, so that they all seemed to have been caught at some gathering, and all had turned to gaze amused, interested, derisive, or apprehensive at the intruders.

Not only sight but sound too contributed to the fantasy. The cavern had strange acoustics. The soft pad of their own feet had gone ahead of them and echoed back. So that the idea came to Melanie that the figures had, till their coming, occupied the centre of the gallery, then retreated quickly to the wall.

'You could swear they were alive!'

'So they are, in a way.'

She walked forward. Tiny palpitations of sound sped ahead of her, echoed back from the stone, so that faint footsteps seemed to come out to meet her. 'Look at those clothes! Trouser suits, chunky jewellery and see-through blouses. I've got some like that. They could walk down from the wall and be fashionable now.'

177

Roy rested his hand on her shoulder. 'A thousand years is nothing.'

'So it seems.'

'We come and go within time. The past is now.'

'The future?'

'Now.'

She sighed. 'I *wonder*. I like the idea, and yet I don't.' She glanced up at him. 'Did you really mean what you said at the bungalow. That you know who you were? Before?'

'Yes.' He walked along the line of portraits. 'Come here and see this one. She's the most beautiful, don't you think?'

He stopped in front of the portrait of a girl with long hair fashioned out of gold leaf, a small pointed face, and large indigo eyes.

'Well,' Melanie said doubtfully, 'she looks as if she had a mind of her own. I hope he didn't have *her* executed.'

'Certainly not. She was Kasyapa's favourite. She followed him into his last battle. He made the mistake of descending to the plain.'

Melanie made a clicking sound with her tongue, not sure whether she wanted to smile at Roy's obsession with history, or whether for some inexplicable reason to feel afraid. And yet, of what was there for her to be afraid? Nothing except the faint, dusty and suffocating, almost pregnant atmosphere of the gallery itself.

'When he was killed, she found sanctuary here. And like a good wife threw herself from the platform. Of her own free will.'

'Poor girl!'

'Oh, I don't know. They were together.' And then smiling, 'I think she looks like you.'

Melanie held her head on one side, judiciously.

'See, you're almost the same height!' Playfully, he slid his hand up from her shoulder to the back of her neck, bending her forward so that her forehead touched that of the painted portrait. The rock felt warm to the touch and smooth as skin.

Melanie shook herself free. 'I can guess now who you think

178

you were.' She laughed. It was all playful surely? Yet the playfulness slightly missed, like a chord struck slightly off key. Like the feel of his strong hand on the back of her neck. Playful surely? But with a degree more of strength than play.

He smiled, shrugged and walked away from her a couple of paces. Along here the rock that roofed the gallery was split with thin faults through which sunlight came splintering down in hard bright needles. Walking in and out of this distorting light, his face seemed to change—now familiar, now a stranger's.

'Shall we go on up?' he said, pointing to a flight of metal steps leading up the far end of the gallery. 'Notice,' he flicked a glance over his shoulder, 'how their eyes follow us?'

'Yes. I saw that before. That's a portrait painter's art, isn't it?'

The effect of the heat, the climb or her own imagination made her heart quicken. Her voice struggled for normality. The strange sense of terror she had felt on the platform touched her briefly again. For looking back, the eyes of the favourite that followed them were blanched of colour, the whole face pale and blind.

'Now we come to the really splendid part.'

They were emerging from the iron staircase on to another wide platform of rock unroofed, with nothing above them but the huge curling crest of the overhang. By straining her head backwards, she could just glimpse the ruins at the summit silhouetted against a sky of hazy blue and cream-white cumulus heads. A clump of bushes, black in this light, waved gently in the slight wind of altitude.

Her head swam with the heat, and the savage reflection of the sun bouncing off the rock. But as if receiving a message from a long way away, her mind seemed to fix on the cumulus clouds. '*Should* we go to the top today?'

'Of course. When we've come all this way. It would be silly not to.'

'How do we get up? Knock on the stone and say Open Sesame?'

'Something like that. Come round here.' He took her hand

179

and guided her round to the right. 'Nearly two thousand years ago, they found the one and only way up.'

At first she could see nothing except two huge boulders, thinning into what looked like columns which disappeared into the overhang.

'Look again.'

Screwing up her eyes against the hard light, she walked forward. Closer to, she saw that each boulder was carved into the shape of a lion's paw, bone and sinew faithfully etched, the long claws smooth and polished as if made of nail. The columns were legs, and between them, but further back where the belly would be, was a steep staircase carved out of the rock which disappeared into the stone above.

'The famous lion staircase. Go on! Those claws can't hurt you.'

She hesitated. Apprehension, intangible, but clutching as cobwebs, returned. She wanted to turn back. Yet as Roy had said, it seemed silly not to go on now. When she turned, he was smiling at her, very easy, very relaxed, very English, very comforting.

'You're *still* afraid of heights. You won't be, when you get to the top, I promise.'

He put his arm round her waist, and step by step, side by side, they climbed up the first few stairs together. The rock was hot to her feet. The light diminished as they ascended into the shadow of one huge leg, then further up and into the beginnings of the lion's body. Now the steps felt moist and still warm. Below she could see the sun glittering on the paws. Diffused light sifted up, but none came from above.

Then a turn of the stair, and the light went out altogether. They were in total darkness. They had to feel their way slowly. And as they climbed, *something*—the vibration of their movements, the wind of height, or the scuttering of lizards disturbed in their sleep—made the whole moist dark womb-like cavern pulsate with heat and life. Horizonless, the curious illusion came to her that they were descending instead of climbing, and in a sudden flash of insight or terror, she didn't know which, she thought she recognized that they were taking part in some ceremonial of rebirth. She and he were being expelled from some pulsating stone womb.

Into what?

Abruptly she squirmed and wriggled and tried to get herself free, but his grip tightened. She opened her mouth to scream, but firmly, he put his hand over her mouth. And like that, bounded with her up the last twist of stair till the sunlight burst over them. They were at the top, with Ceylon all around and only the sky above them.

Her dress was clinging wetly to her body. Her face ran with sweat. She drew in the cooler air in gulps, wiping her face with her handkerchief. I am half in a dream, half in a nightmare, she thought. This strange place, with its ruins of palaces and temples and its scented flowers and bathing pools and trees, cut off from everywhere like a land at the top of some stone beanstalk, that awful staircase, Roy himself.

She was aware that he was watching her. 'My poor sweet.' There was an expression of drowsy sensual satisfaction on his face.

'You really didn't like that staircase, did you?'

'No.'

'But it's really very harmless.' He pointed downwards, and now looking at it from this angle, the whole thing looked quite short and innocuous.

'Anyway, sit down.' A step or so forward, there was a stone-flagged platform half covered with blue flowery creeper, on which was set a pink granite throne. 'This is *gal asanaya* . . . the Lion King's throne.'

'Look!'

As she sat down, Roy waved his arm. The gesture was arrogant, dramatic, proprietorial. This, the gesture said, is totally mine. All the jewel colours of the island—the sapphire of the irrigation tanks in the north, the emerald of the paddy fields, the silvers, pinks and cornelians of the ruined cities seemed from this far-off height to do a slow rotation round her head. She remembered thinking that there was going to be a storm. Sea and sky were merging. The horizon, all horizons blurred.

'You see,' Roy said, 'as I told you, height no longer bothers you.'

'It's not the same up here.' She put up her hand to her head. The long climb up, the shimmering heat, even hunger perhaps, made her feel dizzy, cut off from reality. She had suddenly great difficulty in remembering where she was, when this was, who in fact she was. Time had shimmered under the heat of the sun. She was herself, she was not herself.

She was aware that Roy had come over and was standing beside her. His hand descended heavily on her shoulder. Only taut ribbons of sunlight glistened down from between the dense storm cloud. The air was very still, and over-sweet.

'Marry me, Melanie.' His voice came very loud and startling in her ear. She turned her head, looking up at the profile lit by the eerie silky light. I am now *in* the nightmare, she thought.

Slowly he turned his head and looked down at her. The sunlight turned the face that regarded her to a glittering tawny colour. The nose was foreshortened, the jaw widened. The whole face flat, animal, ferocious. The hand on her shoulder pressed harder till she could feel the bite of claws.

As in a nightmare, she couldn't move. She opened her mouth soundlessly. Down came the face, closer to hers. The eyes widened to golden slits with narrowed pupils.

Then with an audible splash, the first rain fell on the flagstones. The dream, the nightmare broke with it.

The sunlight had gone. And as if it had projected a film no longer there, normality returned. When she looked up at him, Roy was smiling ruefully, was hastily taking off his jacket to put round her. The effect of the sun and too much climbing, she remembered thinking. Or perhaps as Reeves said, Jamie's neurosis *is* catching.

When Hannaker left Melanie Grey in the dining-room of the hotel, he walked straight to the station and caught a train for Colombo Pettah. Gunn was up and dressed, and the apartment tidy. The chaise-longue was cleared of rubbish and the table was drawn up in front of it, with the cigarette box placed on it, a map, and some paper, and a couple of glasses and a can-opener.

'Looks as if you're preparing for a board meeting,' Hannaker said. 'Expecting someone?'

'Yep mister.' Gunn went to the cupboard, opened it and took out a stack of cans. 'You.'

Hannaker set himself down, and raised his brows questioningly.

'We-ell,' Gunn padded over to the table, drew up a chair and sat opposite to Hannaker. 'Yesterday we didn't exactly find much to beat the tom-toms over.' He held up a hand, 'Jest a minute, mister. I know exactly what you're gonna say about negative evidence. Yes*sir*! But this time round, jest a bit too negative for my way of reckoning.'

'Or mine.'

'Exactly, mister.' Gunn clipped open a can of beer, and divided it between the two glasses. 'That's why I figured you'd be back to thumb through the bits. 'Sides, I got that little gadget I told you about. Cost you six hundred a day, like I said.'

Hannaker took a gulp of beer and said, 'Actually I had an idea.'

Gunn looked as if he might have made a facetious response but couldn't quite rise to it. He waved his glass in polite invitation for Hannaker to continue.

'You were pretty smartly on the scene of the crash, weren't you?'

'Me, mister?' Gunn narrowed his eyes and asked softly, 'Is that a question or a statement?'

'A statement.' Hannaker smiled. 'You took a number of photographs. The *Ceylon Daily News* published a couple of them.'

''Sright. Now wait a minute! You're not trying to say *I* spotted the gold, lobbed down and picked it up and off, are you?'

Hannaker shook his head. 'No. But now you mention it, did you?'

183

Equally matter-of-factly, Gunn answered, 'Hell, no. Straight stealing's not my line of territory.'

'What *is* your line?'

'Haven't they told you, mister?'

'I'm asking *you*.'

'We-ell, that's real kind. But sorry, mister, I'm not answering. Not right now. Mebbe some place, some time. But not right now.'

Hannaker inclined his head in a gesture that both understood and accepted. 'What time of day did you take those photographs?'

'First light.'

'Did you *see* anything?'

'Plenty, mister.' He took a long gulp of his beer and looked away. When he set the glass back on the table his hand shook slightly.

'No sign of the gold boxes?'

'They weren't exactly exercising my mind then, mister.'

'Nothing else that might help me?'

'No.'

'It struck me you might have taken more photos than were actually published.'

'That's correct.'

He suddenly jumped up, and began pacing up and down the room, brows lowered thoughtfully. Hannaker went on,

'You take a whole roll, don't you? That's the usual thing?'

'Yep.'

'What is it? Vertical or oblique?'

'Oblique.'

'Who developed it?'

'Me, mister.'

'And have you still got the roll?'

Anticipating the next question Gunn stopped his perambulations and stood in front of Hannaker, hands on his hips, 'What d'you reckon it's gonna tell you?'

Hannaker smiled faintly, 'If it's like everything else, nothing.'

'That's what I figured.'

'But there's just a faint chance that if we could look at it

184

through a projector—I take it you've got a choice of lenses—we *might* just see something.'

Gunn narrowed his eyes, nodded slowly several times but kept silent. After a while Hannaker added, 'If nothing else, I might get a better idea of the trajectory of the cargo that way. Though most of course won't be visible because of the trees.' Hannaker drank some more beer and let Gunn chew over the idea.

'Well, come on, mister,' Gunn seemed suddenly galvanized into action. 'Don't jest sit there. Let's get rolling.'

He led the way across the living room to the passageway, and past the kitchen-cum-bathroom on the right. Further down the dark corridor was another doorway, closed, this time not just covered with a bead curtain, but with a heavy wooden door. Gunn took a key out of his pocket, and turned the lock.

'Gotta do this,' he apologized, as if conscious that somewhere at the back of Hannaker's mind he had noted the locked, hitherto undeclared, room. 'Real strange guys these Sinhalese. Tell 'em keep out, an it's jest like sending a Limey's gilt-edged invite to Buckingham P.'

'When I came here that first day after the crash,' Hannaker said gently, 'you didn't mention you had a room down here. You said search the place. But you didn't take me in here.'

'When you reckoned I might've slipped it in a can of cat food?'

'Yes.'

'Modesty. No, that's not correct,' he laughed, without humour, 'I didn't want *you* poking your collar's nose in right then neither.' He opened the door. 'Darkroom, see, thass all.' He pulled a switch. The room flooded with the light from a green-shaded bulb. ''Sokay. Nothing on the pins, jest now.' He opened a metal cupboard, whistling, apparently unconcerned.

Hannaker glanced around. The room was equipped with two deep stone sinks, draining boards, lines for drying prints, a large easel and what looked like expensive cameras and projecting equipment. On the wall was a screen.

'You got the collar's occupational disease.' Gunn emerged

from the cupboard with a cylinder in his hand and poked Hannaker with it lightly in the ribs. 'Comes up like moral belly ache.'

'What does?'

'Suspicion, mister.'

'It's more endemic and persistent than that,' Hannaker said. He toyed with the idea of asking Gunn where the hell he got the money from to buy stuff like this, and having bought it, was it worth while for the odd picture he got printed in the Ceylon newspapers. But first things first. He had learned, more thoroughly than Gunn would ever have given him credit for, to put his suspicions to rest, till it was prudent to wake them up again.

'O.K.' Gunn switched on a small lamp on the work bench and doused the main light. Hannaker watched him flip the roll into the projector and select a suitable lens. 'How big, mister?'

'Big as you can make it. Big as the screen.'

'Make yourself comfortable then. It's gonna be a long hot summer. O.K. Ready to roll?'

'Ready.' Hannaker hauled himself on to the work bench.

'Kill that light then, mister.'

In the hot steamy darkness a cone of light from the projector filled the screen with a dark smudgy blur. Gunn's hand came forward over the lens and gently adjusted it, until the dark cauliflower tops of the jungle heads sprang into focus, and the swathe of the bent and battered vegetation.

'Just say when you wanna turn the page, mister.' Gunn shifted his position behind the projector so that he too could peer at the blown-up shot. Slowly and methodically, first an over-all stare at the picture, then a meticulous square search from left to right. Nothing visible there, except the very beginning of where the aircraft had struck.

'Move on, please.'

The projector clicked softly. More damage on this picture. The swathe widening and deepening. A man's sodden overcoat hanging on a branch of a mahogany tree. What looked like petals or confetti on a matted spiky-leafed tree just beside it.

'Mail, I reckon,' Gunn said, seeing Hannaker lean forward.

The beginnings of the marshy lake. 'There,' Hannaker pointed, 'what's that?'

'Too big for a gold box. Most likely a trunk. Yep. You can jest make out the handles at the side there. Move on?'

'Might as well.'

The slow progress of the blown-up roll continued. Time ticked away to the faint whirr and click of the reel. Inside the darkroom the air got warmer and staler. Hannaker could smell sweat and rubber and the sharp smell of fixative and processing fluid. Tiny dust motes floated in the yellow cone of light. Gunn kept wiping the sweat off his forehead with the back of his hand. All the scrutiny of the blow-ups revealed was that the freight and baggage had fallen in a funnel-shaped pattern fretted by the different weights of the objects.

'We-ell,' Gunn said, scratching himself. 'We're coming up to the end, mister. Final shot.'

The last exposure showed in vivid daylight the crash site much as Hannaker had first seen it, except the milling figures, the fire engines and the ambulances were gone. What remained was the aircraft itself in bright relief against the forest background, and in the foreground the churned up mud where the vehicles had been.

'Can you focus up the foreground?'

'Sure.'

Hannaker stared at the screen. He felt a curious tightness in his throat. His heartbeat quickened. He felt that curious prescience, that sixth sense of the professional, that now he was on to something.

'Negative evidence in more ways than one, mister?' The shadow of Gunn stretched his long arms lazily above his head. But Hannaker didn't hear him. He was staring fascinated at the tyre tracks in the foreground. A great mass of them all curving left towards the road that led towards Colombo. All except one set. Just visible in the lower foreground of the photograph were a set of tracks, of heavy-duty tyre tracks, that turned right, away from the direction the rest had gone.

'Not quite,' Hannaker said slowly. '*Not quite.*'

Half an hour later, Gunn came through into the living-room, and laid an enlarged print of those tracks in front of Hannaker on top of a survey map of Ceylon. Hannaker stared at it closely. Then he moved it slightly—first at one angle and then at another. It was too grainy now to show much more detail, and it was still damp and smelled of hypo.

Nevertheless as he studied every mark the certainty that he was on to something stirred again. Out of all the welter of negative evidence had come this fragment of the positive. The curve of tyre marks away to the south was short, but unmistakable. He looked back to the map, and then to the print again. He was aware that Gunn was watching him closely. He could feel, and did his best to ignore, the other man's subdued excitement.

'Would you say,' Hannaker raised his eyes after a moment, 'that those tracks were made *before* most of the others?' He lifted the print carefully by the edges with his right hand and pointed to what seemed to be ingoing tracks overlaying part of the curve.

'Yep. That's what I figured.' Gunn's voice was a hoarse whisper.

'What sort of tracks, would you say? Ambulance?'

'Could be. Could be the type used for jungle terrain.'

Hannaker thrust out his lower lip thoughtfully. When he spoke, it was with deliberate cool pedantry. 'If, and it's still an *if*, there was an unknown vehicle at the crash site, it is likely that it made off with the gold.' He paused.

'It's a strong thought, mister. But I reckon you got something.'

'If . . . an even greater *if*—the print's too weak to be certain —it left *before* most of the others arrived,' Hannaker drew a long deep breath 'there seems a possibility that whoever was in it knew the aircraft was going to crash.'

'Or made it,' Gunn said.

Angrily—his only concession to any emotion—Hannaker pushed the chaise-longue back from the table and stood up. He walked across the room to the window. He wanted to shout out these things could not happen. But, God, he above all people knew that they could and did. Aircraft blown up to collect a few thousand pounds of insurance, to get rid of an unwanted wife, to even up a trivial grudge.

Hannaker turned suddenly, came back to the table, folded the map at the portion south of the crash site, and beckoned Gunn to pore over it with him.

'If it wasn't going to Colombo, where was it going to?'

'Jest one place.'

Hannaker went on staring at the map. Gunn folded his arms over his chest and waited for Hannaker to ask him to explain. He changed his weight impatiently from one foot to the other. 'Don't you wanna know where?'

After a few minutes Hannaker said very slowly, 'I think I can guess. Laughton's place. Sinha Radio.'

'We-ell, it's south all right,' Gunn said.

'And it's a large complex of buildings, a village on its own almost.' Hannaker made a little circle round the place with his fountain pen. 'Very efficient, so I'm told. Plus import-export organization.'

'*And* he has an ambulance.'

Hannaker turned suddenly and stared keenly at Gunn, his dark eyes sharp and narrowed. It struck Gunn then that for all his calm scrupulous ways Hannaker would be a ferocious customer to be up against.

'You're sure of that?' With an obvious effort he kept his voice steady.

'Sure I'm sure. It's part of his model factory set-up. Medicine for the workers.'

'Have you actually seen it?'

'Yep. Been there often enough. Done business with Laughton.'

'Do you still do business?'

'Sure. If I get anything he might be interested in.'

'How often?'

''Bout once a year.'

'Is it difficult to get into the factory?'

'I'll say it is! Except on Visitors' Days, which are carefully controlled.'

'But *you* can get in?'

'Yep.'

There was a long pause while Hannaker carefully, un-hurriedly considered several possibilities. Going to Inspector Fonseca. But with what? A blown-up print of tracks, now long obliterated. To Reeves? To Seneratne? To the High Commissioner? To be laughed out of court on such flimsy evidence? Would they not say, as part of his own mind already said, that he was simply too tired, too overwrought, too suggestible to nonsense?

Hannaker drew a deep breath. 'Could you get me in with-out being seen? With the gold detector?'

Gunn's eyes narrowed. A curious expression, something like triumph, crossed his face. 'If that's what you really want, mister. It's your nickel.'

'O.K., mister, if you want my autograph that bad, I'll sign your visitor's book. Though you know damned well your boss is expecting me.'

Gunn's movements rocked the van. The side door slammed. Footsteps came and went. Whispering started just outside the open window. Then came the squeak of a handle turning. The rear doors were flung wide open. Amber light from the setting sun streamed in.

Lying under a black tarpaulin amongst lead piping, pieces of crankshaft and an exhaust manifold, his body curled round the gold detector to protect it, through an eyelet in the fabric Hannaker caught a glimpse of two men in smart blue uniforms, wearing thick leather shoulder straps and belts, revolvers in holsters on their hips—Laughton's industrial police.

There was an up-and-down waterfall of Sinhalese, suddenly dammed by Gunn's slow drawl. 'What about a honey of a Ford crankshaft? It's a real gnat's whistle. Worth fifty rupees. For you, mister, jest ten. No dice? Well, come up front. Got a dandy tool-kit.'

The sunshine abruptly went out as the rear door slammed.

More whispering, fainter now. The clink of money. Gunn's voice again, 'You got yourself a real bargain there.'

High-pitched laughter, the shake of the van as Gunn climbed aboard, the burst of the engine firing and accelerating. Gunn's voice shouting, 'Can't make an honest dime outta you two operators!' More laughter and the squeak of iron gates opening.

Then the feel of the van on smooth tarmac. Gunn's voice, back to normal again: 'You still alive?'

'Just.'

'Emily all right?'

'A good deal more comfortable than I am.'

'Keep it that way. That gal's real delicate.'

The drive was curving round now. The van was going slower as they reached the apex and the main office. The smell of flowers drifted in amongst the stink of oil and dirt and dust.

The van stopped. The engine gave one last convulsive kick and died. The sounds of the handbrake and the opening and shutting of the door. Gunn's footsteps fading into the distance. Silence.

For another half hour, Hannaker lay there listening. It was essential, Gunn had said, to wait for the hooter that sounded the end of the day's work. In the resultant exodus from the buildings, one extra figure would not be noticed. What he did then and where he hid was up to him, as the American could not help with the layout. But darkness fell quickly, and the whole place should be blanketed out by six. . . .

There was a sudden high whine, like an air-raid siren. And immediately afterwards, sounds of opening doors, pattering feet, voices, laughter, the hiss of car tyres. Laughton's employees might be devoted to him, but they also believed, thank God, in downing tools on time.

He gave them another three minutes to be in full flow. Then he pulled himself from under the tarpaulin and into the driving seat, and looked out.

His first feeling was of surprise. After police and guns and iron gates, it all looked so neat and normal. Green palms and bougainvillea bushes alight with blossoms lined the drive, on either side of which were stuccoed factory buildings. A coolie had been cutting the lawns surrounding them with an old-fashioned hand mower, and was now trundling it back into a shed, leaving behind the sweet smell of new-mown grass. A cluster of young girl secretaries in bright frocks, executives in white suits, several Europeans, women in suits and women in saris, some Mohammedans, even a Sikh or two in carefully plaited turbans, a messenger boy on a wobbling bicycle— all went by unnoticing as Hannaker tucked the gold detector under his coat, opened the door of the van and simply stepped out.

Two Sinhalese approached a car a few feet away from him, got in and drove away. Overalled men began clearing the litter-bins. A Burgher woman came down the steps of the offices over which a blue flag bearing the words *Sinha Radio* in gold fluttered in the evening breeze, fussing with a pair of white gloves. Hannaker put his left hand in his pocket and simply followed her down into the multi-racial multitude that was colourfully flowing towards the main gates.

Hannaker had no idea of what he would do or where he would go. He was acutely aware of the detector bulging out at the left-hand side of his jacket. Close behind the Burgher woman in the red flowered hat, he kept his eyes darting to left and right, looking for likely places.

Ahead now was the main engine house, with the factory chimney towering above it. Next to it a long low building which a guard was locking up. Then Sick Quarters, fully lighted with neons, and through the wide plate window a nurse and doctor could be seen in a chromium antiseptic room. Outside there was a large white ambulance which Hannaker studied carefully. He wasn't near enough to see the tread of the tyres, but they looked ordinary enough heavy-duty to him —the tyres one would expect to see on a vehicle of that size. Hopefully he looked for mud stains, but the whole thing was spotlessly clean and very antiseptic. All matter-of-fact, with nothing to hide and in full view for all to see. As he watched, two white-coated ambulance drivers with red crosses on their sleeves started up the engine and began slowly backing the vehicle into its capacious garage just behind—clearly simply putting it to bed for the night.

Next door there were fuel tanks, sheds, garages and petrol pumps. Then the biggest building of all, still blazing with lights both upstairs and downstairs. If the stuff was anywhere, it would be there, Hannaker thought, and he edged to the left of the crowd, sidestepping three clerks in earnest conversation. But when he looked inside, everything seemed to be like a well-behaved factory back in England, only more so. Caught in these prosaic and pretty surroundings, with the tropical night coming in fast on a sweet-smelling breeze, Hannaker began to feel out of place, the more so because no one was taking the slightest notice of him. He left the main crowd, Sauntering now, he was making his way up a small slope when he heard behind him the sound of tyres on the tarmac, and turning caught a glimpse of Gunn's face through the side window of the van. It was quite impassive, the eyes looking straight ahead. Incuriously the crowd parted to let the van through. This time it was not stopped at the gates. With a sudden pang of loneliness, Hannaker watched it turn left and disappear.

At the top of the slope was a tin-roofed bicycle shed where a plump Sinhalese, wrapping his cloth around him to mount, cheerfully called out a greeting before riding away. Searching round the back, Hannaker found a water tank and beside it a pump in a small wooden housing, with a well to one side where there was just enough room for him.

He took up his position there, hunched up with his head on his knees. There was no one immediately around. Here he could make his plans. In the brief walk towards the gates he had been able to form a rough mental map of the factory. The whole compound was not more than ten acres, surrounded by a high wall on the top of which broken bottles had been cemented in. All the main buildings lay along the drive, with smaller outstations such as this one located at right angles behind.

Above him now a sort of purple, like rising damp, edged up from the black earth to quench the colours of the evening sky. The outlines of the buildings were fading away—just bright squares of lighted windows extinguishing one by one. The flow of people along the drive had dwindled to a dark trickle. Two industrial police flashing torches sauntered by quite close, shouted something across the grass, then went back to the main gates.

The minutes went by. As darkness thickened, all the human noises died away, leaving only the steady croaking of the crickets and the occasional howl of a hyena in the forest beyond. Hunched up in the well, watching the second hand endlessly circle round his watch, Hannaker became stiff and cramped. He had intended to start searching around eleven o'clock when the guards would be sleepy—but driven by discomfort and encouraged by the deserted blackness, he decided to start an hour earlier.

Cautiously he crept out of the pump well, and going outside ran over to the building opposite. The whole northern side was a series of windows, and hopefully he began trying them, looking for a catch that had not been properly fastened. He was beginning to despair of finding one when right at the end he saw one only three-quarters down. Sliding the long blade of his penknife through, slowly he worked the catch up, pulled the window open, hauled himself over the sill and dropped softly on to a vinyl-tiled floor beyond.

He put on his small torch. Long benches, each with its stool and slotted shelves, sprang up out of the darkness. This place was a radio assembly shop—worked on an assembly-line basis. Completed transistor radios about five inches by three inches in brown and black plastic cases were stacked up on a rubber-wheeled trolley for cartage to a packing room beyond.

The place had a metallic antiseptic smell to it, and every-where was as neat as a hospital. Hannaker took out the detector, turned the switch, saw the green light go on, heard the slight hum from the scanner as the isotope sent out its invisible gamma rays. He swung it this way and that, more hopefully than methodically, at the same time keeping a sharp look-out for any sign of wooden packing.

Slowly he traversed the whole block. There was nothing—not the slightest whistle from the detector. In the packing-room a machine automatically covered each radio in heavy cardboard, stacked them up and sealed them in cardboard cases. A door—which was open—led into a covered corridor to the next building which was the main store. If ever there was a place to hide a ton of gold it was here, where cardboard boxes full of radios were stacked in neat trays waiting to be sent away.

He went over the whole place meticulously with the detector —but again there was nothing.

He left the same way he had got in, back through the window on to the grass. Outside darkness and silence greeted him —even the crickets were muffled. One single light at the gatehouse showed up. Nothing moved.

Hannaker ran towards the shrubs lining the drive, and under their cover made his way towards the main office building.

Again the problem was getting in. These windows were high off the ground, and all tight closed. Round the back there was a small wooden door. Hannaker tried it and found it locked and bolted. The place was as secure as a fortress, and through the glass he could see the wiring of a burglar-alarm system. He went round to the front, just on the off-chance the front doors were open. They weren't, but just as he was turning away he saw that on the south side a new main water pipe was being fitted. Screens had been put over the work in progress—but jumping down, he found that the new pipe had not been cemented into the building. By removing it, there was just enough room for him to squeeze through into the basement. There was nothing here, and he went up the stairs to the offices.

This was more like it. This was probably the place. Metal filing cabinets, lockers, cupboards, even safes. He put on the detector, and very carefully and thoroughly went through each room, spending most time in Laughton's office.

But there was still nothing. Not the ghost of a whistle came out of the detector.

He tried accountants' offices, secretaries' rooms, even a conference hall. Graphs and photographs watched him palely from the walls. A map of Ceylon in relief, a small model of the factory, a commemorative silver plaque given to the factory by the government of Ceylon, all stood silent under the torchlight in the small marble-tiled main hall.

Still nothing.

Except for somebody moving outside. Hannaker was just turning away when he saw a bobbing light coming up the drive. Two industrial police going from block to block, trying the doors and sweeping façades with torchlight. He flattened himself against the wall, hearing their footsteps suddenly becoming louder, beams of light coming through the windows and flickering like white bats on the walls.

Had they seen something? Or was it a routine patrol?

They were coming up the steps now. The whole entrance hall was filled with their torchlight. They were trying the windows. Now the door—the handle turned, rattled, the whole door shook. Then silence, and retreating footsteps.

Hannaker breathed again. All the same, he kept where he was for the next half hour. The police were still fussing round the other buildings. It was nearly two-thirty before he felt able to move back out through the work in progress in the basement, and to the big two-storey rectangular block by the gates.

Again he looked for a way of getting in. There was no work in progress here—nothing but high walls and small windows. Then high up under the roof and close to the pipes he saw the fan of the ventilating system. Clearly they had to keep the air temperature inside very cool—this fan was almost as big as the propeller of a ship. With any luck he might just be able to squeeze in between the blades.

The drainpipe was easier to climb than he expected. The main problem was keeping the detector intact and protected. Reaching the eaves, gingerly he transferred himself over, holding now on to the hub of the ventilator fan, dubiously looking at the gap available for his body.

It looked incredibly small—a triangular space, convoluted like a shell. Somewhere he had heard that if you could get your head through a hole, you could get the rest of your body through and now, right up to his neck, he pushed first his arms

196

and then his head, feeling the metal close over him like a tight helmet. There seemed a chance, he thought, so lifting his feet off the ledge, he pushed himself further down, his body adapting to the contours of the propeller, keeping his stomach tucked tight in. At least his arms were inside. His left hand blindly caught hold of the blade of the propeller, and holding the detector in his right he pulled his body painfully through. Then swinging on the inside hub, he jumped and landed easily.

He switched on the detector, and with relief saw the green light come on, heard once more the low hum of the scanner. Then in torchlight he started to make his search.

Somehow he had a hunch it was in here. The white dairy-clean walls, the small barred windows, the antiseptic clean air, gave the impression of a twentieth-century vault. There was an extensive air-conditioning system here—this was obviously where the most delicate work was done in a completely dust-proof clean-air environment.

The whole place was really a radio and television laboratory, where experiments were being carried out. Not particularly advanced experiments, but surprising to find at all in a developing country.

Off the main hall there was a spotlessly clean valve assembly room, and next door to that work was in progress on teleprinters and telephones. Clearly Sinha Radio was in the telecommunications business with a vengeance.

Hannaker moved slowly, the detector like a small animal humming and vibrating in his hands. Inch by inch he covered the first floor.

The time ticked by. He saw it was already half past four. Trying to hurry, he tripped over an electric lead, and cursed softly. Outside the windows, he saw a sliver of intermittent moon between heavy cumulus build-ups, lighting up the slanting lines of heavy monsoon rain. He was just looking away, when he noticed something moving in between the flickering wet pools on the drive.

A dog was trotting slowly up from the gatehouse—an Alsatian with head high and its ears pricked forward.

Hypnotized by its alternating shadow and moonlit fur body,

Hannaker watched its progress, all the time getting nearer. It slackened its pace. It lowered its head.

Suddenly it stopped dead, and started sniffing. Then it held up its head and appeared to be listening. It stayed quite still like that for more than a minute, and then again putting its nose to the ground, slowly and deliberately, sniffing all the time, it began moving towards the two-storey block.

Almost in slow motion, not knowing what to do, feeling trapped and helpless, Hannaker watched the dog come nearer and nearer. It was as though he knew what the animal would do. As though there were some sort of wave, some radio communication about the future, a film of the dog's movements already present in the ether before it made them—so that already in some strange way Hannaker knew that the dog would stop sniffing and look up towards the ventilator. He knew that it would start pawing the ground, that its tongue would come out, and it would pant—and then that suddenly it would throw back its head and send a howl—an eerie, ear-splitting sound—out into the wet darkness.

Then it started to bark, loudly and without interruption—moving to the main door, which it started to scratch at with its claws.

From the gatehouse immediately there were movements. Shouts and calls came reverberating through the rain. The moon had been blotted out, but even so, Hannaker could just see dark figures running up towards the block.

Hannaker was obsessed now with one need—to get out fast. He ran up the stairs. At least, they would be coming in through the front door, he could get back out through the ventilator.

Jumping up on one of the laboratory benches, he got hold of the hub of the ventilator with one hand—and was just hauling himself up, when suddenly the whole place was bathed in neon light. His eyes were blinded in the brightness. Just above him, he heard a high whine, slowly at first and then with an ever-increasing acceleration, as the air-conditioner propeller began to rotate.

He let go, fell on the floor, and picking himself up in the

shadowless light, he made for the basement. Under the stairs he had seen a niche, and instinctively he made for it now— where at least it was dark, and he was out of sight.

He flattened himself against one wall—and listened.

He heard the main doors opening. The dog stopped barking, and there were the sounds of quick padded feet. Sinhalese voices—high and chattering. And now, as well, a slow, measured low-pitched voice, speaking English—Laughton's.

Now they were going upstairs, and Hannaker recognized this as his only chance. He dashed for the hall. In the floodlit brilliance, there was not a sign of anybody—and thankfully he had actually made the open door, when from the landing above him, a voice called down politely in English, 'It's Mr Hannaker, isn't it?'

Hannaker stopped. The dog came for him down the stairs, red tongue hanging. Excited, it bounded up at him, barking and snapping.

'Down! Down, Prince!' Laughton issued the command without raising his voice. The animal left Hannaker alone, stopped barking, and went up to Laughton as he reached the hall, wagging his tail furiously. 'Good dog! Good dog! Don't be frightened of him, Mr Hannaker. He doesn't mean any harm.'

The two industrial police just behind Laughton were unobtrusively putting their revolvers back into their holsters, after he had spoken briefly to them in Sinhalese. All three of them were wearing mackintoshes.

'Glad you managed to take me up on my invitation here.'

Laughton smiled. Hannaker had still not said a word. Dazzled by this curious electric scene that was now being played, Hannaker was seized with the wild idea that perhaps he could match Laughton's insouciance, that he need do no more than go along with the attitude that it was the most normal thing in the world to be found in someone else's factory at five o'clock in the morning.

'I'm sorry about all *this*. . . .' Laughton apologetically indicated the guards now leading the dog away, 'But we're plagued with thieves.'

He led the way to the open door. The rain was still sheeting down, but the whole factory was ablaze with light.

'One can get a pretty good idea of the place from here. But I'm not sure what you've seen already. What about my offices? You've had a look? Well, let's try the medical block, if you don't mind putting your head down and making a dash for it. . . .'

With meticulous thoroughness, just as Gunn had done over his own tiny apartment, Laughton escorted Hannaker over every part of the factory that he had not seen. Finally he asked 'Now is there anywhere else you'd like to go? Anything else you'd like to see?'

Hannaker shook his head.

'I suppose you're going back the same way you came? With Gunn?'

Hannaker kept the surprise at Laughton's omniscience out of his face, and simply nodded.

'That's all right then. We fixed the appointment at nine o'clock. Gives us time to go and have early tea. Oh, and that reminds me, I must show you round the bungalow.'

As with the factory, Laughton insisted on showing him every niche and cranny in the bungalow.

As the ayah, smiling a toothless welcome, came in bearing a tray on which was paw-paw, toast and tea, for the first time Laughton appeared to notice Hannaker's soaking jacket.

'Christ, man . . . you better take that off! Catch your death!' Laughton began pulling the jacket away from Hannaker's shoulders, edging it off his back in spite of his protests. With the other man dragging at his lapels, he could no longer contain the detector crooked below the fabric on his left side, and it fell to the floor between them with a loud clatter.

'You seem to have dropped something.'

Laughton bent down, picked it up and examined it professionally. 'Interesting little job. Only the second one I've seen. Hope it's not broken.' He switched it on, saw the green light, listened to the hum. 'No, it's all right. That's good! Keep it safe!' He handed it back to Hannaker with a broad grin on his face. 'I'm afraid a thing like that's a bit wasted here, Mr

Hannaker. We do give good value in our radios . . . but we don't plate them with gold!'

'What I can't understand,' Laughton said, 'is why *me*? Whatever possessed you to think I could do a thing like that?' He drained the last of the tea, and pushing his breakfast cup away from him, wiped his mouth carefully with a napkin. 'It was Gunn I suppose. He must have put the idea into your head. But I mean . . . you're an intelligent sort of chap. Why ever did you fall for it?'

They were sitting together on the verandah, looking out at the lemon and orange trees in the garden. Laughton was in a high good humour. Far from taking offence at Hannaker's suspicions and trespass, he was sympathetic over his situation, was aware of the mystery and the need for a solution, and was making every effort to help analyse the position.

'Pretty well everybody who was anybody in Ceylon knew about the gold movement. I'm not surprised at the government. Nor shocked. The monetary system of the world is so ludicrous, why shouldn't they buy gold in quantity at the standard rate and then flog it for four times the price on the free market? It's better than relying on foreign aid, with all its donor conditions and fluctuations. Though you can understand why its being kept out of the papers. Embarrassing to explain to the World Bank.' He laughed. 'I can just imagine the politicians' faces. They want to believe the gold is at the bottom of the lake, from where it will be recovered eventually.' Laughton gave Hannaker a long searching look. 'But you say this is impossible?'

'As near as you can say anything is impossible.'

'Then you think somebody's got it?'

'Yes.'

'What about . . .' Laughton paused. 'Gunn? Did you know he'd been in the gold racket?'

Hannaker nodded. 'He told me so himself.'

'Poor old Gunn! Got quite a soft spot for him, you know . . . even though he did diddle me on a radio spares contract.

Typical Yankee beachcomber type. Ruined a couple of good careers through his own fault. And now has a chip on his shoulder a mile high. I try to help him whenever I can . . . for which of course he can never forgive me. That's why I said I'd talk business with him on this load of American cathode-ray tubes he's supposed to have. . . .' He shrugged his shoulders and laughed. 'And all the time it was just to smuggle you into my premises to see if I'd made off with a cool million in gold.' He laughed again. 'As you see, I've got more than enough money now. What could I gain from having more? And I'm not at all sure whether I'm supposed to have been conveniently passing with an empty vehicle——'

'You were in the area.'

'—or whether I'm supposed by some sort of magic to have lured the aircraft to destruction.' He took a small thin cigar from a silver case and lit it thoughtfully. 'I would have thought pilot error was by far the simplest and most logical explanation.'

'It is.'

'But you don't agree with Seneratne?'

'No.'

'And you believe that if you solve the mystery of the missing gold, you'll solve the mystery of the crash?'

'Yes.'

'Any evidence?'

Hannaker shook his head. 'Only a hunch.'

'*Another* one?' Again Laughton laughed. 'I hope you have better luck this time! But seriously . . . let's put our heads together on this one. I mean, I know Ceylon like the back of my hand . . . the people, the customs, the religions, the superstitions. Between the two of us, we should be able to sort it out.'

'I'd be glad of any help.'

'Right then! Let's accept your theory that someone's got the gold. Who could it be?' He began chewing at the end of his cigar. 'The whole area has been guarded by police since the crash. You can take it from me that they're too stupid to know what to do with it, even if they were clever enough to steal it.'

He paused. 'What about the crash crews?'

'They've been investigated and cleared.'

'Seneratne's men?'

'Still a possibility, but I don't think so.'

'Well then . . . *who*?' Laughton leaned back in his chair and stared up at the ceiling. 'Gunn? No . . . no. Reeves? He must have been the only one in Ceylon to know that particular flight was carrying gold.'

'I can't see Reeves——'

'No, no . . . I do so agree with you. But what does this leave us with?' Again Laughton fixed Hannaker with a long penetrating stare. 'Of those who were at the scene of the crash, I mean?'

'Well,' Hannaker said slowly, 'there are the priests from the temple.'

'Of course! Of course! The Brahmin and his brothers! I'd forgotten them.' For several minutes, Laughton kept silent, still staring at the ceiling. Then he said, 'You know, Hannaker . . . you may have got something there. Have you had a word with the Brahmin?'

'Yes.'

'He's supposed to be a very holy man.'

'Yes.'

'Did you know he had resisted the building of Tallaputiya? That he thought it was sacrilege?'

'Yes.'

'And that he prophesied disaster?'

'Yes.'

'But d'you know much about the religions here? About the Sinhalese Buddhists and the Tamil Hindus?'

'Apart from the fact that they've been fighting each other for two thousand years, not much.'

'Then you won't know about the mystic power of Eastern religions? Moving mountains, that sort of thing?'

'I know about the spells, the devil-dancing. . . .'

'That's nothing to the power of a *sanyasi* or a holy man . . . the power of their thought and prayer. To our western mind, such things don't happen. As an accident investigator, you would accept that a plane can be brought down by bullets or a lightning strike but not by the power of thought.'

The words struck chords in Hannaker's mind, memories of the market, of talking to Melanie about just this same thing. He stirred uneasily. 'I wouldn't necessarily dismiss it.'

'As someone who has lived here all his life, I would look at it the other way round. I have *seen* unbelievable things actually done. Now let's consider the priests. They were there on the scene almost straightaway. And in the confusion of taking the bodies to the temple, couldn't they have taken in the gold, too? It's quite possible, isn't it, that *none* of the gold fell out before the crash?'

'It's certainly possible.'

'And the police haven't searched the temple, have they?'

'No.'

'Nor would the Brahmin let them, you can be sure of that.' Laughton stubbed out the end of his cigar. 'In addition of course, Fonseca is a deeply religious Hindu.'

'So you think the gold may still be in the temple?'

'Well, I'd have said it's the most obvious place. After all, the area has been ringed by police ever since.'

'It's not much good to them, stuck in the temple. You think they'll simply wait until the police guard goes?'

For a few moments, Laughton said nothing. Then: 'No . . . I don't. I think they'll try to get it out. And for a very good reason.' He paused. 'You see, I think there'll be another crash. If something lucrative works well, the instinct is . . . wouldn't you say . . . to do it again? Now if only the Tamil Hindus, who have always been poor in comparison to the Sinhalese Buddhists, could amass a treasury of several million pounds, they would at last be able to put forward their position on more equal terms, might even come to dominate the island. And one more gold cargo hidden in the innermost sanctuary where the first is now would suffice.'

Laughton stopped, and then smiled. 'You think I'm carried away with my own imagination? Your mind boggles at the idea of mystical forces, I suppose you might call them, bringing aeroplanes down from the sky? Yet Westerners still believe in ghosts, bad luck, good and evil places. The Easterner is far more pragmatic and realistic about it. His whole life, he knows, is dominated by these good and evil influences. Do you believe that?'

Reluctantly Hannaker said, 'I don't disbelieve it.'

'Well . . . perhaps Ceylon has taught you something then.'

'Ceylon has taught me a lot. But I still don't understand . . . as far as your theory is concerned . . . how the Brahmin would move the gold out of the temple.'

'That's what I was going to explain to you. Hindus have a sacred procession which the Brahmin leads. There's a legend that the local god Skanda . . . to whom the Bharratu shrine is sacred . . . came to Ceylon and had an affair in the jungle with a beautiful Veddah milkmaid called Dahili. And every year . . . it's the day after tomorrow actually . . . a gift is brought him on the back of an elephant from the shrine down the sacred way to a clearing in the forest. And from the middle of the jungle, a smaller elephant representing Dahili is led by mahouts to the same clearing. And there, while thousands watch, the two elephants meet. Kapuralas transfer the gift from under the silk-curtained howdah on the Skanda elephant to the howdah on the back of the Dahili elephant.'

'And what's this gift?'

'Nobody knows. One can guess of course, at its fertility origins, but no one is allowed to see.'

'It's kept hidden?'

Laughton nodded, 'As secret as the gold that's been stored in the temple since the crash. You haven't been allowed to look there, have you?'

Reluctantly Hannaker said, 'Not yet.'

'Well, don't you see? That's how the Brahmin will get it through the police. The Kapuralas will simply move it over to the Dahili elephant. Then back goes the Skanda elephant to the Bharratu shrine—and off goes the Dahili elephant taking the gold into the middle of the jungle. And who could challenge it?'

'You say this procession is the day after tomorrow?'

'That's right . . . the day before new moon.'

For a whole minute, they sat there saying nothing. Then Laughton said, almost as though dismissing the whole thing, 'Well . . . it's an idea, a theory.' He laughed. 'At least it's a little more worked out than pinning the whole thing on me. I still don't quite know how you worked out how I was supposed to have brought the aircraft down . . . or hadn't you got around to that?' He gave Hannaker a slightly mocking sideways look, and then not expecting an answer, looked at his watch and stood up. 'Nine o'clock.' He smiled again. 'I have an appointment with our mutual friend.'

They walked down together through the bungalow gardens, and into the factory. Sauntering up the drive, up the steps, into the office, Laughton took things easily.

But so did Gunn. If he was surprised to see the two of them together, he said nothing. He had brought the first consignment of cathode-ray tubes in the back of the van. Laughton examined a sample, pronounced himself satisfied, and bought the lot. The whole deal was over in minutes, and Gunn and Hannaker were back in the van, being this time smartly saluted by the guards at the gate.

They were half-way to Colombo before Gunn said anything. Then: 'You drew a blank?'

'A blank.'

'Emily work all right?'

'Emily worked fine. A wretched dog discovered me. Then Laughton insisted on escorting me through the factory, go wherever I wanted.'

'So it's not there?'

'That's certain.'

'Well, let's see . . . where the hell else could it be? Seneratne . . . possible. Fonseca . . . possible. Reeves . . . no, not possible. My bet is it's one of the big boys in the Cabinet. Gooneswami, he's a possibility . . . lives in a big house close to the Cinnamon Gardens. I know one of the servants. We could get in there easily enough. What d'you say?'

The van's tyres sizzled on the melting uneven tarmac. The

forest gave way to mud huts thatched with palm leaves. Then Hannaker said, 'I'd like to think about it.'

He thought about it all the way to Colombo. He was still thinking about it when they drove up the small slope to the portico of the Mount Lavinia hotel. And all that time, it was as though he was being pulled this way and that, like a pilot coming down through the overcast to the runway on a dark and stormy night. First the ILS needle pointed this way, then that way—first at Laughton, and now, after his good-humoured attitude, right over the other way, this time towards the Brahmin and the priests.

He wondered if he should tell Gunn of Laughton's idea—and then decided for the time being against it. He was not quite sure now who he could trust and who he couldn't. The horizontals and verticals of his horizon had tilted. He was floating in unreality, in a magic world, unrelated to present existence, in an island full of superstitions, demons, gods. Laughton's theory, full of mystique and mystery, seemed beyond possibility. . . .

And yet, just before the van turned into the hotel entrance, suddenly into his mind came that ancient wisdom, old as man himself—*with gold, all things are possible*.

As the van went slowly up the drive, Gunn glanced across the seat to the west, and remarked conversationally and apparently inconsequentially, pointing out the thin white fiinger-nail low in the sky, 'The ol' moon's surely over the yard-arm.'

'Yes. Not much left.'

'D'you figure,' Gunn changed gear slowly, 'that the moon's got a 'fluence?'

'Tides, that sort of thing? Of course. Well, you know that better than I do.'

'Not jest that. On everything. I reckon that's why they have their moon festivals. The Perahera at the full. The Tallaputiya ceremony the day after tomorrow at the new moon.'

'I suppose it might bring heightened awareness,' Hannaker shrugged. 'Wolves howl at the full of the moon.'

'Weirdies get unglued.'

'And when the tides rise, the dying go out with the ebb tide. Or so,' Hannaker added slightly smiling, affirming his own scepticism, 'people say.'

'Specially in this zoo,' Gunn eased the van over the road to the kerb in front of the hotel. 'Though mebbe they're not the only ones. I guess there *is* somethin' about the moon phases.' He pulled on the hand brake and switched off the engine, and leaned back in his seat. Softly he added, 'Something inevitable.'

'What do you mean by that?' Hannaker paused before slamming the car door behind him.

'Me, mister?' Gunn opened his eyes innocently, 'Hey now, don't flip your raspberry. Jest me fannin' the breeze.'

He pulled the door out of Hannaker's hand, and as he did so, he gave Hannaker a long cool steady stare. Part warning, part assessing. The way Reeves sometimes looked at him, but more than that, Hannaker thought, walking over to the lift.

Back in his room, Hannaker had a wash and shave and a change of clothes. Then he sat on the end of his bed with his notebook on his knee, and made a short report on the night's fiasco. Then he read all his notes, mentally weighing every category of every clue.

The net result was a blank. No, not entirely a blank. A mist. Somewhere behind the mist there was something. But the mist remained thick, and time was not on his side.

Restlessly, he walked over to the window, and stared out at the inky water of the Indian Ocean, flecked with white spume, glittering and gently steaming in the sun.

The sliver of moon was lower in the sky.

Soon it would be the new moon period, Ammawaka. There would be no moon visible for four days. It was the time of darkness when the sky was left to the clouds and the stars. This was the time he had arrived in Ceylon, coming round again— a month since the crash.

Were things ordered by the relation of the heavenly bodies to the earth and each other? Did things happen in the same apparently ordered and mathematical way that governed the universe? Were certain events as inevitable as the coming of the

208

rain and the seasons and the waxing and waning of the moon? Out here it was infinitely more easy to believe that this in fact might be so. Laughton sincerely believed it. Even Gunn gave the idea some credence.

'It'll happen again.'

Did Laughton equally sincerely believe that? And if he was so convinced, why didn't he do everything in his power to stop the use of Tallaputiya as an airfield? Though, Hannaker knew, it would be banging his head against a brick wall. The tide of human stupidity could be stronger than in any ocean, and more inevitable than any pulled by the moon's light.

Hannaker examined the innocent blue texture of the sea and sky, watched the still heads of the palm trees and the curve of the sands. Tomorrow would be the same as today—the same hot sun, probably the same monsoon rainstorm moving in at night. And though the sky was left to cloud and darkness, the unlit moon would still be there.

It was exactly the same with the cause of the Whisky Echo disaster. The reasons must be all there—the factors, the clues, the motives, the interrelation between the crash itself and the missing gold—if only he could *see* them, separate them from the mass of conflicting detail. Momentarily, as he stared at the sunlit ocean, his mind seemed to stretch to almost touch and bring down some illuminating thought. His heartbeat quickened with a sense of impending revelation. But like a name on the tip of his tongue, the thought refused to come to the forefront of his mind. The feeling left him.

Doggedly, he went over the unanswered questions. If the crash was humanly brought about, *how*? And for what motive? Revenge? Power? Robbery? Robbery and power together?

And if it was humanly brought about, how could it be *one man*? One thief could carry only a small amount of gold. And one man disposing of any amount would attract attention to himself. Some gossip would have reached someone's ears. Huge thefts required large organizations with international connections. And these, in Ceylon, were at a premium.

Hannaker returned to his notebook.

The government, though such things had been known to

happen, would hardly in this instance rob itself. And now that Laughton appeared to be in the clear, the Brahmin and his monks moved up into a Class A category. The alternative in fact that Laughton himself had pointed out.

Impatiently Hannaker shut his notebook, and lay back on the bed, his hands folded behind his head. He was reluctant to believe that any human being, let alone a so-called holy man, could cold-bloodedly bring down an aircraft with eighty-one people on board. Yet if he, Hannaker, was right *someone* had done just that. And what was human life perhaps, if it had desecrated a sacred shrine? He had all the time been looking for motive. Was this not it? To purge the blasphemy. To restore the quiet at the temple. To fulfil prophecy. And the gold?

Hannaker sat up suddenly. Of course! An offering to the god in recompense. The gift this year would be infinitely more valuable. Many more prayers could be said. Many more temples set up to assuage an angry god.

And if it was the Brahmin, how had he done it? Was it the power of thought? Had he the ability to beam his thoughts on to those of a tired man at a moment of acute mental strain? Now he came to think of it, had the Brahmin not unconsciously demonstrated that power to Hannaker himself? Had he, Hannaker, not been convinced while he spoke with him, of the High Priest's absolute sanctity?

Hannaker covered his eyes with his hands. He felt suddenly very tired, almost light-headed. He was desperately in need of sleep, and yet he knew if he tried to, his mind would keep him awake. He was aware that he seemed to be going round in circles. Perhaps he was, as Reeves had hinted, teetering on the edge of a breakdown. The horizontals and verticals through which he viewed the world had collapsed, and he was looking at everything through a distorted framework. And now he was doing what he had always believed an investigator should never do—latching on to an explanation because there didn't seem to be any other possible.

Gritting his teeth, he willed himself to try to hold on to some rock of reason, while being swung this way and that by conflicting tides. Whether he succeeded or not he didn't know. All he was certain of was what he must do next.

First, he went downstairs, and to quell this curious light-headed feeling of unreality, ate a small portion of cold lunch. Then he walked along to the taxi office and hired a car to take him to the temple. And as if the meticulous performance of everyday routine tasks would somehow restore to him normality, he queried the price and succeeded in knocking the driver down by thirteen rupees.

But once back at the temple, there were no routine tasks to help him. The afternoon sun was high and unrelenting. Light and heat bounced off the white walls. The temple tree sent out its insidious deathly smell.

There was a devotion going on, the same bowed monk as before told him. Yes, he might wait, but the wait would be very long. There was much—here the ever-fluttering hands flew outwards—preparation for tomorrow's procession. If Mr Hannaker would honour the monastery with a visit in two days' time, then all would be quiet, the Brahmin would have his time less . . . how did you say . . . ?

Hannaker said coldly that he would wait. The little bent monk nodded, but did not invite him inside, not even to the room where the bodies had lain. A few seconds later he reappeared with a small wooden chair, which he set against the wall of the courtyard, in the shade of the tree, and smiling widely, waved to Hannaker to seat himself.

Time drifted by in a perfumed, almost complete silence, underlined by the distant hum of the insects in the clearing below, and occasionally broken by the brief pealing of a bell, the quick scutter of a sandalled foot beyond the open doorway.

Inevitably, Hannaker's mind harked back to the night of the disaster. Inevitably, too, the scented quiet and the hard wooden seat accomplished what the comfortable hotel room could not. The last time Hannaker remembered looking at his watch an hour had gone by. After that he must have dozed off.

He was back in time and yet moving forward. The court-yard was full again of the smell of death. The only sound was the slap of the stretcher-bearers' feet as they brought up the bodies. The lights of the lanterns were flashing in his eyes, flinging the High Priest's shadow on the floor, illuminating briefly a dead unknown face. Yet all the time he knew that either the next, or the next or the next, would be the face he did know. Melanie's. It was coming now. He knew he must stop them bringing her in. But the priests were holding him back. He felt their strong hands on his shoulders. Then, just as the lantern was about to illuminate her face, Hannaker woke.

'My son . . . ?' The Brahmin's hand was on his shoulder. His face, in shadow, bent over Hannaker. The expression was inscrutable but the voice was concerned and kind.

'Are you ill?'

'No.' Hannaker struggled to his feet. The sweat was pouring down his body, his legs felt weak. His mouth was as dry as the courtyard floor. 'I am not ill.'

They were all ganging up on him. Reeves, Laughton, even Gunn and now the High Priest, to dismiss everything as some sickness of his mind.

'Well then, my son?' The holy man walked a few paces away, and stood deliberately, it seemed to Hannaker, at the head of the steps where they had brought the bodies in, and with his back half turned to Hannaker, waited.

Tired, dizzy after his sleep, Hannaker searched for the right words for what seemed now an impossible request.

'I have reason to believe . . . ' he began and then stopped as the holy man slowly turned and regarded him.

Somewhere within the monastery, muted by the walls, a bell tolled softly but rapidly, its urgent rhythm matching the beat of Hannaker's heart.

'You have much reason to believe, my son.' The High Priest tucked his hands in the sleeve of his dhoti, and releasing Hannaker from his solemn stare, gazed down instead at the rough baked floor of the courtyard. A bloodhead darted in and out of the crevices of the wall. The holy man appeared to regard it with benign and, to Hannaker's thinking, exaggerated concentration.

'I didn't mean that sort of belief,' he said sharply.

'That I recognize, my son. You spoke without intention or

212

forethought. From within.' Out of the sleeves came one thin parchment hand and touched the rough stuff of his garment in the region of his heart. Then disappeared again within the sleeve. 'And with truth.'

'What I meant to say was that I have reason to believe that the missing go——'

'Do not say it then, my son.' The High Priest held up his hand imperiously. His voice remained soft but its curious hypnotic quality deepened.

Hannaker clenched his hands. Once again he felt tired and dizzy. Though the temple tree spread its shade over most of the courtyard, the sunlight reflected off the white walls and drew out the sickly sweet scent of its blossoms. Hannaker turned his eyes towards it. Once again the smell carried him back to the night of the disaster. Once again the smell of the flower became the smell of death.

'Life,' the holy man said as if Hannaker had spoken aloud, 'you are looking at the symbol of *life*. The tree. We believe,' he gently shook the branch and a few petals fell, 'that the tree of life has its roots in heaven but its branches on earth. We try, though feebly,' he sighed and dropped his hand, 'to grasp them.'

Beyond the silence, with a weird subliminal insistence, the soft temple bell kept up its tolling. 'It must continue now until the Feast of Skanda,' the Holy Man said, answering Hannaker's unspoken question. 'It is telling the seconds of the appointed time.'

Time. Time passing. Time gone. Out of his depth, bewildered and tired, Hannaker seemed conscious now only of one supreme urgency, that he must do something and he must do it fast. The urgency hammered in his head like the tolling of the bell. And in an unnaturally loud voice he heard himself blurting out, without preamble, 'Father, give me permission to see inside the shrine.'

There was at first no reaction at all from the High Priest. He continued to stare at the blossom-laden branches of the temple tree, his head held slightly on one side as if still listening to the tolling of the inner bell. So quiet did he remain that at first Hannaker wondered if in fact he hadn't spoken at all or that if he had the Priest hadn't heard him.

'No, my son.' The voice sounded gently regretful.

'Why not?' Hannaker said sharply. 'If there is nothing to find . . .'

'There is, my son, everything to find.'

'Except,' Hannaker gave a bitter little laugh, 'what I am looking for?'

The Brahmin inclined his head but said nothing.

'In that case,' Hannaker said, 'why not?'

The Holy Man drew his shoulders high in a long sighing breath, 'Because your suspicions, my son, would . . .' he paused as if searching for the exact word.

'Desecrate.' Hannaker suggested harshly.

'No,' the Holy Man frowned. 'Diminish the holiness of the place.' He pressed his hands together, 'Furthermore, today we have the gift within the shrine. Vigil is being kept. No one else may enter.'

'This gift is what?'

'The gift from one God to another, my son.'

'But what is it? Itself?'

'That, my son, I may not tell you.'

'Do you know what the gift is?'

'Yes, my son.'

'And I suppose,' Hannaker said, angrily feeling his face redden with frustration and exasperation, 'that it's of great value. It would have to be, wouldn't it?'

Perceptibly the High Priest paused before answering. 'Yes, my son.'

He suddenly looked at Hannaker. The dark eyes gleamed with something very like compassion. Hannaker had the sudden certainty that beneath the rigidity of his own religious discipline the old man was actually sorry for him. That in some way he was sorry that he couldn't help him. Sorry—no, perhaps that was the wrong word—for what he had had to do.

'Listen, Father, please,' Hannaker took a step forward. He had a sudden impulse to get hold of the old man and wring the truth out of him. Perhaps he was, as Reeves suggested, already slightly mad. 'Tell me one thing. That gift, is it what I am looking for?'

For about ten tollings of the bell the High Priest said nothing. In that span of time Hannaker knew he had somehow got through to the old man. He bowed his head and when he spoke it was hoarsely and haltingly. 'My son, I should not tell you what the gift is not, any more than I can tell you what the gift *is*.'

Then he looked up and stared at Hannaker's face. Gently he shook his head. 'But you are distressed, so I will answer. No, my son.'

Yet as certain as Hannaker stood there, the very expression on the Holy Man's face told him that the true answer was 'Yes.'

'The first lucky break today.' He had just come back from another fruitless day in Colombo when Melanie appeared round the corner. 'Where've you been?'

She held up her shopping basket. 'I'll give you three guesses.' He took the basket from her hand and smiled for the first time that day with relaxed and uncomplicated pleasure. 'I thought I'd do my shopping and then have a rest.' She preceded him up the front steps. 'Anyway, I looked for you yesterday.'

He frowned. 'I was out.'

'So I gathered.' She smiled tentatively, but didn't actually ask him where.

He held the glass door open for her. 'You're still on that Hong Kong trip tonight then, are you?'

'Yes,' she stepped inside the foyer and stood in front of him, brows raised questioningly, her eyes travelling over his face. 'What's up?'

'I wish to hell I knew.' He put his hand under her elbow, moving her forward. He walked heavily and ponderously, funereally, he suddenly thought to himself. 'I also wish you weren't going off tonight.'

He glanced at her profile. He saw her expression deepen into concern. But somehow the wrong sort of concern. Concern not for herself, but *him*. Melanie too, he thought bitterly, running his hand through his hair.

She forced a small dry laugh. 'Don't you always wish I wasn't going off?'

'Of course.'

'But there's an extra reason tonight?'

'Yes and no.'

'You haven't found out anything?'

'Ditto. Yes and no.' They had reached the lift. He dropped her arm, and pressed the button. Why, he wondered, did he feel that he had done all this before? With only small but devastating alterations. That time was looping back. That disaster was going to happen again, only this time, the loop like a noose would gather in different heads. Knowing that he shouldn't, ashamed of his own question before he uttered it, he asked. 'Can't you get out of going tonight?'

She tilted her face up to him. There was a puzzled, slightly apprehensive expression behind her eyes. But her mouth was smiling and yet determined, 'What do you mean? Swap with one of the other girls?'

'Put like that, no.'

'What then?'

He clenched his fist and brought it down on the open palm of his other hand. 'I wish I knew.' And as the lift came graciously sliding down, 'What time are you off?'

'Six.'

'Let me get a taxi and take you there.'

She nodded and smiled. 'It'll be like old times.' Then immediately knew he wished she hadn't said that.

'See you down here about what time?' He handed her the basket.

'Five thirty. Then you can buy me some tea.'

'Doesn't give you much time to rest.'

'It'll be enough.'

Standing in the lift before the doors shut between them, she said, 'I don't know about me, *you* look awfully tired. You try to get some rest, too.'

'Will do.' He raised his hand as the doors clashed shut. He

heard the wheezing of the cage taking off, but he didn't stop to watch. It was altogether too symbolic. Or he was getting altogether too superstitious. Instead, he walked over to the telephone, got through to the airport and asked for Reeves.

'Mr Reeves is in conference, Mr Hannaker,' the manager's secretary said.

'How long d'you expect him to be?'

'An hour, maybe more.'

'Will he be working late?'

'Oh, very likely, sah. He will want to go over the minutes of the conference.'

'Then tell him I'll look in at his office about seven.'

Though what good that would do Hannaker didn't know. He tried 'phoning Seneratne. It was the afternoon for secretaries. Mr Seneratne, too, was in urgent conference. He tried Fonseca. The Inspector was not in.

'In conference, is he?' Hannaker asked.

'Why, yes sah.'

'At the airport, I presume. The conference on the crash?'

'Yes, sah.' The voice smiled with relief that no explanations needed to be gone into.

Hannaker declined to leave a message and put down the receiver. He thrust his hands in his trouser pockets and walked out on to the balcony, staring at the gently undulating sea. So if it was a conference on Whisky Echo, why hadn't he been invited to sit in on it? As if he didn't know. You were out when we tried to get you, we didn't see fit to leave a message. Poor Hannaker, busy chasing his will-o'-the-wisp nightmares while the real investigations had to be done by them. Reeves would explain about the long-overdue holiday. He hasn't seen fit to take one for donkeys' years. His own worst enemy.

Hannaker felt the invisible web of sympathetic disbelief closing in on him.

And if it was a conference about Whisky Echo, what was going to be written in the minutes? Pilot error and gold in the lake. The official enquiry would be a mere formality. All would be neatly done *now*. No one's fault really. A split second's loss of concentration. Could happen to anyone. And the gold?

Well, when Brahma and Vishnu and Siva willed, the lake would give up its gold. All you needed were patience—and God's good time.

Time.

The word was still hammering in Hannaker's head when Melanie appeared. Her hair was scooped up. She was spruce in her uniform. Different somehow, already a step away from him. Committed to a routine over which he had no control. He found he couldn't say any of the things he wanted to say to her. Nothing in fact except whether she wanted anything to eat with her tea.

'Nothing, thanks.' She sat herself at a table by the balcony rail. 'Did you get some rest? As if I didn't know.'

'Do I look as bad as that?'

'You look,' she smiled at him over the rim of her cup, 'as if you'd been up all night.'

'I was.'

She raised her brows. Before he went on, he remembered wondering, belatedly now it seemed, if after all the factor of jealousy had not been one of the strongest in his suspicions about Laughton.

'Actually I was searching your friend's factory for gold.'

'Roy Laughton's?' There was no mistaking the quick flicker of fear that crossed her face.

'Yes.'

She put down her cup. Her expression was solemn. 'Did you really think he'd stolen it?'

'Then . . . yes.'

'You didn't find any?'

'No.'

She looked at her watch and glancing over to make sure Hannaker had finished his tea, got up. 'I'm glad you didn't.'

'I hadn't realized,' Hannaker said, slightly irritated with her as they crossed the foyer, 'that you'd be so much on his side.'

She then made a remark which he dismissed at the time as no more than feminine perversity. 'It's because I'm on *your* side that I'm glad you didn't.'

218

He settled himself in the taxi beside her, 'Well, it doesn't make sense, but it's nice to know.' He glanced keenly up. Already, early as this, cumulus clouds were curtaining the sky, and a few drops of rain had begun to fall. They made an impatient rattling sound on the roof of the taxi like the drumming of fingers. Though it wasn't yet sheeting down as it had done that first time. Nor were the gutters yet running with ochre-coloured water, and the windscreen wipers could manage to keep the driver's vision clear. The inside of the taxi smelled the same. Mouldy upholstery and mildewed leather, and again, Melanie's perfume, carrying him back as no other perfume could have done.

But even as he thought that, he recognized he was wrong. There was one other perfume more powerful. The scent of the temple tree's blossom.

'Who's the captain?' he asked, to break free from his own melancholy.

'Dewhurst.'

Hannaker took some comfort in that. 'Good pilot, I imagine.'

'Very.' She seemed distant again, absorbed in her own thoughts.

Hannaker watched the driver switch on his headlights, the cones picking out the glistening pencils of the rain. The drumming on the roof intensified. On their right the white lead-in lights came up, and the blazing artificial suns of Tallaputiya airport.

A rising breeze was tautening the spotlighted flags on either side of the gates. As they turned in, Melanie said, her eyes on the stylized yellow lion on the maroon ground of the Ceylon national flag, 'He has an obsession about the Lion Race, you know.'

'Who has? Dewhurst?'

'No. Laughton. I think he believes . . .' then she smiled suddenly and shrugged. 'Oh, it's too long to tell you now.' She was already putting her hair straight in the mirror made by the driver's back. Though her eyes remained gentle her smile was one of professional brightness. She hitched her bag on to her shoulder as the taxi stopped outside the terminal block.

'Take care of yourself,' he held on to her hand.

'You take care of *your*self.' Her eyes darkened. Again she hesitated. From behind, the official crew car honked its horn. Melanie was galvanized into immediate action.

'Well,' she smiled, and planted a perfunctory kiss on his cheek. 'This is where I leave you.'

He sat for a moment before going off to find Reeves. He would just then have given everything he had for her not to have said just that.

Reeves's office smelled of black cheroot smoke and only faintly of peppermint. The conference, then, had gone extremely well.

'Come in, come in, Hannaker! Just the man I want to see.' Reeves's wary eyes belied the hearty welcome, and his hand stretched out for the Rennies box. 'I've got some good news for you. Sit down.'

'I 'phoned up earlier.'

'Yes, yes. I got the message. If I hadn't, as a matter of fact, I'd have 'phoned you. Do sit down, Hannaker. You look tired, old chap.'

Reluctantly Hannaker sat himself in the VIP chair. He pushed away the ash tray full of the butt ends of cheroots.

'Excuse the fug in here. Kishti and his cigars.' Reeves adjusted the air-freshener. He popped a Rennie self-righteously into his mouth, and sat back in his chair as if he was really going to enjoy this, which Hannaker knew and Reeves knew he wasn't.

'Now, let me tell you why I wanted to see you.'

'No.' Hannaker interrupted sharply, 'I'll tell you why I wanted to see you.' And holding up his hand against Reeves's pink-faced protest, and borrowing Gunn's phrase, 'It's my nickel. I want you to suspend flights till the investigation's over.'

For what seemed like minutes Reeves said nothing. Outside

in the corridor a group of passengers were being herded along towards Customs. Hannaker could hear the sound of their feet, the excited chatter of their voices. Perhaps the load for Hong Kong. Beyond the window a van accelerated, an aircraft's engines started up to a steady high whine.

Then suddenly Reeves smiled, he put his fingertips together. 'I think we can meet you on that, Hannaker.' His smile broadened, 'To all intents and purposes the investigation is over.'

'That,' Hannaker said slowly waving his hand as if to dispel the cigar smoke, 'was what was going on this afternoon?'

'In a manner of speaking. We were breaking the ground.'

'For the Inquiry verdict?'

'Not exactly.'

'But near enough? What is it? Pilot error?'

'What else? Nothing else that it could be. It's all over, bar the official findings.'

'Bar the shouting, you mean.'

'If you wish.'

Hannaker stood up. 'And I shall do the shouting.'

'Oh, I wouldn't do that if I were you,' Reeves said mildly. 'Otherwise you really will offend people just when they're being especially friendly to you.'

Ignoring his remark, Hannaker said, 'And it still doesn't explain the gold.'

'That's not our province. I keep telling you that, Hannaker. If the Ceylonese authorities are satisfied, why would we see fit to question?'

'In the lake, that's the satisfactory theory is it?'

'Of course.'

'And if I happen to know that it isn't?'

'Then you'd be a good deal wiser than everybody else on the island.'

'That wouldn't be difficult,' Hannaker said and wished he hadn't. It sounded, even in his own ears, a megalomaniac utterance. 'I have reason to believe,' Hannaker said slowly, 'that the monks may have got it.'

Reeves's little eyes blinked disbelievingly for a few seconds.

But when he spoke his voice was mild, friendly, soothing, 'Well, of course one never knows with these chaps. I can't say I really trust 'em. Maybe if they found the odd bar they might keep it. A gift from Allah, eh? Manna from heaven?' He laughed boisterously, his pink cheeks blowing themselves out like tiny balloons. 'Seriously though . . .'

'I'm deadly serious.'

'That's Fonseca's baby. In more ways than one. And he is satisfied it's in the lake.'

'He's also a Hindu.'

'Is he really? I didn't know he was religious. Now where were we . . .'

'I was asking you to suspend flights till the *proper* cause of the crash is found. In particular, the gold flights.'

'But there's only one more, Hannaker. Which brings me to what I wanted to tell you. No, allow *me*. You've had your crack of the whip. Seneratne. George. He's been very friendly about you. The Ministry here has sent a very kind letter to your Masters in London. So has the High Commissioner. Sir Arthur Atcherley has been particularly gracious . . . thanking them for the loan of you. Saying what a help you've been. And,' Reeves popped the peppermint into his mouth and crunched rapidly, 'reminding them about your overdue leave.' He swallowed and smiled warmly. 'They couldn't do better than that, could they?'

'Not if they'd tried.'

'And I have done my little bit, too!'

'Very kind of you.'

'I've got you a seat home. On Wednesday. First class, I may say. Compliments of Oriental Airways.' He laughed coyly. 'Though I shan't tell you who the stewardess is.'

'I haven't had my recall.'

'Oh, but I understand it's in.' Reeves was innocently blinking, but sweating like a pig. He really does think I'm round the bend, Hannaker thought, and I'm not making it any easier for him. 'The High Commissioner said so.'

'At least,' Hannaker said, 'I want to stay till the last gold flight is in.'

'Well'—with huge relief—'that you shall! I'll let you into a secret. As I told you, we leave it as late as we can to make it firm. It's the day after tomorrow. The return of the Hong Kong flight that's going out now. Dewhurst himself is bringing the last lot in.'

NEW MOON

Ammawaka

'HARO HARA! Haro Hara!'

The sun poured down the jungle track like white-hot lava. On either side the leaves of the forest trees hung limp. Hannaker didn't need the spikes through the cheeks of the matting robes that some of the pilgrims wore. The heat, the rough rutted uphill track, the choking billowing dust kicked up by thousands of feet were enough. Jostled on either side by worshippers and penitents, Hannaker wondered for the hundredth time why the hell he had come.

Why in fact had he?

Because of Laughton's tip-off? For that was what it amounted to. Partly that. But Laughton's tip-off wasn't all. Because time was running short, or Hannaker believed time to be running short? That again was part of the reason.

But there was something more. Something that had convinced him he would find what he sought here. Something in the interview with the Brahmin. Briefly and yet certainly Hannaker felt he had read the mind of the so-called holy man. For all the old man's denial, what he, Hannaker, sought would be in the gift, to be brought out of its temple hiding place, protected by sacred customs from prying eyes. Past the police cordon and transferred from the elephant of the god Skanda most lovingly to that of his milkmaid mistress. Then through the jungle, up-country and over the narrow straits to the markets of India. Leaving the temple cache empty and ready to accept the new and last cargo of gold.

'Haro Hara!'

The deep-throated cries of the crowd increased as the path steepened. One of the laces of Hannaker's sand shoes had come loose and he wanted to bend down to tie it up. But the crowd pressed him forward. His shoulders touched those of a young man robed in white on one side, a woman who looked, God forbid, as if she might be heavily pregnant on the other. At every step the young man in white threw back his head and shouted, 'Skanda,' and beat his chest, and gabbled some sort of prayer.

Skanda was the local god whose procession it was. That much Hannaker knew from Laughton. Skanda was number one suspect, Hannaker thought, pounding forward grimly, his chin almost touching the sweaty blood-stained skin of a man wearing steel shackles.

'Skanda! Skanda! Haro Hara!'

Like a river flowing uphill instead of down, coloured the brown of skin and the white of penitential robes, the saffron of holy orders, the red of blood and betel juice, up they climbed, their feet scuffing and slip-slopping. Sometimes the low deep-throated murmur was broken by higher screams—monkeys and parakeets from the jungle, the human cries not of pain but of penitence.

Hannaker tripped over the root of a mahogany tree, swallowed a mouthful of dust, and swore under his breath. But no one seemed to notice him, nor did his dress appear to make him conspicuous. Some of the younger men wore trousers and shirts. An old woman with her face half covered, the red circle of high caste on her forehead, carried a plastic cape in case the rains came again tonight.

About a quarter of a mile ahead some children began singing. The clearing was in sight. Hannaker struggled a hand free, dragged out his handkerchief and mopped his brows.

'Skanda! Dahili!'

Jumping up on his toes, Hannaker could glimpse the enormous clearing where the traditional meeting between the elephant of Skanda and that of Dahili his mistress was to take place. Already the huge area was thronged with people. The procession ahead of him had broken into a smart trot, eager to get places as near as possible to the front. Hannaker had every intention of doing the same thing when the time came. But in the meantime he wanted to get away from the press of all these people, and think.

Threading his way in and out of the crowds, past palm-covered boutiques, lit even in this heat by paraffin flares, filled with mangoes, plantains and green oranges. Past a dormitory for overnight pilgrims in which a hundred or so bodies lay unmoving, Hannaker found a small corner at the edge of the clearing where the forest began. A hundred yards away there was a boutique selling palm mats. He walked over, bought a couple for ten rupees, walked back to the place, spread the mats and sat down.

As he waited, the tide continued undiminished up the pilgrims' way. The clearing filled, vibrated with noise and heat and smells. The smell of the jungle, of vegetation crushed underfoot, the smell of sweat and oil and hot fat cooking and spices. Some of the pilgrims had lit charcoal fires, and were cooking rice flour pancakes. All around the flies and insects hummed. The whole area sent up shimmers of heat so that the scene blurred as if Hannaker's eyes had got out of focus.

'Haro Hara! Haro Hara!'

No one seemed to know when the great moment would arrive. Rumour, unintelligible to Hannaker's ears, fluttered through the forest. People craned their necks, pointed, jumped up and down. Then the excitement subsided till the next rumours came along. Now and again a group would break into a Tamil chorus. A coconut would be smashed on a rough stone altar, and as its milk soaked into the ground the crowd would shout 'Haro Hara!'

But the sun had shifted. The shade of the tree under which Hannaker sat was lengthening. Over on the other side of the way men were burning cow dung, rubbing their feet in the ashes and then walking over red-hot embers.

The power of thought, Hannaker watched them wryly. Or was it the undiscovered protective power of burned cow dung? But it was in the power of thought he was slowly beginning to believe now, wasn't it? Why else was he here? If the Brahmin had the gold, it was not by coincidence that Whisky Echo had crashed. And how else had the aircraft been brought down but by the power of thought on the pilot. Or, as Hannaker preferred to call it, auto-suggestion. And if he was right, and

226

Laughton was right, what could Hannaker do about it? On his own, nothing. Unless he could produce tangible evidence.

Hannaker stood up. Cumulo-nimbus clouds were beginning to eat up the golds and greens and crimsons of the setting sun. And with the light went sound too. The crowd had become quiet. Even the children had stopped shouting and laughing. They seemed in unison to hold their breath. Perhaps that first touch of darkness was the signal, perhaps some of them caught from far away the distant beat of the procession's feet. Whatever it was, the crowd knew.

Very quietly everyone began to sway, first this way and then that, all in perfect rhythm, increasing speed, diminishing it again as if under the baton of an invisible conductor. Softly at first, then louder, pipes sounded, now flutes, now deep bass drums. As the last daylight faded the night was lit with the spurts of kerosene fires.

'Dahili!'

Now the beat was not drums, but bare feet on baked earth. Out of the darkness heralded by dancing pompons of frizzy golden light came the devil-dancers of the milkmaid's procession. Hannaker left his place at the edge of the clearing and came forward, thrusting and shoving till he was at the forefront of the crowd. Waving flares illuminated giant coloured masks with popping eyes, flickered on the sweating bodies that bore them, legs bent, feet splayed, convulsively hopping forward, frantically beating the leather drums. A primitive apprehension chilled Hannaker's spine. His heartbeat quickened.

Now the smoking torches lit the penitents who followed the devil-dancers. Hundreds of them, men and women, bodies mutilated with silver skewers, daggers in their cheeks. One who danced in an ecstasy that resembled joy had a knife blade through his tongue.

I am convinced, Hannaker thought, turning away in revulsion, if they could do this, they could also *finally* mutilate *other* bodies. Prostrate men pulled their bleeding bodies forward over the rough sharp stones as they had done for miles, chanting again, 'Haro Hara! Haro Hara!'

Great wens of flesh were pulled taut by chains and ropes

attached to hooks all over hundreds of arms and legs and necks and cheeks.

Hannaker clenched his fists. They were not so different from those other bodies lit by the light of a single paraffin flare. He wanted to rush forward and drag them up. When he saw people detach themselves from the crowd that watched and rush forward, he thought this was what they were going to do. But no. They tore off their own garments, and down they went, over the sharp stones, flat on their bellies, shouting as the blood trickled out of their cuts, 'Haro Hara! Haro Hara!'

While to the beat of the drums and the whistle of the flute, exactly in unison, the crowd cried, 'Dahili!'

'The power of thought,' Hannaker said aloud, but no one heard.

For now symbolically the milkmaid herself was here. Very slowly, so decked and caparisoned in crimson and yellow-embroidered cloths with a shiny jewelled howdah on top that it looked like a giant tortoise, came the elephant that symbolized the god's mistress. She was escorted by men in tricorn hats and silk tunics. There were two more sitting on her back under the howdah canopy. Already Hannaker had begun to count.

Now the frenzy of the crowd intensified. The ground itself shook under the stamping feet. Earthenware pots filled with camphor were being lit, and placed on thousands of heads. Crimson lights danced, flames flickered over sweating transfigured faces. The fumes of camphor and incense and sweat and cow dung made Hannaker's head reel.

Then sharp and sweet, cutting through the noise and frenzy like a scalpel, came the sound of a single silver trumpet.

The crowd breathed, 'Skanda.'

Another peal on the silvery trumpet. Then bells rang. The single trumpet was joined by a hundred others. Drums beat softly.

From the opposite direction, his face lit cruelly by the flickering flares, pointed and peaked the way Hannaker had first seen it the night of the crash, came the Brahmin. He walked alone, well ahead of his monks, and barefoot, his hands pressed

228

together. As he emerged from the forest, the flares illuminated in poison green the foliage on either side of him, sending over his face ghostly muffled incandescence. Everyone was so quiet now that Hannaker could even hear the slow scuffing sound of the High Priest's bare feet.

From the crowd, hands stretched forward to try to touch his holy garment, the moving camphor flares on hundreds of heads cast over his face a stain of crimson. Yet through it all, he walked, eyes down, unmoved, undeviating.

Hannaker, alone of the front rank of the crowd, did not stretch out his hand. Yet suddenly as he drew almost level with him, the Brahmin raised his eyes. For a moment the high priest's glance didn't seem to focus properly. Then, like two men emerging slowly from their separate dreams, their eyes met. Momentarily an awesome, forbidding expression came into the High Priest's face, as if he had divined Hannaker's as yet only half-formed purpose. Then the woman next to Hannaker thrust one arm forward to touch the priest, waved with her other a white coconut oil flare. When Hannaker could see again, the face was glowing in the white light like that of a plaster saint with a neon halo. The eyes were lowered, the mouth calm. Now he was in profile, now he had moved forward and was gone.

The procession of the monks was drawing level with Hannaker. The quiet for the Brahmin had given way to the screams and shouts as Skanda's devil-dancers appeared out of the forest. This is how they do it, Hannaker thought, feeling despite himself the rhythm and excitement tingling the nerves of his own body. They play upon people's emotions like a tune. Now soft and muted and pseudo-holy. Now swelling, thrilling, proud.

Now he knew without looking that the climax was coming. He didn't need the thunderous yells.

'Skanda! Skanda!'

Hannaker could feel the rhythm of the devil-dancers shaking the ground through the soles of his sand-shoes. Ugly masks, splayed feet, beating tom-toms, passed under his eyes in a blurred ribbon of light and sound. And now in the background, all the time, getting louder, came the heavier ponderous sound of an elephant's feet.

Then, tossing its trunk from side to side, materializing like some huge lump of the darkness behind, came the bull elephant. Someone behind touched his shoulder with a dancing torch. People elbowed and jostled and danced. Faces were thrown in the spotlight of camphor flares, eyes rolling, mouths distorted with frenzy.

'Skanda! Skanda!'

As the elephant drew nearer the flares lit up the gold-tasselled howdah it carried, the embroidered hats and garments of the officials, the jewelled caparison that covered the monstrous animal to half way down its legs. Behind the black and gilt mask the tiny elephant eyes gleamed red in the camphor flares. Its trunk swished idly from side to side. Hideous and menacing as it was, the crowd as it passed, fell to their knees as if cut down.

But Hannaker remained upright and alert. Behind the gold-tasselled curtains of the howdah he could just glimpse the *karanduwa* that contained the gift. There were two mahouts on the elephant itself. Four guards were walking along beside the animal's legs.

Now right in front of him Skanda's elephant had passed, reached the smaller one in the clearing. At first they eyed each other with indifference. The devil-dancers of the two processions met, mingled, danced briskly and melted into the crowd. Only the Brahmin, and at a little distance the priests, stood in front of the two elephants. One of the priests handed the Brahmin a silver bowl. Unhurriedly he sprinkled rosewater on each of the elephants. Slowly, with ponderous dignity, the two elephants moved closer to one another. Skanda's elephant raised its trunk, and shattered all the man-made sounds with a tremendous trumpeting. Immediately the smaller elephant answered. The crowd went mad. The omen was good. Even Hannaker felt the hairs on the back of his neck prickle. Clarinets and flutes shrilled, drums beat, bells rang. People joined hands to dance. They were like the religious fanatics of the Middle Ages, caught in an unbreakable galvanic movement. They looked as if, like them, they would dance till they died.

Some of the frenzy was running through Hannaker's nerves. He watched, above the tall screen, the heads of the guards as they struggled to lower the first enormous chest. He saw the black rectangle come from under the howdah and slide slowly down behind the silk screen. Repelled by this tide of cruelty and superstition, yet catching its potent madness, Hannaker was fascinated by the small distance that separated him from the gift. Those thirty yards of hard baked earth lit by the flickering light of the flares drew him. He couldn't afterwards consciously remember deciding to make a rush for it.

All he could remember was suddenly running forward over the ground towards the elephants. He could remember the rough stony feel of the ground under his sand-shoes. He could remember screwing up his eyes against the bright pulsing light. He was caught up in a feeling of total unreality as if in a dream. If he were awake someone ought to be stopping him. But, taking him for an over-zealous devotee, no one laid a finger on him.

He had reached the silk screens, and thrust behind them before anyone seemed to notice. In the front ranks of the crowd someone had begun yelling. An official turned his head. It was a face Hannaker would always remember, its rolling eyes and terrified expression spotlighted in a yellowish white flare.

A hand was on his shoulder but he tossed it aside. He had reached the chest. He could hear his own breath panting. Someone had caught hold of his shirt. He wrenched himself away. He heard the sound of the cotton tearing. He remembered snatching a flare out of someone's hand, holding it high, half as a weapon, half to see inside the chest. With his free hand he thrust back the lid. It fell back with a jarring sound. A collective moan went up from the officials around. For a moment they seemed paralysed. Then rough hands were on his shoulders. He leaned forward. The dream deepened. The chest was empty. No, not quite empty. In the light of the flare there was no gold inside the chest. No jewels or treasure of any kind.

The chest contained a single chaplet woven of temple flowers. Of the kind a Hindu bridegroom gives to his bride. A token of love.

Hannaker could have wept. Then sheer physical pain jerked him into reality. Someone was twisting his arms behind his back.

He became aware that the wrath of a thousand people was directed towards him. The frenzy, the ecstasy had turned into hate, rage. He vaguely remembered the hands of the High Priest held up, painted wax-white, the thin face looming in front of him, the eyes black as coals, the mouth opening to say the one word, 'Go.'

Hands bundled him under the belly of the great elephant between the writhing bodies of the devil-dancers. He grasped a penitent's blood-stained arm, as he was pressed out and out beyond the illumination of the flares. Then he was on the outer edges of the crowd. They were looking past him, pressing forward to see what the spectacle had been they had missed.

The shoving hands had gone. He was alone.

Moving carefully, he edged his way in and out of the crowd, anonymous now. Then he began running, stumbling over the roots, his face lashed by overhanging branches.

Behind him he could see the dancing flares, heard the angry shouts of the crowd. He glanced behind him. The forest was alight with flares and torches. Voices shouted and screamed. They were following him, but most of them didn't know who they were looking for. There appeared to be general confusion. Then someone must have heard the sound of him running. There was a cry taken up all along the edge of the forest behind. Lights danced closer together, clustered round the top of the pilgrims' way. In the concentrated light figures jumped about, arms pointed, shadows were flung. There was much noise. But no one pursued. It dawned on Hannaker that none of the devotees would retrace their steps down the pilgrim's way after him for fear of undoing the pilgrimage.

Hannaker ran on, ducking under trees, twisting further and further away from the camphor-lit darkness. Down below now he could see more lights, bobbing up and down round the village. He could hear voices, and distantly, he thought he heard the howl of a police klaxon. He stopped for a moment to catch his breath. No one came up the track from below. Maybe they feared he was a devil. Grasping hold of the branch of a tree, he rested his weight. A few drops of rain were falling on the thick green tongues of the leaves.

When he was caught Hannaker knew he would be hounded off the island. While he thought out his escape, he was for the moment safe here. Between the uproar on either side it was like the safe silence when a pilot hit the ILS beam.

Abruptly a terrifying enlightenment dawned. It was Laughton who had led Hannaker on to do this as surely he had led Coates on to crash Whisky Echo. He wanted Hannaker off the island. Hannaker was too near the truth. Hannaker had to be *deflected*. Up in the clearing, down in the village, the crowd yelled for his blood but just for a moment Hannaker stood with his eyes closed.

Deflected. That was it! Somehow or other Laughton had managed to bend the ILS beam.

Drawing a deep breath, Hannaker began running at an angle, nearly fell in thick undergrowth, raced onwards. People were following him. Behind him in the forest he heard sounds of cracking twigs, shouts in Sinhalese, the roar of engines. Police cars were after him, Land Rovers were actually coming into the forest.

He knew he would have to go to ground, that in this island there was one place only where he could find refuge. Gunn . . . he had to get to Gunn. As he raced out through the forest, that now was in the forefront of his mind.

It had begun to rain. The heavy clouds were now bursting in the skies above him. The monsoon came pelting down, soaking him to the skin. It was coming down so hard, he could hardly see.

And to make matters worse, the police Land Rovers were using searchlights. They were sweeping through the water-filled air, flickering over the trunks of trees. He had to fling himself down on to the ground hard to avoid being seen as one of the beams came swishing over him.

Lying on the soaking earth, he followed with his eyes the long track of light. And then, as he watched its white length penetrating the wet darkness, like a soundless landslide in his mind, all the happenings and events since the crash shivered, re-focused, and suddenly subsided into place.

The searchlight was mounted on the top of the Land Rover, a mile away down at the far end of the clearing where the rain from the cloud-burst was not falling. The thick bright beam penetrated three hundred yards of dry air—then hit what now amounted almost to solid water. As he watched the effect, school physics demonstrations came vividly to his memory.

The passage of light from one medium to another, reflection and refraction, a ray of light striking a glass prism. . . .

And bending.

For the beam from the Land Rover did just that. Coming out of the dry air, when it hit the wall of water, the beam was bent *downwards*.

Light wave, thought wave, *radio wave* . . .

That was how Laughton had interfered with the radio wave. He had bent the beam, interrupting the ILS glide path signal. Expert in radio, Laughton had known how to do it. With an oscillator in the ambulance—the one vehicle which had a supreme right to be in at the scene of an aircraft crash—he had waited until Captain Coates reported on the glide path over the beacon, and then he had distorted the beam—after monitoring experiments, had bent it the required degree earthwards, beckoning the pilot to destruction. And the ILS instrument read correctly in the crashed 707 because the oscillator had been switched off just before impact.

As he ran through the drenching rain, Hannaker felt the sudden exhilaration of discovery. And then just as suddenly there came into his mind Double Echo that in a few hours time would be setting off unsuspecting from Hong Kong, this time with Melanie on board. Biting his lip, frenziedly he began to run from the searchlights and the Land Rovers, dodging away from his pursuers into the rain-filled darkness and the cover of the trees. . . .

*   *   *

'I should have worked it out before,' Hannaker exclaimed to Gunn an hour and a half later.

He had managed to circumnavigate the village, steering a rough course along the forest paths to the south of the bobbing flares and the searchlights. Luck and his own sense of direction had been with him. Skanda had not been offended enough to have him caught. Yet.

Once on the road, Hannaker had to take the risk of thumbing a lift. He listened in the wet and wind for the sound of a lorry. Luck had remained with him. The first ancient Ford carrying a load of red rock, drew up. The driver was a Moor. A Mohammedan. He seemed glad of company. He spent the bumpy journey cursing the monsoon and the Hindu festival that had already made him late for his ship.

'Salaam Dorai!' He had dropped Hannaker at the corner of the dock road just a few yards from Gunn's apartment.

Gunn was in. Hannaker could see the light and hear the radio from the living-room window. There, he told his story. Gunn had listened unmoved, then given his plain unexpurgated views on Hannaker's interference with the procession.

Hannaker had accepted them without comment.

'But you didn't seem surprised?'

'Me, mister? Nothing can surprise me. 'Sides,' he indicated the now more muted transistor set—one made by Laughton's Sinha Radio—on the table in front of him. 'There was a news flash.'

'When?'

'Coupla minutes before you turned up.'

'Did they say it was me?'

Gunn shook his head. 'But it figured.'

Hannaker nodded. 'Once they do, that's it.'

Gunn said nothing. He walked over to the cupboard, took out a can of beer, opened it, and put it in front of Hannaker. And as Hannaker waved it away impatiently, 'Knock it back, mister. Do you good. Helps you think.'

'God! I need to.'

'Sure.' He scratched his chin thoughtfully, 'Anyone see you come in here?'

'No.'

'When they find you, they'll run you out. By the first tub that floats or flies.'

Hannaker nodded. 'Which is what Laughton wanted.'

'Sure. He snowed you all right, mister. Made you figure I was the villain.'

'Well,' Hannaker smiled faintly, relaxing a little, 'the casting would have looked reasonable.'

'How d'you mean?'

Hannaker pointed to the shoes under the chaise-longue, still caked with the same grey-green mud. 'Those shoes.'

'Oh, *them*!'

'That mud's from the lake.'

'Sure. Went to have a look after I'd taken the photos. Get a closer look-see.' Gunn shrugged. 'With all those police around, jus' got myself bogged.' And then: 'Have you figured how Laughton did it, mister?'

'He picked up the Hong Kong aircraft departure signals and broke the gold code. Then he fitted an oscillator in his ambulance powerful enough to interfere with the Tallaputiya Instrument Landing System and distort the beam downwards.'

'And smack the pilot comes into the hill by the temple, eh?'

'Then the ambulance rushes to the scene and collects the gold from the wreckage.'

'The vehicle everyone would reckon to see there.'

'Of course they would need monsoon weather.'

'Sure. An' what's more, mister, they get it. If the cloud's not on the deck, they bide their time. They got six throws of the dice, remember.'

Hannaker thrust out his lower lip thoughtfully, going over in his mind all possible flaws in Laughton's plan. 'What if the pilot by any chance survived?'

'Who'd believe him? He might not even believe himself. They'd test the beam same as we did. They'd get the black box. Open an' shut case. Pilot error. Besides, it's a chance in a million.'

Gunn had spoken with such suppressed bitterness that

236

Hannaker stared at him for several seconds. Then he said gently, 'But you survived a crash?'

Gunn glanced at him sharply, then slowly nodded several times, spread his hands but said nothing. With an impatient jerk of his head, he signalled Hannaker to go on.

'Then the lake is the perfect alibi. And if anyone asks too many questions, there's the temple. Never trust the Hindus, that sort of thing.'

'Don't forget the general finger-trouble round here, mister. Best alibi of the lot. Mind, I can name you crashes in this day and age. And in the West, mister. Inquiry's brought it in as an Act of God. How scientific is that? Not any different from Vishnu or Skanda or Siva flipping their lids. God, Vishnu, Skanda, take your pick.'

The radio on the table suddenly stopped transmitting music. An excited voice announced something rapidly in Sinhalese, and then in sing-song English.

'This is Radio Colombo coming to you with a news item. Colombo Police are anxious to interview an Englishman, James Hannaker, in connection with the crime committed a few hours ago against the Tallaputiya Festival. Anyone who has information as to this man's whereabouts must communicate immediately with the nearest Police Station.'

'Laughton might guess.'

'He won't give you another thought. You're taken care of.'

'So far everything's gone his way, hasn't it?'

'Not quite, mister. He'd've expected you to get clobbered the second you laid your fingers on the chest. Can't figure out why you weren't. So you'd be shipped off shouting about the monks and the gold. And they'd all know you'd come unglued.'

'But how does he get rid of the gold? It wasn't in the factory. That I'll swear.'

Gunn smiled grimly. Reaching forward, he picked up the transistor radio as if he were going to switch it off. Instead, he tipped it neatly into the empty cigarette box—the one that had once held the gold delivery bar. 'Always said that set reminded me of something real nice. Mebbe that's why I bought it. See. Fits like a glove.'

'But Laughton took me right through the store.'

'You were too late. The stuff had been distributed via all his dealers. They received their quota of radios. But this month, inside the boxes were gold bars.'

Gunn held the receiver out on the flat of his hand. Before he set it back on the table the music broke off abruptly again. They both waited in silence till the voice came on with the English translation. The news flash was brief. The British High Commissioner had, at this late hour, called upon the Prime Minister. It was not known what their conversation had been about.

Gunn switched off the radio. 'I'll give you three guesses.' He scratched his head thoughtfully. 'I reckon, though, mister, you're safe here for a while.' He sighed. 'Least till we get it sorted out. Have you figured out why Laughton's doing it?'

Hannaker didn't like Gunn's use of the present tense. 'As far as I can.' He made a helpless gesture with his hands. 'It's a bit outside my reckoning. I think he sees this as his destiny. Delusions of grandeur. Reincarnation. The new Lion King of Ceylon. He had this obsession, Melanie said. . . .'

Hannaker stopped talking. The minutes were ticking away while Gunn and he were sitting here. Schedules were being kept. Aircraft were being loaded up.

'An' he won't be satisfied with one million if he can lay his mitts on two, will he, mister? These nuts never are.'

'But would he get away with it again?'

'Here? With that amount of cough syrup to hand out? Sure! More important, does he figure he can? Affirmative again. You bet he does!'

Hannaker closed his eyes. Wild impractical schemes flashed through his mind. But all schemes needed help. And how was he, virtually a prisoner here, to summon it?

'When's the next gold flight, mister?'

'Arriving Tallaputiya tomorrow night.'

Gunn whistled.

Hannaker turned round his wrist and looked at his watch.

Never had he felt so conscious of the enmity of time.

'Exactly how long've we got then, mister?'

'What for?'

With a gesture of great force and finality, Gunn swept the perennial clutter off the table. 'For you and me, mister, to figure out a plan.'

'Ocean Control from Double Echo . . . 96 East at 13.15 . . . cruising in the clear at Flight Level 320. Estimating Tallaputiya at 15.10. . . .'

Dewhurst's clipped voice coming out of the transistor balanced above the dashboard sounded so English and alien, Hannaker thought, against the background of humid darkness and tropical forest. Gunn had backed the van into the cover of rhododendrons and banyan trees, a couple of hundred yards from the Colombo side of the road, where they could still see quite clearly the closed entrance to the factory illuminated by a single light from the gatehouse.

'And if he doesn't come out?' Gunn asked softly.

'Either he's been scared off.'

'Laughton doesn't scare.'

'Or he's satisfied with the gold he's got.'

'And he's never satisfied.'

They waited in the stifling air as the minutes went by. Already it had started drizzling—occasional big drops bursting on the windscreen in front. Now and again a hyena howled, but otherwise there was a quietness over everything, and even the crickets were silent. Nobody was about. No cars came down the road. There was just the patter of the rain around them, gradually getting louder.

'That rain,' Gunn said suddenly, 'always gripes me.'

Hannaker glanced at Gunn's face but said nothing. After a few seconds, he asked softly, 'That crash of yours, what was it? Pilot error?'

'Sure. What else?'

'Did you ever try to do anything about it?'

'No.'

'You should have.'

Gunn laughed soundlessly.

'Why didn't you?'

Gunn put his lips to Hannaker's ear. 'Because, mister, that's what it was. Straight up. Weather something like this. And, well, an error of judgment, as you say.'

'We all make mistakes.'

'Sure.'

'They didn't throw you off on that, did they?'

'Nope.'

Hannaker turned to look at Gunn again, taking his eyes off the gates.

'Were you smuggling?'

In the dark, he saw the whiteness of Gunn's teeth. 'Yep. Oh, that wasn't why I bounced her. I wasn't trying to get in because I had a load. But it didn't help me any. . . .' He shifted his position more comfortable, his gaze still on the road. 'Does that shock you, mister?'

'Nothing shocks me.'

'It figures, that.'

Gently Hannaker asked, 'Anyone killed?'

Gunn said nothing for a long time. 'Only me, mister.' He drew a deep breath. 'That's what I used to figure. *Now* . . .' Suddenly he gripped Hannaker's arm. 'Look.' He pointed to the gates.

Very slowly and in mechanical unison, the two high iron halves split open and parted.

A square black shadow detached itself from the night behind them, moved forward, turned left. As the gates closed silently behind, two sidelights appeared. The light spilling out of the gatehouse shone momentarily on white paint. And then quite noiselessly the ambulance slid past them, heading towards Colombo.

'Don't lose him.'

Gunn already had the van started and was accelerating forward. 'I won't.'

'Is Laughton on board?'

Gunn shook his head. 'He'll be picked up later.'

'Like the pilot?'

'Yep. To direct operations.'

'Like last time?'

Gunn nodded. 'One thing's certain . . . he'll do exactly what he did when he won. Superstitious people always do.'

The needle on the speedometer crept round the dial . . . fifty, sixty, seventy. 'And another thing's certain.'

'What?'

'There's a racing engine in that ambulance.'

Through the twisting, winding darkness, they followed the long arms of the ambulance's headlights and the red will-o'-the-wisp of the rear light. Gunn had not put on his own lights, lest he draw attention to the van. At breakneck speed, they rocketed through a tunnel of night. In the arc made by the swishing pendulum of the windscreen wiper, Hannaker peered forward into nothing ahead. 'Can't see a damn thing!'

'I know the road.'

'Thank God!'

'And so does he.'

A village went by, then a small town. The van bumped over a level crossing. Three hundred yards ahead, the red tail lamp still glowed.

The needle on the speedometer crept past eighty.

'Can you keep up with them?'

'Got the pedal hard down.'

The tyres hissed on the road. Going round a corner to the right, they slithered and skidded. Gunn hunched over the wheel, saying nothing, his eyes glued to the red and white lights dancing in the wet night ahead.

A long line of palm trees flickered past, followed by mud huts and bungalows.

'Kalutara,' Gunn said. And then at a cross-roads, 'Thought he would!'

The ambulance had turned sharp right. Suddenly both headlights went out. The driver was not going the direct way through the town where it might be conspicuous. Using only sidelights he had slowed down on this bumpy red laterite byway. Following, the van banged and lurched for over twelve miles, water from deep puddles now splashing up over the bonnet.

Gunn braked hard.

Ahead of them, the red spark had steadied and stopped.

'Picking up the pilot,' Gunn said.

It was raining much harder now, and they could see nothing. Impatiently Hannaker waited for the ambulance to go on, but nothing happened.

'You're sure that's what he's doing?'

'Sure.'

'You don't think he's seen us?'

'Nope.'

'How far's Tallaputiya?'

'Coupla miles.' And then: 'Here we go again!'

Ahead there was a white smudge and the red light began moving again. Gunn started the engine, and the van moved forward into what to Hannaker was total darkness.

'Can you see?'

'Just.'

Still only using sidelights, the ambulance was going very slowly now. Gunn was managing by following the grass verge. The red laterite way ceased, and they came on to a tarmac road.

Ahead the ambulance slowed down almost to a stop, as though it was searching. Then suddenly the red spark disappeared.

'What the hell's happened?'

'It's all right.' Gunn stopped again. 'He's drawn off the road.'

'I can't see him.'

'He's turned all his lights off. But don't worry . . . he's there all right.'

Anxiously, Hannaker screwed up his eyes and concentrated ahead. But there was nothing—just pouring wet darkness. And then suddenly, he saw them, over on the right, white smudges against the streaming night, one almost exactly from this position behind the other—the lead-in lights to the runway at Tallaputiya.

242

Gunn had seen them, too. 'He's lined himself up with the ILS beam. This is it!'

He leaned across the stearing wheel, and turned up the volume of the transistor. As they waited there in the rain, there was nothing but darkness and interference. And then suddenly, loud and clear, Dewhurst's voice again . . . 'Ocean Control from Double Echo . . . 87 East at 14.15 . . . in cloud at 32,000 feet. Now estimating Tallaputiya at 14.58. Request clearance to descend. . . .'

'. . . Double Echo reporting to Tallaputiya Tower . . . over the beacon at 3000. Coming in on runway 28 on normal ILS approach. . . .'

Clearing the last of the coffee cups off the console between the pilots, Melanie heard Dewhurst reporting laconically over the radio. Outside, the rain was a continuous swirl over the windscreen, which the wipers did no more than stir into different and ever-changing patterns of opaqueness. On the flight deck all the lights had been turned off. The phosphorescent numbers on the instruments glimmered like fireflies against the black background of the panel. Dewhurst nodded to his co-pilot, and Fletcher slowly pulled back three levers to disengage the automatic pilot and then began the Field Approach Check. Under her feet, Melanie felt the vibration as the engine power increased.

'Better get to the back,' Dewhurst snapped at her. 'And strap yourself in. We're in for a bumpy ride down.'

The girl hesitated. She felt she ought to warn him. But of what? Inwardly shrugging her shoulders, she walked off, past the flight engineer now concentrating on setting up the switches. Just as she opened the door into the passenger compartment, she heard Dewhurst say to Fletcher, 'If you see me go even one sliver below the glide path, *pull back on that stick.*'

She walked down the passenger cabin, and just in front of the rear galley, strapped herself in beside the Chief Steward, who sat there nonchalantly adding up his bar totals. Watching

him, she wondered if only she were nervous. Whether any of
the crew or the passengers, some reading, some asleep, had
this curious deadly feeling that something was going to happen.

The Chief Steward looked at his watch. 'Caught up a bit of
time.'

She nodded.

'My last trip on this detachment.'

'Are you sorry to go back?' She heard the engine note die
down as the engines throttled back.

'Not really.'

Perhaps, for all his outward calm, he was feeling it as well.
He kept glancing out of the porthole. But out there it was like
being at the bottom of some ocean—very deep where no light
could penetrate. For it was surely solid water they were flying
through that seemed to threaten to put out the flaring jets of
the engines. It was bumpier than ever down here, the wings
vibrating in the uneven air.

She heard the wheels come down, as the aircraft began to
slow. She knew what that meant. They were completing the
procedure turn, and sliding into the ILS beam. She heard the
engine note die down as Dewhurst picked up the glide path
and settled down on a steady rate of descent to the safety of
the runway lights below.

'. . . Double Echo on final. . . .'

Now they had the signal they were waiting for, Gunn and
Hannaker jumped down on to the soaking grass, and under
cover of the forest began running towards the white smudge
of the ambulance a hundred yards ahead.

The rain was sheeting down, and the wind coming off the
sea was tearing at the trees. As they got right up to the
ambulance, Hannaker saw a green glow coming out of the side
window that illuminated an aerial that had been drawn up
high out of its casing, and was now aligned with the runway
direction.

As the two men crept up to the side of the ambulance the
light from inside flickered eerily. The operator was adjusting

244

the fine tuning on the oscillator to get the frequency spot-on to the Tallaputiya ILS. Crouching against the white metal, Hannaker could feel vibration, could see the retractable aerial now pulled out at the operating angle on the frame of the ambulance.

The flickering stopped. The glow steadied. The slight hum became more pronounced as the full power of this private transmitter was brought into play modulated on the carrier wave of the Tallaputiya ILS so as to interfere with the beam and bend its path. Now, invisibly pouring out into the wet black air, were radio signals that would indicate a false glide path, two degrees lower than the true one. Balancing on the thin tightrope of the ILS, trying to keep the needle on his instrument steady and central, Captain Dewhurst would be lured down to crash into the hillock, just as Captain Coates had done before him, by the accuracy of his own flying. . . .

There was a man sitting in the driving seat. Out of the corner ￼his eye, Hannaker could just see him lying back slightly sideways against the window. If the driver turned his head ever so slightly, he could not fail to see the two of them.

Hannaker stood up, flattened himself against the ambulance flank, trying to make himself invisible. He could feel the hammering of his heart, taste the dryness of his mouth, incongruous in all this wet. Taking his cue, Gunn stood up too, and they began edging to the back of the vehicle.

At the rear, there was a small square window. Standing on the step, Hannaker could just see inside.

There was only one green light just above a radio transmitter beside which were sitting two Ceylonese in the uniform of Laughton's industrial police. They were watching the needles of the output dial and tuning indicator. Behind them, Laughton stood in his shirt-sleeves with headphones over his head, intently monitoring the frequency. Now and again he reached forward to adjust the tuning. There were other figures in the darkness of the background, but there was so little light, Hannaker could not see how many.

But now he could hear something—something quite different from the electric shriek and the rattling of the rain.

The whistle of jet engines, gradually getting louder.

For a few seconds he stood there, listening and staring inside, as though paralysed by the iniquity of what he saw. Through his mind raced a kaleidoscopic jumble of thoughts and memories: Melanie the first time he had seen her, the taxi-ride and the looming of Laughton out of the rain, the sight of the crash and the bodies, the inscrutable face of the Brahmin, the scientific fervour of Seneratne, the gold-caparisoned elephants in the Pera-Hera, the radio factory, the snake in the market, the inside of the British High Commission. And over it all the bittersweet smell that came up like a spectre's warning, like the deathwatch beetle, always to remind him of death and decay: the scent of the temple tree. Then, almost as though she was here beside him, Melanie's words when he had seen her off on this trip . . . *he sees himself as the symbol of the new Ceylon.* . . .

The lion—Lord of the jungle.

Lord of this beautiful island. Lord of the Hindus, the Buddhists, the Christians. Lord of the pearl-fisheries, the jewel mines, the immense potential wealth. Dictator and organizer, the new Messiah, the new Buddha in a new world built on gold, the reincarnation of Kasyapa of Sigiri.

Hannaker felt suddenly weak, as though he was drowning. His hands could not grasp anything. It was as though this evil could transmit its own hypnotizing force that resisted attackers, its own poison more powerful than a million cobras. Against it, Hannaker felt so weak and so defenceless.

Yet he must smash it. He must break it. He must summon all the strength he had. And above all—not only for Melanie's safety, but for the safety of everyone—he must make no mistake. Blundering around, blindfold, ignorant, often swayed this way and that, bent from the true path, he had searched for truth. Now he had it in his hands, he must not drop it.

He felt Gunn tugging his wet sleeve. Turning, he saw Gunn's face close to his, five of Gunn's fingers held up in front of his eyes—there were five of them in there, and then there was also the driver. High above the noise of the storm came the whine of the 707.

Gunn took hold of the handle of the door.

'Ready?'

Hannaker nodded.

'Got the safety catch off your automatic?'

Hannaker nodded.

'Right then . . . *now*!'

As the door swung open, Hannaker saw Laughton turn his head towards them. For a second, nobody moved. Time was frozen into a still photograph. Laughton's staring eyes, his mouth half open, the fingers of his right hand still on the fine tuner: the faces of the sitting Ceylonese, two staring figures at the back—all dyed green from the light on the roof.

Then Gunn lunged forward and got hold of Laughton. A shot rang out, then another one. Hannaker flung himself on to the radio operators. The standing Ceylonese whipped out guns and fired.

The green roof light went out. There was only the small glow from the radio. The whole ambulance rocked with the struggling of intertwined bodies, and the air reeked with the smell of gunpowder and sweat.

Hannaker had pitched the nearest Ceylonese down on to the floor. He grasped hold of the other man's shoulders, was turning his pistol to aim at the transmitter, when it was knocked out of his hand. He felt arms round his head, heard Laughton yelling in Sinhalese, and then another two shots from a revolver.

But with this infighting, it was all too close for firearms. There were grunts and heavy breathing. The bodies on the floor were being kicked and trodden on indiscriminately and were screaming with pain. Gunn had Laughton pinned against the radio.

Now high above all other sounds was a squawking and eerie whistling coming out of the radio. The tuning lights were winking and wobbling. How far it was off frequency, Hannaker did not know, but he was filled with the urgent need above all to smash this machine, this false prophet beckoning to death and destruction.

Guarding his head from the pummelling blows of the second Ceylonese, he drew back his arm, and with all his might smashed his fist into the dials and lights.

There was the sound of tinkling glass. All the radio lights went out. The electric hum suddenly ceased.

His right hand had gone numb. He could feel warm blood flowing from his knuckles and his fingers on to his arm. There was no sign of Gunn. The whole interior seemed to be filled with Sinhalese attacking him. Then Laughton had him by the throat, and in the pitch darkness, he began to fight for breath.

He hit out blindly till suddenly he tripped, fell, and then was rolling on the floor, dirt and dust spattering up into his mouth.

Innumerable feet seemed to be kicking his face. Laughton and one of the Sinhalese were on to him, punching his face and eyes and dragging him towards the open door.

Seeing nothing, Hannaker fought back, kicking with his legs in a paroxysm of fury. Under his body now he felt the vibration of the ambulance motor, felt it lurching forward. The next moment he felt himself falling, falling—going down and down into some wet black pit till suddenly he found himself on muddy grass, tasted sand in his mouth.

Six shots rang out, and he heard the soft splutter of bullets burying themselves in the ground around him.

He had been thrown out of the ambulance—which now, blue lamps blazing, alarm bell clanging, all headlights on, as though assuming its rightful identity in a crisis, had swung out of the forest off the road, and was heading up the hill along the rough path to the temple, with Laughton still firing from the open rear door.

He heard Gunn yell from behind him. Hannaker hauled himself up, and then the two of them started racing through the pouring rain, as ahead of them the ambulance rocked precariously from side to side up the rocky path.

As he ran, Hannaker was not conscious of anything but the one obsession that filled his mind. Before he had managed to smash the radio, it had done its work. Too late the false signal had been interrupted. Too late for Dewhurst to correct the instrument glide path into oblivion. There had been another crash. There had been more people killed, and one of them was Melanie. He had failed. He had failed again. The truth he had found he had not used. He had protected no one.

'Don't let him get away!' Hannaker heard his voice yelling in a frenzy, while all the time the gap between them and the ambulance widened. 'Can you. . . . ?'

And then suddenly, it was as though the black heavens had come crashing down upon them. Hannaker was momentarily aware of a huge dark shape above him, trailing three long legs. His ears were deafened with roaring engines, and the wet night was alight with flaring jets.

Then the whole earth seemed to shiver in a shattering explosion. Instinctively Hannaker ducked as the black sky was momentarily lit up by a long row of round suns that as quickly dissolved back into the night.

There was no sign at all of the ambulance.

Hannaker became aware of Gunn beside him. Breathless and panting, together they went up the hill towards the temple.

Just round the corner of the rough stony track, they found it—a sheet of shattered metal and glass flattened by the huge port wheels of the 707.

The steering wheel had been knocked clear, and the back axle lay thirty yards away, almost intact. Already the leeches were beginning to loop up and down in their progress over the wet white skin—but there was no other sign of life.

This, Hannaker thought, was where I came in. The same entrance hall of the Mount Lavinia Hotel. The same clerk at the desk. The same whisper of saris, and the clink of china. the same pouring rain outside.

Hannaker stared down at his now bandaged right hand. Only he seemed to have changed. He felt simultaneously infinitely older and yet curiously young.

Gunn had dropped him here after they had driven away from the wrecked ambulance and alerted the police. The American had gone into Colombo to make a statement to Fonseca, leaving Hannaker to telephone the airport from the hotel.

'I am surprised,' Reeves had said at the other end, 'that you saw fit to phone. Now listen to me, please. Where are you speaking from? If you stay there for a little while Sir Arthur has undertaken. . . .'

Hannaker heard a bell being pressed as if Reeves were urgently summoning some help. He became extremely irritable when Hannaker persisted in asking about the aircraft.

'Of course Double Echo's all right. Of course nothing's happened. Yes, passengers and crew have landed safely. Why shouldn't they? The Chief Stewardess? Yes, Melanie Grey. The port wheel? How did *you* know about the port wheel? Hannaker, what have you been up to again? The ILS? I haven't spoken to Dewhurst yet. But I understand . . . now look, why are you asking all these questions? Now there's whole swarms of police arriving here. I can see them through my window. . . .'

Hannaker put down the receiver without enlightening the Station Manager. Then he walked back to the same wicker table and sat in the same chair as he had done a month ago.

He no longer turned over in his mind the events leading up to tonight. He did not go over the investigation into the crash with a practised professional self-satisfied eye. He simply sat alone and waited.

The ancient hand on the clock over the door clicked round as relentlessly and yet as slowly as it had done ever since Queen Victoria died. The creaking fan above his head sent a gentle slipstream to rustle the palms.

The clerk, still as an idol, snoozed at his desk. Guests murmured quietly as if fearful of disturbing him. The lift cage whined up and down. He stared more absently at the shaft with its flowers and fruits and curlicues. For the first time he recognized its theme. The tree again, with its branches on earth and its roots in heaven.

Then Hannaker leaned forward. Here they came. From outside he had caught the squeak of brakes, the sound of doors being slammed, voices. Behind his desk the clerk came alive, began sorting through keys, snapping his fingers for the bell boys.

The glass doors were pushed open, letting in a flurry of warm wet air. Dewhurst came first, paused to shake the rain off his cap, fingered the little toothbrush moustache. His eyes were slightly more protuberant, his walk more ponderous. Then the First Officer, white as a ghost, the Chief Steward, two other of the stewardesses that Hannaker now knew by sight. He was beginning to think that for some reason she had stayed at the airport, when in she came.

Smart in her uniform, make-up fresh, hair carefully groomed, the shadowed eyes searching the foyer as if she expected to see someone. He didn't go over to greet her. He allowed himself the luxury of watching her, a fair-haired girl crossing the hotel foyer to the Albert Memorial of a lift.

He waited as she pressed the old-fashioned button. He watched the ornate glass cabin descend. He heard the gates clash open and watched her walk inside. Then she turned and saw him and smiled.

He got up from the wicker chair by the palms and walked over towards her. All the time she kept her eyes on him, while with her two hands she held the doors wide open until he was safely inside.

Then the gates clanged shut—and the ground fell away.